OVER THE LINE
BY ELISE FABER

Newsletter sign-up

OVER THE LINE

Copyright © 2023 Elise Faber
Print ISBN-13: 978-1-63749-119-5
Ebook ISBN-13:978-1-63749-118-8

SIERRA HOCKEY SERIES

Over the Line

Caught from Behind

On the Fly

The Big Skate

ONE

Nova

"DRIVE TO TAHOE, THEY SAY," I mutter, squinting through the snow that is falling so rapidly the entire world has been reduced to flecks of swirling white. "It will be fun, they say."

A gust of wind pushes my car on the icy road, and I gasp, my fingers tightening on the steering wheel as I continue driving forward.

The conditions are worse than any I've ever driven before.

Which isn't hard.

I'm a California girl, born and bred—I barely survive driving in a light rain.

Snow? Ice? Sleet—

What *is* sleet, anyway?

I don't know, and I really don't want to find out, though I'm fully aware that may be something I experience in the coming minutes.

Anyway, the point is that snow, ice, and the aforementioned sleet are *way* out of my driving skill set.

And it doesn't help that I don't know where I'm going.

I'm used to that—to being free and loose and going off without a lick of concern to what lies on the road behind me. Moving toward the beauty and excitement in *front* of me without any plan or purpose or direction.

Just forward. Always moving forward.

Only the road is usually absent of snow.

Which is somehow falling even more heavily now.

"You're fine," I whisper, even as I squint and clench the steering wheel tighter. I'm practically crawling along the road, inching toward my destination, and hating the feel of my tires slipping on the pavement, the tension creeping into my shoulders, the way my jaw aches from grinding my teeth so forcefully together.

Normally, I love a drive up to Tahoe.

Winding roads.

Huge conifers.

A snaking river that follows me along the side of the highway, its water broken up by fallen logs and chunks of granite in every size, from pebbles to boulders.

I love getting away from the city and into the fresh air in the summer or spring or fall.

Not the winter.

And not today when it feels like I'm running from the hounds of hell (aka the hounds of my lame, pathetic, miserable life).

"Woof!"

I blink those thoughts away—forward, always *forward!*— and risk a look over to the passenger's seat, where Steve is buckled into his puppy harness. Safety first for my baby boy.

"You're okay," I reassure him before refocusing on the road, and slowing down even further.

No one is behind me.

I can move slowly and carefully for a change, rather than headfirst into disaster.

Plus, the turnoff has to be soon and I don't want to miss it.

I exited the highway what felt like hours ago, so it *has* to be soon—

"*Woof?*" Steve asks in a concerned bark, his doggy eyes so wide they are almost bugging out of his face.

Or, okay, fine, so that's his normal pug face—smooshed nose, goofy ears, bug eyes, and a penchant for snorting and sneezing and *snoring*.

So, basically, Steve is the cutest puppy in the history of all puppies.

He just also looks like he ran into a wall.

Small details.

"We're going to be okay," I reassure him, knowing we have to be. Because no matter how bad the last twenty-four hours have been, we are going to be okay.

Mostly because I am always okay.

Even if I have to fake it until that's true.

And anyway, Steve has plenty of food, his entire collection of squeaky toys and fake bones, *and* his hoard of cozy beds all stuffed into the back seat, so he'll be well-fed and entertained.

He'll be better than okay.

He'll be content and snotty and sneezy and well, fucking perfect.

While I, on the other hand, will be—

Thunk.

I gasp, jerking at the steering wheel and nearly sending us off the road. A quick maneuver has me back inside the lines and I hold my breath as I flick a brief look in the rearview.

A huge branch lies in the middle of the road behind me.

Not a person.

Not an adorable puppy with bug eyes and goofy ears and a tendency to snot in my face when I bend over to kiss him on the head.

Just a branch.

"Thank you, universe," I whisper, clamping one hand to my chest, gaze returning to the road as I resume squinting through the sideways falling snow for the street sign that will indicate our turnoff.

It *has* to be close.

It *has* to be.

"There," I whisper, finally spotting a green sign that is nearly invisible in the furious swirling whiteness. "Forest Bend."

Thank. *Freaking*. God.

I point at it as though Steve knows how to read. "See? It's right there, buddy. We've made it. We're going to be okay."

I slow to a snail's pace, prepare to make the turn—

"*Woof!*"

Steve's bark is so loud, so sharp that I jump, jerking the steering wheel hard to the right.

My tires start to skid.

My *car* starts to slide.

But this time my attempt at getting us back between the lines is the wrong one—too rough, too jarring, too damned quick...and the skid doesn't slow.

The slide doesn't halt.

"Shit," I whisper, pumping the brakes hard.

Note to non-snow-driving self, this is *also* the wrong move.

I might as well be hitting the gas for all that does to slow me down. In fact, it seems to increase our speed, and though the snow is starting to fall even more rapidly, I can see my future with crystal clear accuracy.

The snowbank.

My car.

Me.

Steve.

"*Shit*," I hiss as the side of the road sweeps up toward us.

Slow motion, but not.

Warp speed, but not.

Inevitable, absolutely.

I throw my arm out to the right in true dog mom fashion, as though that action will protect my pup from any and all threats as I wrestle with the steering wheel, still trying to avoid the inevitable even as the inevitable is coming closer.

I pump the brakes to no effect.

I push my arm into Steve, pressing him deeper into his doggy seat, hoping it will keep him safe.

I—

Run out of time.

My car rattles and bumps and lurches forward...

And then it's sliding off the road.

TWO

Lake

BEING a professional hockey player has its perks.

Driving through a blizzard because my coach is an asshole is not one of them.

We've been hearing about this freakishly early winter snowstorm—hell, it's November, so it's not even technically winter yet—for days on end now.

The Snowmageddon that's supposed to shut down the Sierra Nevadas.

So, cool, cool. Thanks, Coach, for keeping us a couple of hours late after practice was supposed to end. Not like we all have shit to do. Not like we've been warned to buckle down, stock up, and brace for the snow.

Not like we haven't just returned from a long-ass road trip which means that we haven't had time to do any of those things before today's mandatory skate.

That he added to the schedule because not only is he an asshole, but the rest of us are too.

Bickering. Fighting in the locker room. All but throwing away a game that was within our grasp to win.

So...a brutal, exhausting extra practice added to our schedule, just for funsies.

Then racing the storm rolling in as I try to accomplish my stocking up.

Milk to buy.

Generators to buy gas for.

Toilet paper to hoard.

The only good thing about the coming storm is that I won't have to talk to anyone.

That's the real perk—not having to interact with any of the assholes who make up the Sierra's locker room.

I have exactly three teammates I like—Knox, Riggs, and Leo. And I have *exactly* three teammates I like because I only have three who aren't total trash humans or emotional vampires or who don't fuck around on their wives and girlfriends.

Three.

Three perks hidden amongst twenty-three PIAs...and I have to win games with those pains-in-the-asses because that's my fucking job as a professional hockey player.

As the captain of this team.

It would be a hell of a lot easier if I was playing with the Breakers or the Gold. They have this player-prioritized, family-first mentality that is not my experience, that has *never* been my experience as a professional athlete.

I'm a commodity. A resource to be consumed until my body gives out.

Always have been. Probably always will be.

Definitely if I stay with the Sierra, that'll be the case.

My phone rings and I glance at the screen mounted in the dash, see that it's my mother, and *so* not in the mood to deal with her bullshit, I reject the call. The wind is picking up and it's been a long enough couple of weeks without thinking about the shit show that is my family.

That's my career.

I get paid an obscene amount of money to carry a puck around the ice.

I also get paid indecently to put my name on a vodka brand, to pitch socks, and to model underwear.

My life is *so* hard.

"Yup. So hard," I mutter dryly, squinting out the windshield of my SUV, glad that I'm almost home. I'll drink some of my "shit-tasting" vodka my friends like to give me a hard time about, put on a hockey game for a team whose schedule isn't impacted by the incoming Snowmageddon, and forget about Coach, about practice, about the fact that, from the outside, everything in my life seems like it's going perfectly, but, inside it, things feel...

Off.

"Fuck!" I growl, whipping the steering wheel hard to the left, nearly sending it into a skid, but thankfully the hockey gods have provided me with four-wheel drive and snow tires, and—since I grew up navigating through exactly this type of shitty weather—the ability to keep my vehicle under control.

Keep it under control and manage to *not* hit the object in the road.

No.

The *person* in the road.

"What the fuck?" I snap, pulling to a halt and throwing my gearshift into park. I hit the hazards as I get out to prevent an accident on the off chance that someone else drives up—fucking unlikely, considering that we're supposed to be buckling down and bracing.

Not standing in the middle of the road trying to get mowed down by an SUV.

In a fucking blizzard.

"What the actual fuck?" I say, somehow madder than I was before.

Because the person is *still* in the road.

Standing there in a hoodie, a pair of jeans, and sneakers wholly unsuited for the weather.

Standing there like it's the front of a fucking Target and they're giving themselves a pep talk to spend less than two hundred bucks inside all while—they hang their head—knowing that it's a pointless endeavor.

That money's going to get spent regardless.

They *aren't* standing there like it's the middle of the road in a snowstorm, where visibility is limited and it's highly likely they could get hurt—

Or say, run over by a large SUV.

Or say, acknowledge the fact that they nearly *had* just been run over by said SUV.

The wind is whipping so loudly that I can't hear anything else—perhaps why they don't acknowledge the almost-getting-run-over—as I stare at the person—at the woman—whose jeans are wet and filthy at least six inches deep from the dirty, muddy snow that's quickly being covered by the fresh flakes falling from the sky. I take a step toward her and feel something inside me still as I see them—see *her*—throw back her hood, sending a swathe of deep brown hair cascading down her back and shoulders.

The sight is...sinful, beautiful, *terrible*.

But I can't focus on the fingers that have just reached into my chest and clenched around my heart.

Because she is launching herself forward and...

Colliding with the side of a car stuck in the snowbank.

A car that's barely visible.

Because it's white and almost completely buried.

The car—no surprise—doesn't move, so she backs up, repeats the action.

"Jesus Christ," I mutter, the sound of her second collision audible even over the wind so fiercely blowing in my ears, cutting through my jacket, my jeans, blowing my hair into my eyes. I move closer and hear her.

"Come"—a grunt as she stops shoving at the car and switches to yanking on the handle—"*on!*"

I move forward. "What the fuck are you—"

There's a *screech* and I have to jump back to avoid getting plastered by the car door that's suddenly swinging toward my face.

I jerk up my hand just in time to slap my palm against the metal panel.

It stings like a motherfucker, pain radiating down my arm.

I ignore it because I'm used to pain.

I ignore it because the woman turns around and—

Those fingers clenched around my heart squeeze tighter.

And...

I lose it.

THREE

Nova

"WHAT THE FUCK ARE YOU DOING?"

I'm sweaty.

I'm exhausted.

I'm approximately three milliseconds away from crying—and this time in relief for the first time in twenty-four hours.

But I still manage to react to the man shouting at me with impressive speed, bending down and scooping up the Tupperware container I had commandeered to use as a shovel and lifting it threateningly. "Back off!" I shout, looking up.

And then up.

And then *up* some more.

The man in front of me is huge.

Like head brushing along the bottom branches of the pine trees that cluster around the road, like he won't fit in the driver's seat of my car, like he'll bang his skull on the tops of doorframes, like he is...*huge* kind of huge.

My Tupperware won't do shit to stop him, but I still hold it like I'm going to wield it as a sword anyway.

I am fierce. I am a warrior. I am...

Going to die.

I consider launching the scoop of snow at him, straight into his eyes, a la a bad guy throwing dust in the hero's in every cheesy action movie I love to watch.

Likely, this man would just swipe it away.

And *then* murder me worse.

Which—God, if I have nothing else (and I didn't have much)—then I at least need to maintain my grammar dignity.

Starting with removing the phrase *murder me worse* from my vernacular.

"What the fuck are you doing?" he snaps again.

"Back"—I lift the container higher and—

He plucks it out of my hands, tossing it to the side in a movement that is almost faster than my eyes can track.

"Hey!" I snap.

I need that. I keep my cookies—the ones I had to gainfully consume in order to free up the container for digging—in there. More than that, it's a good container, and good containers are hard to find.

Or maybe that's men.

Whatever.

Tupperware is expensive and it still has its matching lid and...it's *mine*.

Yes, that's me going full Gollum.

My precious.

The huge—*huge!*—man rotates back to face me, hazel eyes snapping with fire. "You're standing in the middle of the fucking street in the middle of a fucking snowstorm."

"Wow," I snap back, sarcasm so rampant I almost surprise myself, "I hadn't noticed. Thanks for pointing that out."

Sneakers skidding on the ice, I march over to my precious, scooping up the container and cradling it against my chest as I glare at the man and move back to my vehicle.

"I almost hit you with my car," he grits out.

I set the container on the back seat, consider belting her in just to be safe then decide that's a step too far. "Clearly you didn't," I return as I spin back to face him.

Though, with all that spinning, I don't miss the skid marks in the road—mine that are almost completely erased, his that are rapidly being filled in with snow...and lead to a large black SUV.

Yeah, getting hit by that would've sucked.

And likely resulted in more *murdering me worse.*

He growls and I jerk my head from the sight of the behemoth of a vehicle to glance back...

And fall into the prettiest hazel eyes I've ever seen.

I want to grab my camera, want to take a close-up of those irises, to study all the shades of gold and brown and green, the texture of the peaks and valleys beneath his cornea, the—

He blinks and I lose my focus, dropping abruptly right back into my reality.

Which is going great, considering that my car is buried on the side of the road and I just spent the last half hour digging out my door enough so I can get Steve's stuff from the back seat.

A muscle flexes in his jaw. "It's dangerous for you to be out here."

I sigh, bite back my sarcasm, and push down the last supremely shitty twenty-four hours. "Look," I say calmly. "I appreciate your concern—and thank you for not hitting me with your car—but feel free to move on. I'm staying at a house on Forest Bend, and now that my door's open, I can grab my stuff from the back and hike up there."

He freezes, looks me up and then down, and I want to

pretend there's heat in those gorgeous hazel eyes instead of derision. Unfortunately, I would have to pretend *really* hard for that to be true.

"That's fucking stupid," he says.

I blink once.

Then twice.

Expecting him to not actually be calling me stupid.

People didn't seriously do that to each other's faces.

They wait until they're in private and confide it to their best friends, and occasionally their sisters, who they want to be close with, if only their sisters didn't—

Right.

Not the time.

Eyes stinging, I shake my head and turn away from him. "Well," I say quietly. "It's not like I want to stay in my car and freeze to death out here."

"You have a cell phone?" he asks sharply.

I frown, rotate back to face him. "Yes."

"Then you stop being stupid," he snaps. "You call for help. And you"—he leans in, bending at the waist so we're almost nose to nose—"wait in your car so that said help can come and you don't get hit by my fucking SUV."

My frown deepens.

But then my eyes start to sting again.

Because who can I possibly call?

I have no one except for my best friend, Ella, and she's already done enough in arranging for me to stay in her brother's house, has already done enough in plenty of other ways over the years, over the last twenty-four hours.

Rescuing me from my shit.

But I've had enough of this conversation—such as it is. I've had enough getting yelled at, enough scornful words tossed at me, enough disdain dripping in my direction, and I've just…had *enough.*

"Thank you for not hitting me with your car," I say so politely it's as frozen as the snow coating my clothes. I spin back to my open car door and reach for my purse that's fallen behind the driver's seat, slinging it over my shoulder. Then I unbuckle Steve from his doggy seat, coax him to hop back to me, and snag his leash from the floor, intending to clip it on him.

But I don't get it attached.

Fingers wrap around my arm, tug me out of the car.

"What the fuck are you doing?" he snaps.

"*You,*" I say, jerking out of his hold, "are going about your business, which will hopefully continue to include not running over helpless people with your SUV. *I*"—I thump a hand to my chest—"am going to get on with my life." A beat. "*Without* you in it."

"You're going to walk," he says disbelievingly.

"That's none of your business."

A flick of his eyes down again. "You're going to walk through the ice and snow in *those* shoes?" A beat that's filled with contempt. "And do it loaded down with your shit?"

I glance at my feet. "It's not like I'm a magical shoe wizard and can snap my fingers so a pair of snow boots appears." I mean, I have them somewhere in my bags. It's just…they're mixed in with things I don't want to see and—

"Let's hope you can snap your fingers and make common sense appear."

My mouth drops open. "Are you fucking kidding me?"

"You're risking frostbite," he says instead of answering that. "Do you even know where you're going?"

"Of course, I do. I just need to go up that road and—" I

spin, the flakes of snow in my eyes obscuring my vision. Obscuring almost everything. "It's right—" I keep turning.

"Forest Bend is"—the man grips my shoulders, turns me the opposite direction—"over there."

"Right," I whisper, my outrage fading.

My anger morphing into embarrassment.

He lifts his brows expectantly.

Oh, look at that. My anger makes a reappearance.

I try to step back, to pull out of his hold, but his fingers just tighten.

"Look—"

"*Woof!*"

FOUR

Lake

THERE ARE tiny pinpricks of pain in my ankle.

Like a swarm of little bees are stinging me—except all at once, like eight or ten of them have surrounded my ankle to mount a coordinated attack.

"What the fuck?" I mutter, breaking away from the woman's surprisingly captivating emerald eyes—the color of the slender, green needles of the pine trees surrounding this road, when they aren't being hidden beneath the snow that is falling faster by the second anyway.

I glance down and see...

"What the fuck is *that?*" I ask, lifting my ankle, the creature —and apparently the source of those pinpricks of pain radiating up my leg.

The woman gasps and yanks the tiny demon off my ankle, sending razor blades of sensation along my skin—even through my jeans and socks—then cradles the creature against her chest.

"Steve is *not a that*. Steve is a pug and he's the most adorable of all adorable pug puppies in the whole world."

I lift a brow at the smooshed-up face of what is apparently a dog. "He's a puppy?"

She narrows her eyes, hugs him tighter. "Okay, so maybe he isn't a *puppy*, but Steve is still the most adorable dog on the planet."

"Your dog's name is Steve?"

Those emerald eyes narrow further, and her chin comes up. "Steve is a perfectly acceptable name for a dog."

I shrug. "If you say so."

"I—" I smirk and a flash of stubbornness settles across her face. "Just go on with your life, yeah?" she snaps. "And leave me to mine."

"So I can get questioned by the police"—or worse, blasted on social media—"when your frozen body is discovered on the side of the road and people find out that I've abandoned you during Snowmageddon?"

Her head tilts to the side. "What the hell is Snowmageddon?"

I look to the sky. Back at her.

Then to the sky again—to the darkness, to the thick clouds, to the fucking blizzard settling in around us.

And I decide I've had enough of this conversation.

I bend, snatch the creature from her arms—which is snorting and snotting and making noises that belong to a fucking demon and *not* a dog—and then I turn toward my SUV, ignoring her shout of protest as I stride toward my car and dump the creature in the passenger's seat. It growls at me and I narrow my eyes, silently telling it to stay there if it wants to live, then close the door.

Last thing I need right now is the little shit running off into the snow.

I'm not a total asshole.

I'd go after it.

But I'd be pissed off about it—or *more* pissed anyway.

The tiny demon's head appears in the window, teeth bared, but I ignore the sight that should be in a horror film and move back to the woman.

"What the fuck are you—?" The rest of her question cuts off with an outraged gasp as I snatch her purse over her head, reach past her, and grab a bag from the floor of the car.

I walk away, toss the shit in the back seat of mine.

"—doing?" she exclaims as I come back, look to see if there's anything else.

When I don't spot anything, I slam the door and glare at the annoying woman with those emerald eyes and a butterfly stud in her nose, and ask, "Anything in the trunk?"

And yeah, I can see she's definitely got something in *her* trunk, and it's a big, juicy ass that tempts a man.

Just not enough to tempt me.

"I—" She frowns. "What?"

"Anything." I pause, glance toward the back of the car. "In the trunk."

Wide eyes on mine. Then she seems to shake herself. "My suitcase is—"

I'm moving before she finishes the statement, wrestling with the trunk's latch for far longer than I want to, the cold already settling heavier over me, sinking into my hands.

She has to be freezing in those fucking sneakers.

Finally, the latch pops open and I grab the bags filling the inside.

"Hey," she exclaims. "Don't touch—"

I sling them over my shoulder, look back at her as I slam the trunk. "Lock your car and come on."

A long, slow blink.

I ignore that she looks pretty when she's a little discombobulated.

The world is full of beautiful women.

She's nothing special.

Plus, her dog is ugly.

I open the door, chuck the bags in the back seat with the rest of her shit, and slam it shut again.

When I turn around, she's standing there, just inches away, and I catch the slightest hint of cinnamon on the air. The snow's still falling and the wind is still blowing, but in that moment, it seems as though the world has quieted.

I shake my head once hard, sending that sensation from my mind.

The wind rushes back in, the world intruding abruptly.

Coldly.

I glance behind her, see that her car appears secure—or as much as it can be when it's sitting in a snowbank on the side of the road, rapidly being covered with even more of the white fluffy shit.

Good enough.

I open the passenger's seat, dodge the dog that takes a run at me, snot flying, teeth bared, and order, "Get in."

She narrows her eyes at me, but—thank fuck—starts to climb in.

I react without thinking, grasping her hand, steadying her as she steps onto the slick, black running board.

Her head whips around, deep green eyes locking with mine for a moment.

Time stilling. The wind quieting again. The cold fading away.

Her skin is soft, her fingers fit in mine like two pieces of a puzzle coming together.

Sparks of sensation along my palm, up my arm, toward my heart—

"Woof!"

I shake myself, all but shove her the rest of the way inside.

Then, fingers flexing, that prickling awareness acute, I step back.

I glance down at my hand, expecting...it to look different.

But it's just the same.

The wind gusts and I plummet back into reality—ankle hurting, temperature dropping by the second, snow falling harder. Sighing, I ignore the woman and dog tossing twin glares at me through the window, round the hood, and get into the driver's seat.

Thankfully, she's clutching the dog to her chest so it can't take another run at me.

I grind my teeth together as I buckle in, jabbing at the button to turn on the engine, putting my car into drive, and reaching forward—

There are fucking bite marks on my steering wheel.

FIVE

Nova

HE DOESN'T LOOK at me as he buckles in and reaches for the button to turn on the ignition.

Yup.

A button to turn on his car.

Meanwhile, when I splurged for the new-to-me sedan with just short of a hundred thousand miles currently resting in the snowbank, I was excited about finally having electronic locks.

Oh, and airbags.

Meanwhile, this man has a button to turn on the ignition, leather seats, a space-age-era computer in the dash, and...

My butt is warm.

Cozy and *warm*.

I casually sneak my hand down, press my palm to the leather.

Yup.

Warm air is blowing through it.

I don't realize how cold I am until that warmth begins to

sink through my clothes, glides over my skin. A shiver skates through me and my teeth begin to chatter. Cold or adrenaline letdown or...

Steve's wet nose brushing my throat.

I shudder but don't push him away.

I could have seriously hurt him if the crash had been worse, could have lost him.

That has me shuddering again.

The man flicks his gaze to mine, and our stares connect in a way that sends my pulse skittering. He's intense and big and those eyes of his are deep pools of brown and green and gold, as beautiful as a vein of granite I stumbled upon once when I was out hiking in the summer. The hillside seemed to have cracked open, maybe from an earthquake, maybe just because we had a lot of rain that year. Either way, that cross-section of earth had frozen me on the spot for long minutes.

Only when a bird chirped in the distance had the spell broken slightly.

And then I wanted it back.

I took picture after picture, trying to commit the beauty of that moment to memory, to capture every unique facet that had so completely captivated me.

The gold specks sparkling in the sunshine.

The way the green seemed to race the bands of brown from side to side, top to bottom.

The rough texture that was also somehow smooth.

The way nature made something more beautiful than any art I had ever seen.

I filled an entire memory card during the hours I spent there.

And when I got home, I found the pictures I took couldn't do that spiritual experience justice. They weren't three-dimensional, didn't make my heart race, didn't lift goose bumps on my arms.

I learned then—

Or maybe had it pounded home.

That sometimes, special moments in time are impossible to capture, impossible to hold on to, impossible to keep close.

And sometimes the heavy, dark, *terrible* ones stay bright. They never fade away.

They remain tattooed on my mind forever.

No matter how hard I try to erase them.

I shudder a third time, struggling with the barbed thoughts.

He breaks his stare away, reaches for a button on the dashboard, jabs at it several times, and hot air fills the inside of the SUV.

"What about my car?" I ask as he shoves the gearshift into drive, eases off the brake and we start to roll forward.

"I'm not the fucking Hulk," he mutters, gaze pointed at the windshield.

Even from his profile, I can see he's scowling.

I wonder if he has any other expressions.

Given the lines between his brows, around his eyes, probably not.

"I don't know what you're talking about," I say when he doesn't expand on his superpower abilities, and I mean, I get that he's big, but it's not like I'm going to confuse him with the giant green guy.

"Join the crowd," he mutters, wiping his sleeve on the steering wheel before slowly maneuvering around the snow piling up on the side of the road.

I frown. "*I'm* not the one talking about the Hulk."

"Your car is buried in the snowbank," he clips out, slowly and steadily leaving my car behind us. "I don't have superhero strength, so it's going to stay there." A beat. Another flash of those hazel eyes on mine before he looks out the windshield again, jerks his chin forward, as though indicating the ever-thickening blanket of snow around us. "Same as this storm. It isn't going anywhere any time soon."

"Because it's Snowmageddon," I say softly.

"Yup," he mutters on a sigh. "The storm of the century and I'm stuck out in it, rescuing your ass when we're supposed to be bracing and buckling down at home."

Hurt coils through me, but only for a moment.

Because then my anger is back.

It's a weird sensation.

I'm not a woman who gets angry. Not much bothers me. In my life, I couldn't survive if I let all of the small things pile up and weigh me down. They have to skate down my back like water, wash away and not impact me.

But this man...

Oh man, does he grind my gears.

And I've known him for all of ten minutes. Tops.

"I didn't *try* to get stuck on the side of the road, you know," I mutter, crossing my arms around Steve and drawing him tight against my chest.

He licks my chin, snuffles against my skin in the typical pug way.

A flick of those hazel eyes toward mine again, judgment in golden green depths. "Regardless," he says the words, sharp spikes of ice hurling through the air, "I'm not the Hulk and I can't singlehandedly rescue your car. We're going to have to wait for help to dig you out"—he turns right onto Forest Bend, navigating the snow and ice like a professional (and maybe he is)—"and you're going to have to deal because that's going to take at least a couple of days."

I blink once.

Then again.

Not hours, but "Days?" I exclaim.

Steve woofs.

The man just says, "Snowmageddon."

And look, I'm not a woman prone to violence, but I very much want to reach across the console and throttle him.

Of course, that would probably cause us to end up in *another* snowbank.

Sigh.

"I'm not letting you freeze to death," he says, taking the hill with a speed that has my free hand gripping the seat, my other arm wrapped tightly enough around Steve that he snorts disapprovingly against my chin. But then we're up and over the hill, moving slowly and steadily along the road. "Too much fucking paperwork."

"Let?" I ask dangerously.

A danger he ignores, just driving forward without answering me.

"Paperwork?" I ask, tone even icier.

He flicks on the radio, keeps driving, and I debate hurling myself out the door.

But...Snowmageddon.

And Steve.

And hurling sounds like it would hurt.

So, when he keeps driving, the soft rock music playing in the background, I settle into my seat and do what I always do.

Let this latest fuck-up roll off my back.

And then I hug Steve a little tighter.

SIX

Lake

THE DOG IS DROOLING on her chin, but it doesn't seem to bother her.

I do, though, judging by the glares she tosses my way repeatedly during the short drive to my house. "If you're an ax murderer, I swear to God," she mutters, still holding on to the little demon dog like it is the most precious object on Earth.

And not a tiny terror with a smooshed-up face.

I'm almost tempted to ask her to finish that sentence.

But that would mean talking to her more.

And I can't decide if she's annoying as fuck, or...kind of amusing. And, frankly, I'm worried I'm settling on the side of amused, which is a complication I really don't need.

Hence why it's tempting to stop my car and order her to get out.

Unfortunately, I'm an asshole with a bit of a conscience—or else I wouldn't have rescued her from the side of the road in the first place—so I can't dump her out in the snow to turn into a human popsicle.

As much as it pains me, the only place I can take her is my house—

Wait.

She said she rented a place nearby, and—

"Where are you staying?"

A narrow-eyed glare in my direction. "1262 Forest Bend."

I blink.

Then frown.

Because...what the actual fuck?

"You're mistaken," I say sharply.

"I'm not." She shakes her head, reaches around and grabs her purse from the back seat, and pulls out her phone, jabbing at the screen. "My friend arranged for me to stay at her brother's place, and...see?" She points the cell in my direction and since there are no other idiots driving around in this shit storm, I brake and pull to a stop in the middle of the road, staring down at the screen as I scroll through the conversation.

> Good news, my brother says you can stay at his place.

> What's the address?

> 1262 Forest Bend. There's a spare key under the green pot on the porch.

> Is he sure about this?

> Yes, he's sure. He's never home as it is.

> I don't know, Ella. I feel weird about staying at a random guy's house.

You've met Knox before. You know he's a good guy. Just accept that someone is willing to do something nice for you for once, Nova, and take this time to get your head and heart together—

Knox.

Knox.

How many assholes in this world are named Knox?

I'm not a fucking genius, but there can't be that many.

Probably as many as women that are named Nova.

I glance up at her, at *Nova*, and decide that the name suits her. There's something bright about her, an inner light and—

What the actual fuck am I talking about?

An inner light?

Have I just been booked to chat on a shitty, woo-woo podcast?

It's a name, that's all.

And she's a woman. Which means that she's trouble—a trouble I don't want.

Unfortunately...

"1262 Forest Bend is the address of *my* house," I say, shoving the phone back at her—and nearly getting my fingers bitten off by the little demon named Steve in the process.

Silence. A long, slow blink. Then, "But you're not Knox."

"No," I mutter. "I'm Lake. My asshole teammate—who doesn't even live on this side of town, by the way—is Knox."

More silence.

Wind buffets the car and I start forward again, though I'm tempted to turn around, to drive over to Knox's apartment and dump Nova on his porch. It's too late. We need to get somewhere safe and out of this weather.

"The address is for *your* house," she whispers.

I hit the gas, knowing that the snow is building up and I'm

going to need the speed to get up the final hill, ignoring that her little gasp makes me want to reassure her that I know how to handle my car, my street, that I've been driving in the snow for as long as I can remember.

I just stay quiet and keep going.

And then we're approaching the entrance to my house, the driveway that slopes down into the garage. I hit the button and wait as the wide metal and wood door slowly opens, then pull inside, hitting the button a second time.

The storm is slowly closed away behind us, and when I shut off the engine, a hushed sort of quiet surrounds us.

Quiet except for the snorting from the little demon.

"This is your house," she says quietly.

I just look at her and get out. "The garage is insulated, so if you want to camp out here and call your friend to figure out what the fuck is going on, feel free. But"—I pop open the door, allowing in a rush of cold air that cuts right through my clothes and sends her shivering again—"it's clearly not warm." I nod at the door to the house. "Come in when you're ready."

I climb out, slam the door behind me, and go to the trunk, pulling open the hatch, grabbing a couple of bags of groceries, and heading toward the house, but when I reach for the knob and start to open the door, I happen to glance back.

And she's sitting there.

A stunned look on her face.

"Fuck," I mutter, shoving into the kitchen and setting the bags on the counter.

I go back for the rest of them.

She's still sitting there. Head down, shoulders slumped.

Doesn't matter.

I load up, walk by the closed passenger side door, refusing to look through the glass as I move into the house and drop off my second load of groceries.

But when I start to turn away, start to peel off my now stifling layers of clothes in the heat of the house, some demented part of me takes over and pulls open the door. I pop my head out, telling myself it doesn't matter what I see out in the garage.

Only...she still hasn't moved.

"Christ," I mutter.

I stomp back out and yank open the passenger's side door, reaching for her.

Steve growls like the little demon he is, teeth clicking together as he lunges for my hand.

I bat him away, snag her arm. "Come on already," I snap.

She blinks, glances up at me. "It's your house."

"Yeah." I reach over her, scooping up Steve and tucking him under my arm like an unruly football as I unbuckle her seat belt. "We've established that."

Then, trusting that she'll follow since I've stolen the tiny demon, I turn for the house again.

Steve calms the moment I step over the threshold, nose working—and covering my arm in snot—as he takes in his surroundings.

"You pee or shit on something," I growl at him, "and you're out."

If it's possible for a dog to look at me derisively, this mutt has done it.

Calling my bluff in a second.

Little asshole.

But I just set him on the floor, let him go off and explore.

And probably chew up something valuable.

Because just like I can't leave a defenseless woman on the side of the road, I'm not going to put a tiny demon dog out in the snow during Snowmageddon.

Even *if* he looks like he ran into a wall.

SEVEN

THE DAMNED MAN has stolen my dog again.

Just plucked Steve out of my hold like my little pupper wouldn't try to bite him again, then had looked nonplussed when Steve had made the attempt.

Tucking my dog under one strong arm.

Walking away.

Walking into the house I am supposed to stay at for the foreseeable future.

With a man who clearly despises me.

And I can't even leave.

Because apparently, it's fucking Snowmageddon.

This is the point where I really wish my powers of letting things slide off my back hadn't been damaged, maybe permanently.

No problem that this man hates me for no reason.

No problem that my best friend arranged for me to stay in his house.

No problem that he's stolen my dog and my car slid off the road and...

I drop my chin to my chest, suck in a breath, then get out of his SUV, straightening my shoulders, marching into the house.

There's a storm outside. My car is stuck in a snowbank.

There's nothing I can do about either of those things.

At least I'm warm and safe—so long as Ella hasn't arranged for me to be temporarily staying with an ax murderer.

I take the two stairs that lead up into the house, turn the handle, and push inside, warmth immediately surrounding me like a cozy blanket. I exhale, something settling in my belly after the unnerving drive up into these mountains, just because I'm safe and warm and have a roof over my head.

Knowing that I'm not going to walk into the other room and find Ashley and George—

"Woof!"

I blink, shake the image that's burned into the backs of my eyelids out of my head, and move toward the sound, hustling through the narrow mudroom with deep green cabinets built into the walls. Hooks and drawers and shelves and solid front doors are pretty much a blur as I hurry into the other room.

If he's hurting my baby...

The kitchen has me halting for a heartbeat—it's huge with rich people appliances, as my friend Ella and I always joke—the fridge and dishwasher hidden behind wooden cabinet fronts. It's the type of space where I have to search to find the trash can because it's not white plastic—or, if you are *really* fancy—a stainless steel can shoved into the corner.

He even has one of those microwaves that's mounted into the bottom cabinets like a drawer instead of sitting on the counter, and *also* shoved into a corner, usually surrounded by half-eaten bags of chips and dog treats.

Or maybe that's just my life.

Because everything in this space is...pristine.

Expensive.

Way too fancy for me.

I reach for the stone countertop, run my fingers across the surface. It's sleek, clean, a crisp white that contrasts with the navy-blue cabinets. But then Steve barks again and I'm startled out of my stupor, tearing my eyes away from the large swathe of shining stone and hurrying out from the massive room.

But I don't go far before I find it hard to keep my feet moving again.

This time drawn in by a massive family room with a huge fireplace that's covered in stone from floor to ceiling.

"*Woof!*"

"Focus," I whisper, gaze whipping through the room, spotting the hallway on the other side of the enormous space and hurrying toward the sounds of Steve's outrage.

"Woof! Woof! *Woof!*"

I turn and look, spot Lake scowling at the end of the hall, just outside an open door.

And he's shirtless.

Sweet baby Jesus, I'd *never* seen a man with a body like that —not outside of an underwear ad anyway. It's like he's my own private peep show as I move closer. He's got his hands on his hips, expression brooding, jeans riding low and giving me a glimpse of the tight black waistband of his underwear.

Boxers? Briefs? Or boxer briefs?

Any of those options would be a gift.

Nothing at all would be better.

"Grr!"

Steve darts around him, and I see now that he has something gray in his mouth.

"Give it back," Lake snaps, bending, and...

Holy fucking shit.

That ass is...

Heaven. Hell. Twin handfuls—and then some—of sin.

"*Grr!*"

"Give it to me, you little—" His head shoots up and he glares at me over his shoulder. "Want to help me, or are you going to keep staring at my ass?"

Keep staring at his ass.

Hands down.

"*Nova!*" he barks.

I jerk my head away from said ass and focus on his face—though, in fairness, that's not much better, even with the beautiful features scrunched up into a fearsome scowl. "Yeah?"

"Want to give me a hand with your asshole of a dog?"

"Steve is not an asshole," I say, lifting my chin and elbowing my way past him, bending, intending to reach down and scoop up my baby—

Who decides right then...to be an asshole.

He darts away from me, straight in through that open door...and slips beneath the huge bed that takes up most of the far wall.

I sigh, gaze accidentally connecting with Lake's. He lifts his brows, as if to say, "See? Asshole."

But I don't engage, just move into the bedroom, kneel next to the bed, and peek beneath the mattress. "What does he have?"

A long pause.

Then, "My underwear."

"Boxers, briefs, or boxer briefs?"

Silence, hot and terse, and I want to melt into the hardwood floor right then and there. I actually said that out loud.

Out. *Loud.*

And because I am a glutton for punishment, my stare can't stay away from those pretty, pretty hazel eyes.

I get lost in them for several tense moments.

Then he flicks his brows up again, this time as if we're playing a game of Chicken.

And maybe we are.

"Boxer briefs," he says, tone a challenge.

Sweet baby Jesus. My favorite.

I can't stop my gaze from flicking down, from wondering exactly what that ass would look like clad in tight gray fabric. It would definitely put gray sweatpants to shame.

Focus.

On his ass? Or his penis lovingly cupped in skintight cotton?

"Woof!" Steve barks, focusing for me.

Because I know the tone of that bark.

It's the *I'm staying under this bed until I'm good and ready to come out* bark.

I bite back a wince and manage to climb to my feet. "It would probably be best if we let him come out on his own," I say. "Steve has a bit of...an underwear fetish."

"Don't we all," Lake says dryly, walking by me like he hadn't just made a joke.

He disappears behind another door, the wooden panel shutting with a decisive *click*.

I sigh, peek back beneath the bed. "Steve, baby. Come out with the mean man's underwear."

"Woof!"

Lake is right.

My dog *is* an asshole.

EIGHT

Lake

I COME out of the closet, shirt on and half expecting her to be stripped down naked and lying in my bed, legs spread, breasts perky and on display like an offering to the sex gods.

Or maybe that's just what I'm hoping for.

But there's no sign of her.

The dog, on the other hand...

The tiny demon growls when I bend and look under the bed, still going to town on my underwear.

"Pervert," I mutter.

"Grr."

Straightening, I shake my head and walk into the hall, looking for the troublesome woman. She's not there—something that's easy to see because the doors are all open and the rooms are all empty.

"Did you get your furniture repossessed or something?" she asks when I clear the hall, finding her standing in the center of my living room, arms akimbo, body slowly rotating as she surveys the space.

I did the same thing when this room was still a shell—all two-by-fours and rafters and exposed plywood.

Huge with lofted ceilings.

No sheetrock or insulation on the walls.

No electricity or lights or stone on the fireplace.

I just stood on the naked wood floor and looked up.

Sitting in the knowledge that this is more space than I ever dreamed of having in my name, let alone in my house, in one *room.*

But it's mine, and I've worked my ass off for it.

Even if there isn't any furniture filling the space.

So, I don't tell her and those judgy eyebrows that construction finished on this place all of a couple weeks ago, that I haven't yet had time to go furniture shopping because I was on the road with the team, and that while I might have shelled out big money for this house and all the expensive finishes and fancy perks inside, the designer can fuck off with her twenty-five-thousand dollar couch and rugs that are costly enough to fund a small country.

The reason I *have* money is because I don't drop it on shit like twenty-five-thousand-dollar couches and rugs that make my eyes water when I look at the price.

I don't tell Nova any of that.

"Your dog's a pervert," I say instead, marching by her and back into the kitchen, starting to sort through the groceries, putting the refrigerated and frozen stuff away, then shoving the rest onto empty shelves in the pantry, both of which are mostly stocked up, with the exception of the boxes of some staples like cereal and pasta and Twix I find space for. And not a bag of those small, pathetic fun-sized ones either, but a full box I grabbed from the checkout line because I might run out of cereal and milk and pasta, but I sure as shit am not going to run out of Twix.

I shove a bag of brown rice next to my stash then go back out into the kitchen, stopping when I spy the rest of the bags unpacked, my canvas shopping totes folded and nicely stacked, the rest of the items grouped by type.

Efficient.

Much better than me just grabbing shit and shoving it onto the shelves, and yeah, I'm talking to you, brown rice.

But I don't say anything, just ignore Nova standing there, and snag some basics I'm not too much of a bachelor to have picked up, and disappear back into the pantry.

She's still standing there, albeit not looking at me—eyes trained on the microwave, of all things—when I return for my third and then my fourth (and final) trip to fill up the shelves in the pantry.

And by fill up, I mean fill up all of three whole shelves.

Sighing, I flick off the light, wondering how much food it will actually take to make the space look lived in.

More than I can eat on my own, that's for certain.

If my mom got a single glimpse of how empty my pantry is, she would brave the storm and buy out the local grocery store and my shelves would be *packed.* I would be able to survive a hundred Snowmageddons if she was stocking my kitchen.

But she isn't.

Same as she isn't buying my furniture—something that's a good thing because it wouldn't stop at furniture. The shelves on either side of my kickass fireplace would be loaded with trinkets and tchotchkes, an explosion of crap and belongings as messy as her life, her marriage, her relationships.

I love her—she *is* my mom—but I don't want that shit in my life.

Nova pushes a button on the microwave.

I hear a soft beep and the drawer slides open.

"What are you doing?" I snap.

Her head jerks up, a guilty expression on her face, and I hear the quiet beep again, the drawer sliding back in. "Nothing," she says quickly.

Women.

I go back to my tried-and-true method of dealing with them.

Ignoring.

I ignore Nova as I head back into the garage to grab her shit from the back of my car. Only this time, she doesn't freeze and stare off into space, ignoring me right back. She follows me into the garage, too fucking close, that hint of cinnamon in my nose again.

More shit to fucking ignore.

I yank at the door handle, pull the metal panel wide, and lean in to grab her shit.

"Here," she says, trying to reach past me, "I've got—"

I straighten, nearly taking her head off with my elbow in the process.

Luckily, she ducks and I lift my arm in time to avoid disaster, but she's still all up in my fucking space. "Christ," I mutter, deliberately gripping her shoulders and setting her away from me. "Back up."

Hurt in those pine green eyes. "I'm just trying to help," she says softly.

"Yeah," I mutter. "That ship has long sailed."

Now the hurt disappears and she glares at me instead. "They're my things, and—"

I turn my back on her, reaching for the bags, looping the handles around my wrists, yanking them toward me, nearly taking her out a second time—only this time it's with the bags. "Are you *trying* to be annoying?"

"I'm *trying* to get my stuff," she snaps, lifting a hand and extending it in my direction, flicking her fingers a la *The Matrix*. "Give it here."

I'm not Agent Smith.

Or Malfoy.

I'm not going to be goaded into this fight.

Except, she doesn't let me go that easily.

She grabs at the bag, tries to tug it down my shoulder, reaches with her other hand and seizes the duffle hanging from my wrist.

"I've got it," I say, turning my body from hers and starting for the house.

She doesn't let go of either bag.

And I don't stop walking.

Rip.

I frown, not registering the sound as I take my next step—

RIP!

That I register, and though I stop walking, I don't do it in time.

The bag explodes—paper and photos and trinkets flying in all directions. I see a handwritten note flutter to the garage floor, watch as a journal bounces off my foot and is lost beneath the tool bench. A tin of thumbtacks drops, the top opening, the tiny pins scattering on the concrete.

It's not the bag of someone who's planning on spending a couple of days in the mountains.

It's a bag that's holding a person's life, their memories and hopes and dreams.

A picture drops onto the floor in front of my feet, and Nova gasps, leaping for it.

I reach for her. "Don't—"

But I'm not fast enough.

She drops to her knees.

Right on top of the tacks.

NINE

Nova

THE PAIN in my heart is so intense that, at first, I don't feel it everywhere else.

Then it begins to creep into other places. My knees. My shins. My palms.

I manage to tear my eyes from the photo of me, George, and Ashley, arms thrown over each other's shoulders, sand on our bare feet, waves and the setting sun in the background. I look down, and—

"Fuck."

But it's not me saying that, even though I'm the one with thumbtacks sticking out of my body.

I try to sit back on my heels, to find a way to stand, but I'm being jabbed all over.

And suddenly, there's an arm wrapping around my middle, lifting me straight up and out of the tangle of my belongings, going tight around my belly and leaving my arms and legs hanging loose as Lake starts walking forward.

Pictures and notes are scattered by his bare feet and he somehow avoids the tacks when clearly, I couldn't.

Not a surprise considering I hurtled myself toward them.

And then I'm not looking at the notes and pictures and memories.

I'm being carried into the house like I'm a stray piece of luggage.

Or Steve misbehaving.

"Sit," Lake mutters, setting me on the counter. "Stay," he adds, turning for the cabinets and pulling open a door. He grabs a bowl, a bunch of paper towels, and sets both at my side.

"I—"

Hazel eyes flicking to mine, their furious depths freezing me in place. "*Stay*," he says again, the gruff order at odds with the gentle way he wraps his fingers around my wrist and lifts my hand toward him.

"I'm not a dog," I mutter.

His eyes are on my palm. "You behave about as well as that demon you call a pooch."

Outrage in my belly. "Steve is not a demon."

He turns my hand over, still handling me in a gentle way that has my heart squeezing. "*Steve* is currently eating my underwear and won't come out from beneath my bed."

Since this is true, I don't acknowledge it, and instead say something even more dangerous, "Which brings us back to the fact that you only have one bed."

He carefully removes a pin from my palm, the slight pinch of pain almost immediately disappearing when he rubs his thumb lightly over the small hurt. "Who was in the picture?"

I still. "No one."

"You launched yourself at the photo like it contains the nuclear codes."

"It doesn't," I say.

Another twinge of pain as he removes another tack, setting it in the bowl next to me, the slight *plink* of the metal against ceramic not masking his question as he slips the photo from my fingers and moves on to my other palm. "Who's the dude in it?"

The slight ache from him continuing to remove the pins is nothing like the agony slicing through my heart. The last twenty-four hours have been the worst of my life—and I've had plenty of times before now where I thought that was true.

But none of those times top going home yesterday and finding Ashley and George—

I inhale, hold it for a second, then let it out silently, trying to allow that pain to slide down my back. To tuck it away. To move forward. *Forward.*

But it all flashes through me again, running to Ella's, pretending I was staying at her place for a girl's night, sneaking back this morning and packing my stuff.

Then the drive from hell.

And the snowbank.

And now playing pincushion and being tended by a big, brooding man who can't stand me.

And my dog is a pervert.

"He's no one," I say, using my pin-free hand to reach down and start plucking thumbtacks from my shin.

He moves to my other leg, begins doing the same, though he's still moving carefully, with precise movements that speak of control instead of my herky-jerky attempts to hurry toward escape.

Which bears the question: what else does he like to control?

I shiver, but deliberately don't meet his eyes when he looks at me for a long moment, just concentrate on the thumbtacks, on making sure they're out of me and landing in the bowl.

"Who's the chick in it?"

I snatch the photo, folding it in quarters and shoving it in my sweatshirt pocket. "No one."

Plink. Plink.

Those hazel eyes lift again.

Oh look, he has one of those fancy dishdrawer dishwashers. I saw them on HGTV once and thought they were the coolest thing ever. Of course, I'd been single then and liked the idea of not having to waste water by running a full cycle for a small load—

Of course, I was single now.

Alone.

Like always.

Blegh. I'm a strong, independent woman. I relish my alone-ness. I gild it and wear it like a fucking crown.

"No one, huh?" he asks, smoothing his hands over my legs, and I have to remind myself that he's just searching for pins.

That he doesn't like me.

But as those big, broad palms skate higher, I find it hard to remember that.

Especially with him so—

"Hey!" I exclaim, reaching for his arm but too damned slow.

He's snaked a hand into the pocket of my hoodie and snatched the photograph out, stepping back as he unfolds it. "Doesn't look like no one to me."

"Give it back—" I jump off the counter and immediately squeak in pain.

He curses again, scoops me back onto the counter, lifting my foot, peering at the bottom of my cheap sneaker. "Jesus," he mutters, plucking a tack out from the sole and dropping it into the bowl.

I loved these pushpins when I picked them out a couple of months back. They have cute sparkly butterflies topping the short silver tacks, and I used them on my bulletin board we had in our kitchen, used them to display the bright, happy moments I thought would fill my future.

Memories that are tarnished now.

Because of Ashley and George.

I loved them—the tacks *and* two of the most important people in my life—before today.

I hate them now—the tacks, *not* the people, though I want to—and not because they were poking at the bottoms of my feet, pricking into the skin of my hands, jabbing at me through my jeans, not because they hurt me.

I'm used to pain.

But I can't stand to stare at that glittering beauty and know it's all bullshit.

"Stay," Lake repeats, pressing on the tops of my shoulder, dropping the unfolded picture into my lap before retracing his steps out to the garage.

I stay—better than Steve ever has.

Because when Lake walks away, he's left the photograph on the counter and our faces are looking up at me—Ashley's, George's, my own—smiling like the future is limitless. And back then, it had been.

Now it's...

Different.

Painful.

Not what I want.

But what I have to accept anyway.

There's noise in the hall, and I look up, see Lake coming in with my bags over his shoulders, including my old duffle whose zipper had busted. It's open, and I can see from my spot on the counter that it's been filled back up, Lake having seen God knew what while shoving my shit back inside.

My nape prickles with embarrassment.

And shame.

But I shove it down, lean forward and search for any sparkling butterflies with sharp points ready to jab me.

When I see the floor is clear, I hop down, ignoring the sparks in Lake's eyes as I move toward him, clutching the photo in my hand. I open my mouth, intending to thank him—something I should have done a while ago, if I'm being honest, but just then, Steve runs down the hall, moving toward me with his adorable little smooshed-in face.

I scoop him up, clutch him close. "Lake—"

He sidesteps me, sets my stuff on the counter, turns back to face me.

I open my mouth again.

"I've got shit to do." An abrupt announcement as he turns away and disappears down the hall, the bedroom door shutting with a decisive *click*.

Leaving me alone.

With a painful, gaping wound in my chest.

Steve licks my chin.

"Right," I whisper, hugging him close and heading for my things. "Not alone. It's you and me, bud."

But not even Steve can heal that hole in my heart.

TEN

Lake

I'M A DUMBASS.

Pushing for details I don't want.

I recline back against my headboard, phone in my lap, the tape I need to review already in my team inbox.

Most of it is from the last road trip—a mix of plays from my line, plenty of fuckups I made, a few—and only a few—things that went right (because Coach doesn't much believe in positive reinforcement). My memory is such that I remember every fuckup with crystal clear accuracy. They're on replay in my head, the good stuff barely a blip in my thoughts—there and gone in a flash because I can't get better by focusing on all the things I do right.

I can only get better by fixing the bad shit.

I review some contract offers—sponsorships, promotional events for the vodka company I'm the face of, check the dates of a photoshoot for the underwear brand I work with (and that

Steve likes to destroy), and then I look through the workout plan that's been sent over for me—made in collaboration with the team's PT staff and my trainer, Ivy. She's a tiny redheaded dynamo who busts balls and has no problem standing up to grumpy hockey players *and* kicking our asses in the weight room. Since I won't have access to my normal gym if we're all snowed in, she's made some changes and modifications to my typical workout so I can exercise here at the house, with the limited equipment I have on hand, for the next couple of days.

And it better only be a couple of days, I think, sniffing the air and catching the faint scent of something cooking—

Or maybe something burning.

"Christ," I mutter, clicking the button to lock my phone and tossing it onto the nightstand. It lands with a clatter as I push out of bed, feet hitting the floor and—

I curse, sidestep immediately and glare down at the piece of my wet, chewed-up underwear.

"Fucking demon," I grumble, bending and snatching it up, marching to the bathroom and shoving it in the trash can. Then I'm out in the hall, the scent of burning getting stronger and—

I come to a halt at the mouth of the hall.

What. The. Fuck?

I'd left the kitchen organized. Clean. And now...

It's a fucking war zone.

I move toward the chaos, drawn like a rubbernecker at the scene of an accident.

A pan is smoking on the stove—on my new fucking stove I haven't even had the chance to use yet. Plates are stacked in the sink. Boxes are open and shoved haphazardly in different places in the kitchen—seemingly half of what I just stocked into the pantry...and some shit I haven't.

Hers?

I shake my head, take in the remainder of the chaos—this being caused by a small woman and a tiny demon dog.

"Just. Give it. *Back,*" she mutters from her hands and knees, shapely ass in the air, arm extended toward—

I frown.

My cabinets.

She flops to her side, feet curling as they press into the floor, body contorting. I can't see her top half because it's crammed into the corner cabinet, but I can see enough.

Ass. A strip of skin revealed by her shirt sliding up, showing off a sliver of soft, feminine curves.

But her voice—or maybe I should say, her groans and grunts —as she somehow shoves even more of herself into that cabinet is what has me stopping and staring.

My dick twitching.

"Steve!" she hisses and I blink, ignoring my cock because clearly, I haven't had enough quality time with it of late, and reconsider that face-down-ass-up position from a different perspective.

The demon dog.

Christ.

"What the fuck are you doing?" I snap.

Her body jerks and—

Thunk.

A blip of something—not my cock this time—slides through me, but I push that away as I move over to her, shoving my hand into the cabinet, positioning it between her head and the underside of the counter so she won't bump it a second time. Then I wrap my other arm around her, slide her out of the cabinet and take her spot.

Demon dog has something in his mouth again.

I sigh, maneuver out, flick off the knob of the stove, turning off the burner. Whatever has turned to a black tar-like substance in the bottom of the pan smells like ass, so I take it to the sink, load it up with soap and water.

Then I spin back to face Nova, who's rubbing the back of her head.

She catches me looking and winces.

"What's the demon dog have?"

A scowl. "Nothing."

Swear to fuck, this woman is contrary just to be contrary.

I lift an eyebrow. "That's why you were trying to play Oscar the Grouch?"

Her nose wrinkles. "He lives in a trash can."

"*He's* a puppet," I say. "And you're a liar. Is the pervert trying to eat another pair of underwear?"

"No," she snaps. "Steve's not used to his surroundings, you know. And he had a scare earlier and he's—"

"An asshole," I finish for her, reaching in, and, using my longer arms to my advantage, I pluck him out of the cabinet, figuring rightly that with his mouth occupied, he won't be able to sink his tiny fangs into me.

He snuffs and snorts, but he doesn't bite me as I plunk him into Nova's lap and shut the cabinet door.

"What does he have this time?" I ask, leaning back against the counter as she wrestles it out of his mouth.

Her eyes come to mine then dart away, but she doesn't answer as she keeps struggling with the dog, trying to simultaneously open his mouth and reach in to retrieve—

He coughs and—

Splat.

Something bright blue and black ends up in a puddle of whatever fucking disgusting liquid the dog spits up. Nova reaches into it like it's no big deal, extracting what had been in the demon's mouth and lifting it, slimy strings still attached.

I gag.

She looks at me and rolls her eyes. "Tell me you're a prima donna without telling me you're a prima donna." She carries the object over to the sink, turning on the water and spending enough time cleaning it off that I know it has nothing to do with *her* being a prima donna and everything to do with her dog being disgusting.

Case in point?

The tiny demon licking up his own...*fluids.*

I gag again but reach for the roll of paper towels on the counter, showing how much of a *non*-prima donna I am by clearing up the mess in the face of the growling, snotting beast.

At least he doesn't try to bite me.

I dump the dirty paper towels into the trash, ignoring the sight of a blood-stained one that tells me she tended to her wounds while I lounged in bed watching hockey videos.

The dog glares at me.

I glare right back.

Until I realize that the water is still running, and Nova's shoulders are slumped.

Even Steve realizes that something is up, whining softly and moving to the sink, leaning against her leg with a soft huff.

Tiny demon with a soft spot for its owner.

The contact startles her and I watch as she wipes the blue and black object on her pant leg then shoves it into her hoodie pocket. A second later, she's pushing her sleeves up and going to town on the pan.

"I was trying to cook you dinner," she says. "And Steve was being..." A sigh. "Steve."

"I don't need you to cook for me."

She glances over her shoulder, eyes narrowing. "I'm sure you're fully capable," she says. "But I had food in my bag that needs to be used today and you're letting me stay and"—a quiet sigh—"you rescued me from the side of the road."

"So...what?" I ask dryly. "You're repaying my hospitality with a meal?"

Her brows dragged together. "Why do you sound like that?"

I scowl. "Like what?"

"Like the thought of that makes you want to suck lemons."

ELEVEN

Nova

"I DON'T KNOW what that means," he says.

I wave a hand in the general direction of his face. "It means that you look like *that*." His sour lemon scowl deepens as I reach for the sponge (still in the plastic wrapping), open it, and start scrubbing at the burned butter in the bottom of the pan.

I do this fast and furiously.

Mostly because it takes my mind off the damaged butterfly in the pocket of my hoodie.

Steve really is an asshole.

Teeth marks in the wings. One of the tiny diamonds missing. The metal scuffed up.

My heart convulses. My eyes sting.

Just another thing to chalk up to this shitty ass day.

But the good thing is that all my furious scrubbing means that the pan comes clean relatively easily and, before long, I'm dumping the extra water into the basin of the sink and searching the drawers for a dish towel to dry it.

"What are you doing?" he asks sharply.

"Looking for a towel."

"Why?" Suspicious now.

"So I can stuff it into your mouth as I murder you," I say, looking up and hefting the pan like I'm getting ready to swing it at his head. "I'll have to get a stool to reach your thick skull with this first, though."

His eyes narrow and he marches out of the room.

I'm heading for the paper towels when he comes back with a huge plastic shopping bag in his hands, reaching in and pulling out a pack of towels still with the plastic hanger secured at the top. "Here," he says, shoving it at me.

I look at the towel then up at him. "You're not going to wash it first?"

"It's a towel. It's clean."

"Um," I say, gently placing the set of plain blue cotton on the counter and reaching for the paper towels. Not ecofriendly, but at least we won't get cholera. "It's not clean. It's been in a factory and then it's been packed in boxes and shipped to stores and then unpacked and hung on the hooks in said stores while shoppers take it off and look at them before putting them back or little kids with their grubby hands touch them before someone like you buys them—at which point they are then put on a conveyor belt and touched by a cashier and a bagger before they finally end up here." I shake my head. "So, not clean. Very *not* clean and you should wash them before you use them."

He lifts a brow. "You have a problem with my towels when you just stuck your hand into dog throw up?"

I glare, hating that he has a point. "No," I snap. "I'm just smart and think things through and—" Here I falter because that's not me at all, because I never really thought about this stuff until my sister gave me the same long spiel enough times for it to stick because *she's* the germaphobe and—my heart convulses—she's not in my life any longer. "And it makes sense to wash stuff like this before you use it."

His hazel eyes held mine for a long moment. "Do you operate a washing machine better than a stove?"

"What?"

"Do you know how to use a washing machine?"

I huff out a breath. "I think my rant about using clean towels indicates I do."

"Good." He reaches toward me, snags the pan from my hands then shoves the towels at me. "You wash"—a nod to the huge bag—"I'll cook."

*** *** *** ***

I DON'T REALIZE until I'm halfway through my meal of brown butter pasta with bits of broccoli and peppers and blackened chicken breast and a dash of red pepper—a meal that's significantly fancier than the Rice-A-Roni and ranch chicken I was going to make.

Not that mine wasn't going to be tasty.

It's just...me.

Maybe a little bland, forgettable. It fills a need if necessary, absolutely, but it doesn't dance along the taste buds, doesn't make them sing.

It's halfway through this meal—me plunked onto the counter again, Lake leaning on the opposite side of it, conversation stilted and ringed with insults, though he doesn't seem to be putting much effort into them, when Steve looks up at me with his big puppy eyes and whines, reminding me—

He hasn't eaten dinner yet.

And he may have been a bit of a jerk since arriving in Lake's house, but he's still my baby boy.

And he's hungry.

I set my plate to the side, glance down for any stray tacks—because I've decided today is the day where I can't be too careful—then hop down, moving to the other side of the massive island, where my stack of bags sits.

My clothes.

My belongings from the apartment, everything that means something, everything I couldn't leave behind.

Steve's bag of blankets and toys.

Steve's...

I frown and look around, searching as though the tote bag where I had his water and food bowls, his bag of kibble, his treats and the supplements that make his coat shiny is going to magically appear in the empty house.

Then bend and look under the counter, thinking it could be in the little opening where barstools would go—if the man had them.

Which he doesn't.

Which also means I have a clear view of the space beneath and can see the tote bag isn't there.

Also, I have to be real, if that food bag was anywhere in the vicinity of Steve's reach, he would have been headfirst in it, snarfing down the entire package of kibble, eating until he made himself sick.

Instead of sitting like a good boy, whining up at me with big puppy dog eyes.

"What are you doing?" Lake asks.

I straighten, nearly bonking my head again. Thankfully for my smarting scalp, I stop in time, carefully maneuvering out as I say, "Nothing." Then I'm snagging my plate and separating the chicken from the pasta. I stack a couple pieces of broccoli with it too because Steve's a chonky boy and can use some veggies. Then I start cutting them up into bite-sized pieces.

I'll have to get back to my car tomorrow, get him some real food.

Tonight though, I reach down and start giving him my chicken.

And broccoli.

And then some of my pasta because he's looking up at me with big, soulful eyes and my chonky boy is still hungry and—

"That doesn't look like nothing," Lake says, and swear to God, for such a big man, he moves quickly and silently and all ninja-like.

I jump, nearly upending my plate—something Steve would have loved—then look up at Lake guiltily.

Is he going to get pissed at me for feeding his masterpiece to an *asshole?*

"Don't you have food for him?" he asks.

"I do," I snap. "It's"—and just as quickly, my anger fades, worry invading, taking its place—"I must have left it in the back of the car."

His brows tug together.

"I'm just giving him mine," I say quickly, guilt pooling in my belly. "I'm not going to get more and give it to him."

TWELVE

Lake

I SCOWL.

Does she seriously think I'm going to get pissed about giving the mutt a few scraps of chicken?

I yank the plate from her hand, stomp over to the pan and scoop some more onto it. Then I reach into the cabinet, grab out a bowl, and pick through the pasta for some chicken to feed the damned demon dog.

He snuffles at my feet, clearly knowing where the food is and being impatient about it. I look down, clock those rolls on his back and neck, and decide to throw in some broccoli too.

Dog needs some greens, some exercise, and some manners.

I can help with the first tonight.

Tomorrow, I can haul his fat ass to Nova's car and get him his damned food.

Narrowing my eyes at him in a silent warning to eat his vegetables, I set the bowl on the floor then walk back over to Nova, shoving the plate at her. "Eat as much as you want."

She has tits and ass, but her face is drawn, her collarbones jut out above the slouchy neck of her sweatshirt. Plus, I lifted her, carried her into the house. She's light as a fucking feather.

She looks—and feels—like she hasn't had enough food in... maybe ever.

And fuck that.

The pan is full enough. There's plenty of food in my house. We're not about to go full Donnor party. She can have seconds. Hell, even the demon dog can too.

I shake my head, fill up my own plate for a second time, and glare at her until she starts eating again.

"Were you just nice to me?" she asks softly.

My eyes flick up, catch on those damned collarbones again. "No," I mutter.

We fall silent—well, silent except for the sound of the dog's slurping and our forks hitting the ceramic and the soft sigh she lets out when her plate is clear.

Somehow mine is too, so when she reaches out, says, "You cooked, I'll do the dishes," I let her take the plate and walk away from me.

"Who's in the picture?" I blurt.

Like a fucking idiot.

She freezes, the plates hovering over the sink for a moment before she sets them in the basin and turns on the water, almost drowning her out when she says, "My ex-boyfriend and my sister."

There's way too much information in that short sentence, in those few words.

They're screaming out for someone to ask more about them —for *me* to ask since I'm the only one here. But I can't bring myself to actually form the words.

Then I don't need to.

"I found them together in my bed," she whispers.

I blink. Because that is pretty much the last thing I expect her to say.

"Yesterday afternoon."

I blink again.

Okay, I stand corrected. *That* is pretty much the last thing I expect her to say.

"I went home early because I got fired—"

Fuck.

"And there they were, naked and having such a good time that they didn't notice me." All the while, the water is running and Nova is scrubbing at the dishes and her shoulders are going higher and higher, creeping toward her ears. "The lease wasn't in my name," she whispers and I have to move closer to hear the rest of her words, "so I went back this morning, packed my stuff, and left." She turns her head to the side. "There's no point staying where I'm not w-welcome."

It's that break in her voice that does it.

I reach past her, turn off the water, and do something supremely stupid.

I pull her into my arms and I hug her.

She sniffs but doesn't do as I half expect—doesn't burst into tears, doesn't collapse against me, doesn't do the typical M.O. of a hysterical woman. She just stands there in the circle of my arms for eight seconds (*exactly* eight because I'm counting) and then she awkwardly pats my back once before stepping away, head turned to the side, eyes diverted. "Right," she says. "That was weird—"

I scowl, nape going hot, stomach twisting.

"And unexpectedly nice." She clears her throat, keeps her gaze turned away as my scowl deepens. "Thanks." Her voice drops. "I'll just finish the dishes and—"

A yawn.

Getting late.

Thank God.

The sooner this night is over the better.

Because it means she's another moment closer to getting the fuck out of my house, leaving me to my peaceful existence that's devoid of women—which means it's also devoid of the trouble and drama and bullshit they like to sprinkle into my life.

I have friends who are happily paired off, and once I thought that might be my future too.

But I've learned.

That shit isn't real.

There are always hooks and barbed wire and concrete shoes and fucking *angst*.

My mom taught me. Olivia—

Well, she could have taught my mom more than a few things.

Luckily, I learned that fun little tidbit about her in time. And just like with hockey, I fix shit and never repeat my mistakes.

Never.

Olivia's gone.

My mom lives on the opposite coast—thus, is relegated to occasional phone calls and surprise visits.

So, my friends can enjoy their delusions of grandeur when it comes to happily ever afters and fidelity and relationships that last longer than a viral TikTok.

I'll enjoy my peace—

"Woof!"

However much of it I can carve out, anyway. I glare at the tiny demon, but instead of growling at me or attempting to gnaw off my ankle for a second time, he just sniffs at my foot and licks my sock.

Apparently, the key to the tiny demon's heart is food.

He's still ugly.

And an asshole.

I grab the rest of the dishes, help her load them into the dishwasher and then stand there awkwardly as she dries her hands on a paper towel. "Do you have a leash?" I ask when she flicks her eyes to mine and away for the fourth time.

Her brows draw together. "Why?" she asks suspiciously.

"The demon has to go out and do dog stuff before bed, doesn't he?"

Her expression clears. "Oh," she whispers. "Right. It's—" She moves to a duffle that's full of toys and extracts a leash and harness, clipping both on Steve with no small amount of effort. Apparently, the little asshole likes his walks.

"If you go through the garage," I tell her, "there's a side door that has a covered pathway where he can do his business."

She frowns up at me.

"What?" I ask shortly.

"You're being nice again," she mutters, "and I don't like it."

Wow.

"You've known me all of a couple of hours."

"Yeah," she says. "And I think that's told me enough."

Jesus Christ.

"Just walk the dog or don't," I growl. "But I'm not cleaning it up if the demon shits or pisses in my house."

Her deep green eyes on mine. "That's more like the Lake I know." She scoops up the end of Steve's leash, turns away. "Come on, baby," she croons.

And she walks out the door.

Swear to God, the tiny demon sticks his tongue out at me as he prances through the door behind her.

THIRTEEN

Nova

GETTING my dog to use Mother Nature as his bathroom is a struggle on a normal day.

Squirrels and shadows, wind picking up and sending a plastic bag crinkling across the road. Other dogs. Cars. Bikes. People. Kids. Frisbees. *Anything* is a distraction.

Add in snow falling rapidly, the flakes gathering into huge piles that are larger than Steve and are shifting in the cold wind that is cutting right through my clothes, and my pupper is *not* a happy camper.

He looks up at me and whines.

"We can't go in until you use the potty," I tell him.

He whines again, puppy eyes going even puppier, but I stand strong on this one. My pooch might be a pain in the butt who is energized by causing trouble, but I refuse to let him get away with using the bathroom anywhere but outside.

He can't sit or roll over and he's a terror on a leash who won't give me his paw, even if I bribe him with a thousand treats, but he hasn't had an accident inside since he was four months old.

That streak isn't ending today.

Mostly because I don't want to see what Lake's eyes will look like if Steve leaves him that kind of present.

I mean, I kind of do because Lake brings out the devil in me.

But my dog parenting standards can't be put aside just because I want to bust someone's chops.

Tempting though, especially when Steve looks at the snow falling and then back at me and whimpers softly.

I shore up my spine, put on my grumpy face, and say, "I'm not budging, love bug. We can stand here and turn into popsicles, but you have to go to the bathroom outside."

Steve moans, but he finally stops shooting those puppy dog eyes my direction and starts sniffing at the pile of snow.

Eventually, he does his business and shivering, we make our way inside. I stomp my snow off as we go, trying my best to not make a mess inside, considering the man doesn't have furniture or rugs and apparently uses towels without washing them first.

Speaking of that, I let Steve off his leash and move the towels to the dryer.

Then I walk back into the kitchen.

And...this is where I ran out of steam.

Because the man didn't have any furniture. Not a rug. Not a couch. Not a corner-mounted dinette set I can curl up in. No furniture in the common areas of the house or in the rooms. No furniture anywhere...except his bedroom.

Well, shit.

I nibble at my lip, decide that I'll wait for the towels to dry and make myself a nest in front of the fireplace with my clothes and those warm towels. Steve will cuddle up with me and maybe I can convince the grumpy Lake to let me borrow a pillow. He has about twenty of them on that giant bed of his.

Okay, great.

Good plan.

I nod to myself, start to take a step forward, and—

"He do his business?"

My head jerks toward the hall, watching Lake walk toward me like he's the hero in a teen romantic movie, shirtless, muscled, and no way he's under eighteen or what I'm feeling should send me straight to hell.

Then he's standing a couple of feet away from me, the overhead lights gilding his skin, turning him into a Greek statue.

I exhale when he stops, bending to scoop up Steve, who's apparently tabled his aggression toward Lake and starts kissing his chin.

Lake scowls, holds him away. "You were licking up your own vomit not that long ago, dude," he says. "I don't want kisses."

Steve squirms as he tries to get closer.

Likely because he's now identified Lake as another potential source of food.

Hazel eyes come back to mine, a dark brow lifts. "Yeah," I say, "he did his business."

A nod. "Good. Come on."

He turns, starts walking back across the room, Steve still in his arms. I watch him go for a moment—because, holy hell, the back view is as good as the front—but then I realize he's walking away from me again with Steve in his arms.

For all that the man calls my dog a demon, he certainly walks off with him a lot.

"Wait," I say, hurrying after them. "Where are you—"

But Lake's already at the far end of the hall, walking

through the wide door of his bedroom by the time I start making my way to the mouth of the opening.

"I—" I whisper before breaking off with a shake of my head, hurrying after them, walking into the bedroom, and stopping.

Not because Steve is making trouble.

He hasn't stolen a pair of underwear, hasn't crawled under the bed.

He's currently turning circles at the foot of the bed, getting comfortable in that quintessential dog way—spinning around and around, digging in the blankets, spinning some more, and then finally collapsing with a huff.

Lake shakes his head then disappears behind a door while I stand there, flat-footed and on edge, wondering what's come over him. The last thing I expected is for him to offer me up his bed—and certainly not without a lick of a complaint.

Perhaps Steve is growing on him.

Or, more likely, he feels sorry for me.

I pause, toes digging into the soles of my shoes, not liking that thought at all, hating how it makes me feel, but I don't have much time to sit in that shame because then Lake is out from behind that door, walking across the room, his arms full of blankets.

"I can't let you give me your bed," I say softly.

He stops, frowns. "Who says I'm giving you my bed?"

Now *I* frown. He's got blankets in his arms and my dog is settled in his bed and he told me to follow him down the hall.

If I'm not sleeping in his bed then what the hell am I doing standing here?

"I—" My gaze goes from Steve, already snoring, to him, his arms full of blankets, and back to the bed. "No one, I guess," I whisper.

He tilts his head to the side then shakes it as though I'm the most confounding creature on the planet—and I suppose to him, I am. He drops the armful of blankets and sheets onto the bed and turns to fully face me, frown deepening, hazel eyes sparking.

"You think you're going to sleep in my bed."

"I—" I shake my head again. "Never mind. I'll just grab Steve and—"

"*You're* not sleeping in it," he says.

"Yeah," I mutter. "Reading that loud and clear—"

It'll be me and my clothes and towels and maybe Steve if I can coax him from the bottom of the bed.

Fine.

Whatever.

I can deal.

I always do.

I start to turn away.

"We're sharing."

FOURTEEN

Lake

SHE SPINS AROUND, mouth dropping open. "Wh-what?"

I went from feeling generous and a little bit soft about this woman who'd clearly had a shit twenty-four hours to being annoyed.

In a second.

Or maybe defensive because I'm a dumb fuck who was feeling soft about a woman I didn't know—and had been about to offer to sleep on the floor in another room while she took my bed. But then she'd gone ahead and proved she's a woman who's exactly like the other women in my life, present and past.

So, I'm a dumbass for that blip in the space-time continuum, for that moment of soft.

Now, I'm moving on.

Soft is gone. Asshole is back.

She's going to hate me.

The thought is crystal clear and piercing through my brain.

Whatever.

It doesn't matter if she likes me—or if her little dog does too.

In fact, it's better if they both despise me.

Which is why I double down. "You can either share"—I wave an arm at the bed, an eastern king because I'd bought absolutely the biggest mattress I could get my hands on—"or you can find another flat surface in this house to sleep on."

"I wasn't trying to take your bed," she says quietly.

I lift one shoulder, drop it. "Sure seems like it."

She glowers at me. "I just thought you were going to offer and it's—" Her teeth clamp together before she shakes her head and huffs out a breath. "Never mind." A sigh, chin lifting. "Am I allowed to take one of those pillows and maybe a blanket?"

Asshole, that's me.

I nod tersely, and she moves toward the top of the bed, taking one of the pillows—taking *my* pillow, as in the only one I've slept on to date, as in my expensive as shit pillow that I bring on road trips and don't let *anyone* use. "Not that one," I say before I can stop myself.

She turns, and if looks can kill, I would be dead before my big body hits the floor.

Then she sighs again, extending her hand toward the other pillow. "Is this one acceptable?"

I nod.

She slowly grabs it, eyes on me, as though waiting for me to protest again. When I don't, she moves to the foot of the bed, places her hand on a blanket, lifts her brows at me. I keep my mouth shut, and she picks it up. "Come on, Steve," she says softly.

I expect the tiny demon to ignore her, and though he makes a soft sound of protest, he still gets to his feet, jumps down, and follows her out of the room.

I watch her go, stare at the open door for long minutes, expecting her to come back in.

To make a pass.

To throw a fit.

But she doesn't.

And eventually, the cold seeps in and I creep into the hall.

No sneak attack by a hysterical woman.

No sight of the woman at all.

Until I make it into the family room and spy a pile of blankets and clothes and towels in front of the fireplace.

Which has a pathetically small fire inside it.

Christ.

It's like she got it started with the three logs that were in the basket next to the fireplace itself when I have a full rack of firewood on the side of the house—only she wouldn't know that, would she?

She probably figured that's all the firewood I have and—

My eyes catch on the basket, see there's still a piece of wood remaining.

She didn't use all of it.

She saved one piece.

"Christ," I mutter. This woman is going to be the death of herself. Sighing, I move quietly past her—and the mutt who slits open his eyes and growls softly at me—carefully shoving my feet into my boots and opening the front door. I slip out into the storm, walk to the rack, fill my arms with wood, and bring the logs back over to the fireplace.

She's either an Oscar-worthy actress, or her shitty day has tired her out because she doesn't move as I unload the wood, which isn't a quiet task even though I'm trying to make it one. I pile on some logs, wait for the flames to catch, then stack the rest in the basket.

But as I turn back for the bedroom, I see that she's shivering.

"Fucking hell," I say, grinding my teeth together as I go back down the hall and grab a few more blankets, grab my expensive ass pillow.

I carry them out and drop them to the floor next to her, debating.

Then because I'm fucking tired and I've carried them this far. I shake one out, tuck it around her, trying to cushion her from the cold, hard floor. I spread another over the top of her, and then one more, the heat of the flames already starting to warm the space. Since she's already rolled off the pillow, I prop my good one beneath her, ignoring Steve's warning growl, then start to head back to the bedroom.

But, growl or not, my gaze goes back to the tiny demon dog, and I see he's burrowed closer to Nova, as though seeking out her warmth.

I stop, head dropping back, eyes on the ceiling, shoulders heaving with a sigh. "You are a fucking idiot, Lake Jordan."

But, *idiot* or not, I stride back down the hall, rip my spare blanket from the foot of my bed and I carry it back to the family room.

And I spread it out over the demon pup.

Who sighs and closes his eyes.

I am a fucking idiot.

I still stop and shift the grate, settle one more log on top of the growing flames, then make sure the metal mesh is secure so no dangerous sparks will escape before heading back down the hall.

Into my bedroom.

Closing the door softly behind me.

Then opening it an inch, just in case I need to hear—

"Dumb," I mutter and close it.

But I leave the handle unlocked.

And only then do I go into the bathroom and brush my teeth, do my business.

I crawl into bed, pull the blankets up.

Sleep is a long time coming.

FIFTEEN

I WAKE up with an aching hip, a sore neck, and...warm.

I frown because I distinctly remember feeling cold just before exhaustion had risen up and claimed me.

Steve must be sprawled out on my chest, slowly suffocating me as he's wont to do.

It's the fatal flaw in his life plan of causing as much trouble and eating as much food as possible—if he kills his owner, he can still do plenty of the first, but the last will be difficult.

Unless he starts noshing on my dead body.

And I hold no false notions about him feeling bad about losing me—he'd definitely snack on a dead me, especially if my chonky boy got the hungries.

A bead of sweat starts to drip down between my breasts.

I wince, scrub at it, knowing this is far too much dead-body talk for whatever time in the morning it is—well, really, my dog eating my corpse is too much dead-body talk for any time of the day. As for the hour, I'm not sure what it is, aside from early, based on how tired I still am.

Though, that might be depression speaking.

Exhaustion pulling at every limb, the urge to pull the blankets over my head, to sleep for a thousand hours, every muscle aching.

Either that or I'm tired and sore because I'm sleeping in a nest of clothes on a cold hardwood floor.

"Right," I whisper, peeling open my lids and blinking until my eyes adjust to the light...

From the fireplace.

From a much larger fire than I built.

I frown. Turn my head to the side, doing more blinking when I spy the under-cabinet lights are also on. And...cue more frowning.

I *know* I turned those off before I went to bed.

Same as I know that my fire hadn't had a pile of logs on it, that the basket hadn't been full to the brim with firewood.

That I hadn't been warm.

"What the hell?" I whisper, taking in the blankets—the *extra* blankets that had been draped over me and the...extra pillow behind my head that smells spicy and male and far too much like Lake for my own peace of mind.

I lift my head and Steve grunts in protest, his little head poking out from a blanket that I definitely hadn't tucked over him.

Because I only grabbed the one blanket last night.

The fire. The blankets. The pillow. Steve wrapped up like an oversized burrito.

I either have a temperature fairy—or Lake has proven his humanity again.

Sighing, I sit up, immediately shivering against the cool air, but it also helps wake me up. I need to focus, figure out what I'm doing with my life.

I *need* to figure out what the fuck Ella had been thinking, sending me on a collision course with the grumpy Lake.

For that, I need my phone.

It's probably dead, but I have a charger in my purse.

I'll track both down and plug it in, wait for the bare minimum of charge, and then yell at my friend.

There. Good plan.

Mentally, I clap my hands together and say, *Break!*

But I'm moving slowly as I force myself from the blankets, as I slide carefully away from the burrito that is Steve.

My purse is on the counter, but my phone isn't inside.

And neither is the charger.

"What—"

But I don't finish the question because then I spy my cell *and* the charger—plugged in at the other end of the island.

Something I definitely didn't do last night.

Something that makes butterflies fill my stomach.

Lake.

It doesn't matter.

I exhale, round the counter, and unplug my cell, looking at the screen and seeing a bevy of missed calls and text messages.

But only one is from the person I want to talk to.

I delete the unwanted texts, the voicemails, then jab at Ella's text chain.

Please tell me you got laid.

A bolt of outrage, my shoulders tensing, annoyance gathering in my belly.

Was she fucking *serious*?

I do some more jabbing, this time at her name in my contacts list.

The call rings once before my friend's voice comes onto the other end. "Please tell me that you climbed that giant hockey player like a tree and got stuck on his *branch* like a naughty, naughty pussy cat."

Was. She. *Fucking*. Serious?

"You've lost your mind, Daniela," I snap.

My friend clicks her tongue, sighs sadly. "That's a no then."

"You told me it was your brother's house," I grind out.

"Well, for all intents and purposes, Lake is *like* Knox's brother. And Knox *is* my brother, so..." She trails off then pops her lips. "Ipso facto my brother."

"I don't think you'd get arrested for fucking Lake," I say. "So table your ipso facto, and tell me what the hell you were thinking? Was I just going to use that spare key on the porch, walk in on a man I don't know and be like, *Surprise! I'm here to crash at your place!*"

A beat then, "Well...yeah," she says.

I sigh, rub at the ache in my forehead. "You've lost your mind."

Ella's voice softens. "We needed to get you out of there. Knox said that Lake is a good guy and that his new house is huge. Plus, it's in Lake Tahoe. You love being up in the mountains. I just figured it would be as good a place as any when you told me what happened with George—"

I wince and she somehow picks up on that through the airwaves, or maybe she just knows me far too well.

"—with he-and-she-who-must-not-be-named," she corrects and I know *her* well enough that I can picture her biting at her bottom lip before straightening her shoulders, lifting her chin. "Lake is pretty and successful and he's known for keeping things light and easy and commitment-free. I just figured some horizontal fun time would be good for you after—"

"It's been a day, Ells," I say, heart squeezing but annoyance fading. Because she's trying to look after me. "It's too soon, even for my free love and easy breezy soul."

A long pause. "Right," she whispers, and I know there's more lip-biting commencing. "I'm sorry."

"I know, honey," I tell her softly.

Another moment of quiet. "Is the house at least nice?"

"It's"—I pause and look around at the wood and stone, the painted cabinets, the hand-scrapped floors, the wide windows behind which the snow falls in a flurry—"incredible."

A relieved breath. "There's that at least."

"And what about the room you stayed in?" she asks. "Is it luxurious? Knox says he's spent an ass-ton of money on the place."

"Is ass-ton a precise measurement?"

She giggles and I relax, annoyance gone, worry that *she's* worried fading, and settle into a dishfest with my best friend. I glance at my nest of pillows and blankets, towels and clothes, and tell her, "The house is empty. Well, *nearly* empty," I amend, though this is less shocking now that she's told me this place is new. "He has a stocked kitchen and food in the pantry, a few bags of towels and other stuff from the home goods store, and one bedroom has a bed, but there's nothing else."

A beat. "Nothing?"

"Nothing."

Her exhale rattles through the speaker. "So, my brother sent you up to a house in the mountains with a famous hockey player who's well known for the size of his *branch* and his skills wielding it—"

Probably, I should have realized that Lake is a hockey player sooner.

He's huge. And that *ass*.

But I haven't been on my game since I walked in on my sister and boyfriend fucking so…

"*—and* it only has one bed?"

"Yup," I say dryly.

She cackles. "This is too good."

"No," I say, despite the fact that I've stepped out of the pages of a romance novel. "It is, in fact, *not* good. You and Knox sent me up to Tahoe to the house of a grumpy hockey player who has no interest in sharing his space with me and Steve during Snowmageddon."

"What's a Snowmageddon?"

Yeah, see? I'm not alone in not knowing what the hell Snowmageddon is.

"A giant blizzard that means my car is currently stuck in a snowbank and the likelihood of me being able to leave said grumpy hockey player's house is nil," I tell her. "At least for a couple of days."

Silence then a guilty laugh. "Shit, Nov, we did you dirty."

"Yup, that I know."

"Was his bed at least comfortable?"

"No clue," I say. "He slept in the bed. *I* slept on the floor."

A gasp. "Seriously? What a jerk."

Except, he gave me that pillow he was attached to the night before and covered me in blankets and rolled Steve up like an extra-large burrito…

I open my mouth to tell her that, but suddenly there's a commotion at the front door—a flurry of wind and snow and noise.

I jerk my head up, watch Lake shuffle inside.

"Uh, Ells, honey," I say instead. "I've got to go."

"Everything okay?"

"Yeah," I say distractedly as I see him waver on those tree trunks of legs. "I'll fill you in later."

"Okay," she says. "But don't forget, jerk or not, if you change your mind about it being too soon, he supposedly knows how to use that branch of his and can—"

"Bye," I say.

"Multiple orgasms!" she calls.

I blink, shake my head, and click off. "Lake?" I say, standing up from the stool, taking a step toward him.

Just as he slips and eats serious shit on the hardwood floor.

SIXTEEN

Lake

FUCKING *OUCH*.

"Oh my God!" Footsteps pounding toward me.

"*Woof!*" Nails clicking on the floor.

My ass. Sweet Jesus, my ass.

"Lake, oh my God, are you okay?"

I get my elbows under me, open my mouth to tell her to be careful.

It's too late.

I watch her feet slip out from beneath her and she starts to fall, seemingly in slow motion as I roll toward her, trying to break her fall—

I do.

Just not the way I intended.

I move.

She falls...

"*Oof!*" I grunt.

...and lands right on top of me.

"*Woof!*" Steve launches himself at us, tiny demon paws landing on my stomach.

"*Oof,*" I grunt again.

"Shit," Nova says, pushing against my chest hard enough that I grunt a third time, but then she's scrambling off me, trying to corral Steve who's whining and snotting and licking at my chin with horrific doggy breath. "Steve, baby"—she grabs at the pooch, but he just launches himself at me with renewed vigor—"get off, I need to see if Lake is—"

I sit up, ass still hurting. "Are you all right?"

She frowns. "Lake, you just took a spill and then I crushed you and Steve—"

I reach forward, cup her jaw, forcing her to stop sputtering and panicking and just look at me. "Are you hurt?"

Silence, except for the sounds of Steve's grunts and grumbles.

Then she shakes her head. "No." A wince. "You broke my fall."

"Good." I shove the dog at her, move slowly to my feet and over to the front door, shutting it with some effort, closing out the wind and snow that are being blown into the entryway.

"I'll get some towels," she says, standing too quickly and nearly ending up on her ass again.

I snag her arm, steady now that I'm expecting the slick surface. I grew up with blades strapped to my feet, I can navigate ice and a wet floor...most of the time, anyway. "Careful," I say, guiding her away from the wet puddle gathering near the door, thinking I should have bought some rugs to go with my towels.

And furniture since this woman slept on a pile of blankets instead of a bed.

Not my problem.

So why does it feel like it is?

Steve launches himself out of her arms and I dart forward, catching him before his dumb, tiny demon ass hits the floor. "Careful," I tell him, but he doesn't seem to hear the admonishment at all as he crawls up my chest and tries to lick at my face again.

Nova giggles softly, and I freeze as she steps away, not sure if I've heard her laugh yet.

If I have, it hasn't been like that—hasn't been soft and sweet and...beautiful, so fucking beautiful it's like a clawed hand gripping my heart, forcing me to remain motionless, so beautiful I'm stuck in place as she pats Steve's back and says, "I'll get you some ice and grab some towels to clean up the mess."

I open my mouth to tell her I'm fine, but before I can, she's moving off, bustling to the pile of blankets, extracting a towel, and making me feel like an ass all over again as she carries it back over to me.

I reach for it, but she moves behind me, wraps it around my shoulders. "You're soaking wet."

My ass is, because while I'd worn my winter coat and boots, I hadn't bothered to put on something heavier than jeans.

Something I realized was a mistake approximately two minutes after walking out the door.

But...I couldn't sleep.

I kept thinking about Nova on the floor, kept getting up to add logs to the fire, kept thinking about the way she told me she wasn't going to eat extra after sharing food with her dog.

Food that was in her car.

Food that's now sitting just inside the front door, where it landed when I tried to break my ass on the melted snow I tracked in on my multiple trips to the firewood rack throughout the night.

Something she notices as she goes still on her hands and

knees, the mopping up of my mess pausing, towel stilling, head having jerked to the side.

Then slowly looking over her shoulder at me.

Soft expression. Pretty face.

Lush ass in the air.

This is fucking dangerous.

Steve woofs and wriggles to be let down, probably finally sensing his food is in the vicinity.

And sure enough, the moment I release him, his nails start clacking on the floor again as he takes off for the entryway and his mistress and...

Stuffs his nose in that bag of food.

"I need a rug," I say, moving toward her and bending down to nudge Steve back, to grab the bag with the rest of his things—bowls and chew toys and what appeared to be a year's supply of kibble and treats when I peeked inside earlier—scooping it up, and hanging it on my shoulder.

She doesn't move, just watches me with wide eyes, so I bend again, snagging her arm, helping her up to her feet, and drawing her away from the mess at the door. "Feed the tiny demon," I say, passing her the bag and snagging the towel from her grip. "I'll finish up here."

"You went out in the Snowmageddon and got Steve's food."

I nudge her toward the kitchen. "Yeah, butterfly, but that doesn't matter. Steve's hungry."

A woof from our feet.

I look down and see Steve sitting like the good boy he isn't, pleading puppy eyes on us, expression saying, "Yes, I am very, very hungry. Starving even."

"I don't understand," she whispers.

"It's not complicated," I say, starting to feel a little impatient.

Something she picks up on because her eyes start to clear

and she shakes her head slightly. "You went and got Steve's food."

I pass her the bag, table the impatience, even though part of me hates that she's clearly surprised. Is it because I went and did something that can be construed as nice—that she's shocked I can stop being an asshole for a minute? Or is it that she can't believe someone would do something nice for her?

Considering what assholes her ex and sister are, that can also be playing into her reaction.

But I don't want to think about that.

"Tiny demons have to eat too," I tell her.

She blinks, shakes herself again, but then proves she can take it on the chin with the best of them, her fingers wrapping around the bag, her shoulders straightening. "Steve is not a demon, tiny or otherwise."

My mouth hitches up. "Just a pervert?"

Her eyes narrow and she flounces off toward the kitchen. "Rude." A glare over her shoulder, lips twitching. "Chop. Chop. Get to cleaning."

"Maybe *you're* the tiny demon," I say, shaking out the towel.

"Maybe you're the large one."

The other half of my mouth curves, and I grab both ends of the towel, start rolling it.

She's in the kitchen now, but she doesn't miss what I've done. "Don't you d-dare," she sputters.

"What?" I ask, prowling toward her. "Punish you for your insolence?"

"No," she squeaks as I let the towel shoot out with a sharp *crack.* "You're supposed to clean up the water while I feed Steve."

"Hmm." I set the towel on the counter, lean back against it, very much in her space and not giving a damn. "I don't think that's a fair trade. After all"—I shift toward her, so close that our bodies are pressed together from thigh to shoulder, so close I'm able to feel her arm move against mine as she fills Steve's bowl with food—"you're the one who crushed me."

Her head whips toward mine, eyes flashing. "I didn't mean to crush you. I was trying to help you when you fell."

A beat, trying to keep my amusement out of my words. "And how do you explain your little demon dog trying to claw me to death?"

Her eyes narrow. "Steve was worried, you—you...annoy-ing...annoyer."

I freeze, brows drawing together.

Then laughter bubbles up in my chest, dances across my tongue, explodes out of my mouth.

Her face goes slack, that fire in her eyes extinguished, and the befuddlement that fills her expression is so beguiling that I think—

Fuck it.

I bend down...

And kiss her.

SEVENTEEN

Nova

ONE SECOND, he's stalking me like a tiger, tracking me through the jungle and readying to pounce when I least suspect it.

The next, he's laughing and it's fucking beautiful—a deep rough sound that seems to bounce around the room, that settles over me like one of those thick blankets he tucked over my sleeping body the night before.

I get the sense that he's not a man who laughs very often.

But him giving that to me...

I am *arrested*, frozen in place because it's the most astonishing and bewitching thing I've ever heard and seen.

His smile is wide and free. His skin crinkles at the corners of his eyes. The strong cords of his throat stand out in sharp relief. His laughter is equal parts velvet and sandpaper—gentle brushes over my skin that relax me but also rough sweeps that prickle my nerves, sending me to rigid attention.

I didn't know laughter could be a gift.

But from Lake it is.

Especially as he turns to face me fully, hazel eyes sparking with humor. He's so close now that I can see his pupils have dilated, can see the individual strands of hair in the stubble on his cheeks—

Then I can't see anything.

Because his arm is banding around my middle, bringing my body flush to his.

All of the air in my lungs escapes me in a rush...and then he's breathing for me, or maybe I don't *need* to breathe, maybe I don't need to think, maybe I don't need—

Anything but this man's lips on mine, soft and yet firm as he parts mine, sliding his tongue inside my mouth in such a skillful move that I quickly forget my name, where I'm at, the shitty circumstances that have brought me to these mountains. I quickly forget everything aside from how his hands feel on my body, his lips on mine, the sleek darts of his tongue.

The man can kiss.

Confidently. Without mercy.

One movement brings me even closer. Another has my feet dangling in the air. A third has my ass hitting the counter, knocking Steve's bowl to the floor.

It lands with a distant clatter and I hear Steve's nails as he rushes toward it—and no doubt the mess we've just made—but even that noise doesn't fully snap me out of my stupor. For one, Steve's a great vacuum. For another, Lake has sunk his fingers into my hair, is tilting my head back, his lips releasing mine and moving along my jaw, down my throat. He nudges the neck of my sweatshirt to the side, nips at my collarbone, laves his tongue into the divot at the top of my chest.

I shiver and his lips are back on mine, kissing me into oblivion, kissing me without mercy, kissing me so that the only thing I can do is *feel*.

His other hand goes to my hip, drawing me forward, settling my ass on the edge of the countertop. That hand slips from my waist and beneath my sweatshirt, beneath the T-shirt I have on under it, and the first brush of his warm, rough fingers on my skin makes me gasp, electricity surging through my nerves, moisture gathering between my legs, desire a fire burning out of control in my belly.

Then those fingers keep moving, sliding and shifting until his palm has gone flat on my side, until it starts to sweep its way up.

Yes.

This I like.

This is what I want.

Especially when there isn't any hesitation in his kiss as his hand continues to move and his lips and tongue don't stop and his fingertips reach the elastic band of my bralette...

And he brushes his thumb along the bottom curve of my breast.

Sensation sparks through me, my pussy getting wetter, my thighs clamping together—or trying to, anyway. Because I'm blocked by a narrow waist and strong legs and a man who's slowly lowering me back onto the countertop.

I lose his mouth, but I gain another hand, this one shoving up my hoodie and T-shirt, exposing me to his heated hazel eyes. The counter is cold as fuck beneath my now naked back, but that flashes through my mind and is gone in the next second. Because he grips the elastic band of my bralette, tugs it up with one sharp movement and—

"*Fuck,*" he growls as my breasts pop free.

I'm on the thinner side, I've always been—first because there wasn't much food growing up, and then because I got used to being hungry. Now it's mostly because I'm on my feet all day for work and often forget to eat.

But I have boobs, always have, the pesky things getting in the way when I want to run or reach for something in my opposite pocket or just want a shirt to fit correctly. Bringing far too much attention I didn't want at too young an age. A heavy weight that makes my shoulders ache.

Basically, they're a pain in the ass.

But seeing the way Lake looks at them makes me thankful for them for the first time ever.

Then he cups one—and I forget all the inconveniences, all the pain, all the discomfort and things I didn't want.

Because his touch brings me pleasure.

More pleasure than I've ever known as his pointer finger circles my nipple, closer, closer, tighter and tighter, the tip hardening, begging for touch...which he doesn't give.

Not until he bends forward, lips parting, mouth closing over one taut bud, forefinger and thumb pinching gently around the other, rolling back and forth, back and forth. The combination of tongue and lips, teeth and fingers has me crying out, arching against him, thighs tightening around his waist, reaching for something that I haven't ever experienced with another human.

With my vibrating friend? Definitely.

Multiple times.

With a man who's taking charge of my body like he knows it better than I do?

Never.

"Lake!" I cry, as he rubs his beard over my sensitive flesh, my fingers diving into his hair, the silken locks skating over my fingers.

He grunts, and I realize I'm tugging, immediately loosening my grip. "Not you," he says around me, eyes meeting mine when I lift my head to look down at him. "Harder, butterfly."

Then he flicks out his tongue, sending my worry away, sending my pleasure ramping again.

Especially when he pairs it with suction.

Oh lord, if this is how he uses his tongue, I can't imagine how good he's going to be with his *branch*.

My fingers tighten. "Oh God!"

He grunts again.

My legs wrap more firmly around him.

He sucks harder.

I gasp, draw him closer.

"That's it," he says, kissing his way over to my other breast, his hand coasting down my belly, dipping beneath the waistband of my joggers, my underwear, brushing over my clit and—

"Fuck," I groan.

Because I'm right *there*.

EIGHTEEN

Lake

THERE ARE pinpricks of pain in my ankle.

Again.

And growling in the air.

Again.

But I've got my mouth on the most glorious set of tits I've ever seen and—

"Lake!" she cries out, clenching at my hair, arching against me, pulling my head down as if she can't get enough of my mouth.

And maybe she can't, considering the way she's grinding against my pelvis.

But her calling my name out means that the pain in my ankle increases, the fucking demon of a dog activated to full asshole mode as he clamps down. I grunt and she immediately loosens the hold she has on my hair, the apology already forming on her face. "Not you," I say around her nipple, meeting her eyes, ordering, "Harder, butterfly."

Her fingers tighten.

The sting at my scalp increases and my cock twitches, loving the slight bit of pain, wanting more, wanting everything this woman can dish out.

I press my teeth lightly into the taut bud of her nipple.

"Oh God!" she moans, nails biting into my scalp.

My cock's happy for one moment—and only one moment—because then Steve presses *his* teeth into my ankle. I grunt, and it's not in pleasure, it's not my cock loving that bit of pain. It's because it's a fucking distraction, and it's because that tiny demon is trying to cockblock me.

It's because the little asshole's grip hurts, and not in a good way.

I suck at her nipple, not gently, because she seems to like that bit of pain as well, because the tiny demon is treating my ankle like a chew toy and I need that shit to stop, and *I'm* not stopping until she comes apart beneath me.

I slide my hand down her side, over her belly, shoving it beneath the waistband of her sweats and into her underwear.

Slick, *slick* heat.

Wetter than I expect, sopping, soaking wet, fucking *dripping*.

I forget about my ankle.

I focus on the bundle of nerves at the apex of her pussy, and the fact that she really likes it when I press my thumb to the spot.

That she cries out my name again when I slip one finger into her tight cunt.

She clamps around me, pussy and thighs, hands in my hair, and then I feel it.

Her orgasm closing in on her.

In the gush of desire coating my palm, my finger, making it

so I can slip another in without resistance, can slide a third into that tight sheath.

My name dances off the tip of her tongue.

Her body undulates against mine.

Throbbing in my ankle. In my cock.

I keep working her breasts, keep thrusting my fingers into her pussy, keep pressing my thumb to her clit.

And—

Finally.

She comes apart.

"Oh God," she gasps. "Oh God. Oh my fucking *God!*"

Her body tenses...and then she slumps back onto the counter, limbs going lax, pussy convulsing around my fingers, mouth parting in a soft O, eyes sliding closed. Her sweatshirt and tee are rucked up around the tops of her breasts, shoved under her arms. Her joggers are hanging low on her hips, stretched out with my arm beneath them.

Not even fully naked.

But the most beautiful woman I've ever had the privilege to see.

My dick is hard and aching and I'm desperate to drag her pants down, to thrust into that tight cunt, to feel all that slick heat surrounding my cock, the clasp of her pussy around me.

That desire is so damned strong, I almost do just that.

In fact, I slip my fingers free, need ramping when she gives a soft mew of protest, and grip the waistband of her pants—

"Grr."

The growl snaps me out of my daze, out of the driving need of my cock.

The sharp increase in pressure at my ankle does the rest of the job.

"Fuck," I hiss, releasing her sweats, slipping my hand behind her shoulders and helping her sit up. A sharp tug covers her breasts with that sports bra thing, another has her T-shirt down, still one more has her sweatshirt covering her torso.

Only when I make sure she's steady, do I step back.

I pick up the towel, wanting to go back to the mess, wanting to pretend this didn't happen. Wanting...

To fuck her senseless.

So. *Fucking*. Stupid.

Especially when her eyes flick down, teeth pressing into her bottom lip and need courses through me anew. "Do you want me to...?" she offers with a gesture toward my crotch.

My dick twitches and a little of *my* inner demon comes out, even though I'm spiraling and freaking out inside and trying to come up with any reason why me fucking her right now is a bad idea.

For the record, risking tiny demon bite wounds is *not* one of those reasons.

Neither is the flush on her cheeks.

Or the vision of those lush breasts imprinted on my mind.

What I wouldn't give to see them jiggling as I fuck her hard and fast and—

"I mean," she whispers, "You, um, helped me out and I—" Those cheeks turn a deep shade of red. "I can return the favor."

Fuck, she's cute.

Really cute.

And sweet and gorgeous.

And I want her.

For more than just one quick fuck.

No other thought could have succeeded in cooling my desire as quickly, as completely. One other time in my life, I thought that. One other time and it seriously ended up fucking *me*.

Fucking with my head, my heart, with everything I thought I knew.

I'm not doing that again.

Not now. Not ever.

"No," I snap. "I don't want you to help me with my dick."

Her face falls and I know I'm an asshole. I *know* it, but I can't stop, can't let this continue. Better to remind her how much of a jerk I am here and now.

"Oh," she whispers.

"You've done enough," I mutter and that's the *only* truth in the bullshit I'm spouting. Because she's rocked me to my fucking core, has exposed every weakness to the chilled, snow-filled air.

"Right." Another whisper.

"My dick doesn't like women who barely know how to fuck, who just lay there like goddamned pillow princesses"—I toss her a sneering look, dragging it down along her front, staring at the body I'm so desperate for I can still taste her skin on my tongue, staring at her body so I can avoid the pain in her deep, pine green eyes. "Trust me, I've had better than whatever shitty hand job you're about to offer me."

She gasps and now I can't avoid looking up, can't avoid looking into those eyes.

They swim with tears.

I. Am. A. Fucking. *Asshole.*

But I don't apologize.

I just shake the damned dog off my ankle, turn away, and get the fuck out of there.

NINETEEN

Nova

I WATCH his back recede as he strides down the hallway, thinking it's not nearly as sexy as the night before.

Thinking that this actually hurts—his words, his derision, the sight of him walking away—almost as much as walking in on Ashley and George had.

Thinking that I don't give a fuck if it's snowing outside, I need out of this house, and I need it *now*.

I hop down, nearly landing on Steve, having to do some fancy footwork in order to avoid killing my precious pooch. But nearly committing pupicide is the blast of normal I need. I'm able to focus, to get a series of tasks together so that I can function.

"Breathe, Nova," I whisper, nudging Steve back so I can pick up the towel.

I walk to the door, finish mopping up the puddles gathered there then carry it back and toss it into the washer. On my way back to the kitchen, I spy Steve's bowl and remember hearing it clang to the floor distantly while Lake had—

Made use of skills that weren't his *branch.*

But were as good—*better*—than the rumors Ella had shared with me.

The metal bowl is overturned on the floor, and I lift it up, revealing a few stray kibbles. For the most part, though, I see that Steve has made good of his vacuum skills.

He's eaten.

Now he needs water.

And then he'll need his vitamins and a walk to use the facilities.

Which is perfect. I'll bring my camera, use it as an excuse to build my portfolio to pass some time, to pretend that what had just happened hadn't *actually* happened.

Step one in letting things roll off my back again.

Step one—or two, rather—in regaining myself, my spine, my confidence.

"Yay, me," I mutter, picking up the bowl and setting it on the counter then grabbing the little ceramic basin that serves as Steve's water dish and moving to the sink. I fill it with water, snag one of the dish towels I washed the night before, spread the cotton on the floor, and place the bowl on top of it.

Hopefully, in a place I won't trip over it and spill it everywhere.

That might stain this beautiful wood, might cause some of the gorgeous, hand-scraped planks to swell and morph, to grow misshapen.

That'll serve him right.

I narrow my eyes in the direction of the hall then decide that's not helpful to my pretending this all doesn't hurt, that this all is totally fine and I'm unbothered, so I force my expression to smooth out and go to my bags, pull out my snow boots, snag my winter coat.

I'm not a total idiot—even if I missed the whole Snowmageddon thing.

I knew I was driving up to the mountains in the middle of winter, so I made sure I packed the necessary garments.

Something that wasn't hard to do, considering I was packing up my entire life.

Still, I made sure they ended up near the top of one of the bags, so...winning?

And whether my Bay Area heavy coat and boots will hold up to the blizzard still pumping out snow outside the house is another story.

I'm going to find out, aren't I?

Steve's harness and leash, jacket and booties are next and he drools all over me as I get everything on—remnants of scrounging up those last couple of kibbles and attempting to drink his water dish dry before he heard the jingle jangle of his leash and abandoned all searching for consumables in lieu of the potential to bark at a squirrel or a plastic bag.

I wipe my arm on my pants and decide to swap them out for something thicker.

See? I can think ahead.

Can pause without rushing stupidly headfirst.

So says the girl who was nearly fucked on the counter by a man I barely know all of five minutes earlier.

At least I got an orgasm out of it.

Jeans on. Jacket over my shirt and hoodie. Thick socks on my feet. Waterproof boots on.

Camera over my shoulder, extra battery and memory card in my zippered pocket.

Beanie on my head.

Ready to brave the blizzard outside.

I look down at my baby. "Let's go, Steve."

His tongue lolls as he trots over to me, leash dragging behind him, tags on his harness tinkling as he meets me by the front door.

I tug it wide, feel the cold gust of wind.

It cuts through my layers, a frozen razor blade glancing over my skin. But it's too cold for me to bleed, all of the blood in my body leaving my limbs and coalescing deep in my belly, hidden in that safe spot buried beneath layers and layers of protection.

For a second, I had thought—

Well, it doesn't matter.

I know better now.

I know it's the same as always.

Which is why I snag Steve's leash and we walk out the front door.

❄ ❄ ❄ ❄

HALFWAY DOWN THE STREET, I notice the wind dying down, the snow slowing its fall.

The world is quieting.

I don't know if the storm has passed, or if this is just a break in the winter pounding—which is so *not* a good reference to have running through my mind after Kitchen Counter-Gate.

But the slowing blizzard means that I feel comfortable pulling my camera out from beneath my jacket and framing a shot in my mind, snapping off a couple of photos to test the light and exposure and shutter speed.

Steve huffs out a sigh and sinks onto his belly, head dropping onto his paws, hood from his jacket half falling forward to cover his adorably smooshed-up face.

He doesn't otherwise bug me as I fuss.

Probably because the squirrels are in hiding and there aren't any plastic bags blowing in the wind—or maybe because he's been out with me shooting enough times to understand this process goes a lot faster when he behaves.

I tweak the settings, take a couple more shots then look at the viewfinder.

Nose wrinkling, I glare at the tree, thinking it's not quite right but unable to put my finger on what's wrong.

I shift to the side, letting the leash out so Steve doesn't have to move with me.

And I keep shooting.

Better.

Close to perfect.

Just not...*perfect*.

Another shift, a little less exposure, increasing the shutter speed, and—

Then I have it.

That perfect moment.

The one frame that captures exactly what's in my heart—frost and snow and branches weighed down by the weight of Mother Nature, by the weight of the world, but not all hope is lost. There's a sliver of light that glimmers through the snow still falling, that sends the snow clinging to the pine needles sparkling like glitter.

So much white.

It's all around, from street level to the treetops.

But there's *so much* color in this white—hints of blue from hidden pockets of ice, the pristine, crisp bone-white that's gathered at the tippy tops of the trees, grayish shadows from where the snow has mounded up unevenly and created small pockets of darkness below, green from the pine needles peeking out beneath their frosty coverings.

Together it all forms a storybook showing of a Winter Wonderland.

And once I see those different shades of white, the beauty in the range of coloration, in the variations of Mother Nature herself, I fall into my work.

I lose track of time and space.

I lose track of myself.

TWENTY

Lake

I TAKE A SHOWER, locking down the sliver of guilt as I stroke myself to completion, knees shaking after an angry orgasm.

Angry because I'm an idiot.

Angry because it doesn't do anything to make my dick softer.

How can it?

I've got the smell of cinnamon in my nose, the memory of that slick cunt on my fingertips.

So, yeah, I can come.

But it doesn't do shit to relieve the ache in my balls...in my heart.

Asshole with a conscience, all right.

I sigh and grab the bottle of body wash, go through the motions of cleaning up then shampooing and conditioning my hair.

Something Knox likes to give me a hard time about.

A high-maintenance pretty boy who conditions his hair and gets oiled up on photoshoots.

Both of which are true, but I think I'm far from high maintenance.

I just...like what I like, and I want to do shit my own way.

What's the problem with that?

"Nothing," I mutter, cranking off the water and reaching for my towel. "Absolutely fucking *nothing.*"

I dry off, get dressed, and hole up in my room as I review a few more contracts, book a couple more dates for meetings and shoots and sit-down lunches with potential advertisers who want to "put some feelers out and see if we're a good fit."

This is usually a sign of it being a pain in the ass for me, but money is money, and who knows how long I'm going to be able to play hockey.

I have to prepare for the future.

But hockey is still the bulk of my life now, which is why I have a game on in the background—a weird early start weekend game that I hate playing in myself because it messes up my routine, and if there's one thing that hockey players—and professional athletes, in general—have in common, it's a fondness and strict adherence to our pregame rituals. From a certain workout or food to unwashed socks (*I'm looking at you, Knox*) to taking a nap at a certain time, we all have our quirks.

Early games fuck that up.

But, they're also part of the life—so I've learned to deal.

Still have the lucky underwear, though.

So long as a tiny demon dog doesn't eat them.

I grunt and narrow my eyes at the screen, not wanting to think about Steve or Nova or what happened in the kitchen, so I force my focus on the game, knowing we'll be playing both of the teams in the coming weeks. I always like to check in on my opponents, to see who's really hitting their stride, what lines are working, who's on a hot streak. It's also helpful to see what type of goals are going in, the shit the refs are calling, and yeah, the video coaches can pull all of this for me if I ask, but also, there's a reason I play hockey.

I love it.

I love the speed and intensity. The way I feel like I can do fucking anything when the puck is on my stick.

There's nothing like skating into the offensive zone all by myself, just the goalie between me and fucking *glory*.

There's nothing like lining up and laying out an asshole, crushing him with an open-ice hit.

Especially if he's been harassing our goalie or one of the smaller guys.

Because. Fuck. That. Shit.

I'm lucky. I'm big. I'm fast. I've got good hands, a wicked shot, and I can body most anyone off the puck. I can take my own back—and have had to plenty of times over the years—and while dropping the gloves isn't my favorite thing (I would rather save my hands for actual hockey and not punching fuckers from the other team in their hard ass heads), I do it as necessary.

I'm the player everyone hates to play against but loves to have on their roster.

Because I make a difference in games. Because I score and hit and fight and pass.

But hockey doesn't matter right now when my stomach's rumbling and I can't ignore it any longer.

I'm that big guy. I need food.

Which means I *need* to deal with the woman who's invaded my house.

Sighing, I stand up and shove my phone in my pocket, leaving the TV on, moving to the door and carefully opening it, listening, expecting to hear the snorting, grunting demon who didn't break the skin on my ankle with his earlier antics, but who had left it aching with an array of scratch marks.

Asshole.

Even though I deserve the marks, deserve worse.

But I don't hear any grunting or groaning or snorting or snotting or barking as I pad my way down the hall.

I don't hear anything, and when I make it into the family room, I find it empty.

No smells of burning food.

No sign of the demon.

No Nova anywhere in eyeshot.

Probably taking the beast to the bathroom.

Only, when I peek outside, I don't see her. Or the dog. And they're not out front either.

I start to close the door, to keep the warm air in, and that's when I see it—see *them.*

Footsteps leading away from the house.

I look up at the sky, see dark clouds closing in, feel the cold air getting colder by the second. I think of the woman on the side of the road in wet sneakers and a fucking sweatshirt, the woman on my kitchen counter in sweatpants and that same hoodie.

No gloves. No boots. No jacket or beanie or thick wool socks.

And footsteps—one set of human, one set of tiny demon—heading away from my house, moving down the driveway, moving into the street.

Christ, is the woman *trying* to kill herself?

I whip around, march to the mudroom, grab my boots, my jacket, a fucking blanket because, God knows, the fucking woman—and her little dog too—are going to be popsicles by the time I find them.

The wind begins to blow by the time I make it to the

bottom of the driveway, freezing cold gusts that slice through my layers.

The snow starts to fall by the time I make it to the next block.

Harder before I get to the end of the street and spy Nova's car still stuck in the snowbank, mostly covered now.

But empty.

Relief wars with irritation.

She's not dumb enough to attempt to dig herself out in this weather, or hasn't succeeded and driven off, gotten into a worse accident somewhere down the road.

But then the worry is back, clawing through me.

Because she's not here.

And if she's not here...

Then she's wandering around fuck knows where.

During Snowmageddon.

TWENTY-ONE

I CROUCH DOWN, all but lying flat out on the icy road, camera angled up, aiming between the branches.

"A little more," I whisper. "Just...right...*there!*"

I snap the shot—and a few extras for good measure—and just in time because Steve's lost patience from where I zipped him into my jacket, his little smooshed face poking out from beneath the zipper, cold nose pressing to my throat, tongue darting out and slurping along my skin.

"Ugh," I say, wiping the back of my gloved hand over the spot, using the other to scroll through the shots, making sure I captured that sliver of tree and pine needles and snow, the knobby end of the branch, the divots in the bark, the claw marks from a bear making his territory known or scratching her back or cubs making trouble.

It's there, and it's exactly what I want.

A perfect slice of nature, a small, beautiful moment with a thousand tiny details hidden, almost lost, in the outside world.

But once spotted, it's easy to get lost in that tiny circle that houses an entire world.

It's going to look amazing blown up.

It *would* have looked amazing in the magazine—but since I don't work for one any longer...

I exhale, let my camera drop to the side, the heavy weight a welcome comfort.

The wind has picked up, and the temperature has dropped since I left the house—hence the reason my little pup is zipped against my chest. Even with a sweater and snow booties, it's too cold for him to just be sitting out in this weather. Especially when snow is falling again.

I start making my way back to the house, not having made it far.

Part of that is not wanting to get lost.

Part of that is because Steve isn't a huge fan of walking long distances in the snow, apparently—or long distances at all, really.

Part of it is because these trees right here are beautiful.

Almost as beautiful as the flakes of snow falling like magic out of the sky, playing tag with each other, being turned topsy-turvy by the wind.

I pause, not because I want to.

But because I *have* to.

I lift my camera, start hitting the shutter-release button, letting it fly, filling up my memory card, committing this moment to memory both on camera and in my mind.

The cool biting my cheeks.

The wind lifting my hair.

The tiny bites of cold as the snowflakes hit my nose, my forehead, my cheeks and lips and chin, and melt instantly, forming tiny puddles, narrow tracks as they drip down my skin and off my jaw.

The trees—

"What the fuck do you think you're doing?!"

The moment I'm committing to memory shatters, breaking apart into a thousand tiny shards.

Steve woofs and I turn to see Lake storming up to me, expression furious, footsteps churning up the falling snow. He marches right up to me, those hazel eyes sparking with fire. "It's fucking Snowmageddon and—"

"*Grr!*"

Steve's head pops out again, little crooked teeth bared in warning.

Lake freezes, mouth hanging open, gaze going from me to Steve. His eyes still spark, but his voice eases, the anger cold rather than hot, the volume quieter, barely able to be heard above the wind that is now picking up, starting to gust through the trees. "What the fuck were you thinking going out in this?" he grinds out.

"*This*"—I wave a hand, indicating the snow falling, the wind blowing—"wasn't happening when I came out. *This*"—another wave—"is why I'm heading back to the house."

He lifts a brow. "*That*"—he nods toward my camera—"is you heading to the house? Cause it sure as shit looked like you were standing there lost, waiting for me to fucking rescue you again."

"Re-rescue m-me?" I sputter.

The other brow rises, joining the first. "Are you seriously trying to pretend that isn't the case?"

"Yes!" I snap. Then shake my head. "No! I know where your house is, and I know where I'm going. I was stopping to..." I break off, bite my lip. Because this is going to sound stupid, because I've already spent enough time feeling shitty about myself around this man. Because I'm going to do everything in my power to avoid that happening again.

"...to get lost," he supplies, reaching for my arm. "On purpose."

I dance back, swatting his hand away. "You're a dumbass."

Get lost? On purpose?

Shaking my head, I spin on my heel and start marching toward the house.

I'm responsible.

I'm not a fucking moron.

I'm—

A hand catches my shoulder, turns me back.

I jerk away from him. "I know where I'm going," I snap.

"Yeah?" he asks derisively.

I don't even deign to answer that, just start stomping away from him again, boots sliding slightly on the ice, but making good progress back the way I originally came.

Back toward his house, turning onto Forest Bend, stopping at the correct driveway to toss a glare back at him.

See? I know *exactly* where I'm going.

Then I lift my chin.

Tramp up the driveway.

Ass. Fucking. Hole.

The front door comes into view just as I hear footsteps behind me. Steve growls softly, but I just pat his little butt, murmur, "We're fine."

Then I'm over at the green flower pot, lifting it to reveal the key beneath it.

I take the key, shove it in the lock, wrench it to the side, and open the door.

"Woof!" Steve barks happily as the warmth hits—and I can't lie, the heat feels incredible after being outside for so long.

I feel Lake come in behind me, but I don't turn around, don't acknowledge him.

I just release Steve from his jacket prison then lean against the wall to yank off my boots. My coat is next, the sleeve catching on my camera strap, the two tangling together in a mess that isn't easily unsnarled.

"Nova," Lake begins.

I yank at the strap, at the jacket, desperate now to get away, to end this, to put me out of my misery.

My peace is gone.

That beautiful moment is ruined.

And now my jacket is caught.

My breath hitches in my lungs but I grind my teeth together, don't allow it to escape.

Breathe.

Relax.

But the tangle doesn't magically undo itself, and when I yank harder, my camera strap breaks.

I gasp, lurch for the single most expensive belonging I own —aside from Steve.

Only, I'm not fast enough.

The strap slips through my fingers.

And my camera falls.

TWENTY-TWO

Lake

I DART MY HAND OUT, catch the camera before it hits the floor.

It's instinct.

It's also because I don't know her, but I saw her bag of belongings, saw that they aren't expensive. Her coat has a hole in it near the hem, the laces of her boots have clearly broken and been knotted back together in several places. The dog has a hundred toys, plenty of food and treats, and what looks to be a brand-new leash.

This camera is expensive.

She must have sacrificed a lot to buy it.

I tighten my fingers around the strap, lift it close enough to cradle carefully against my chest.

I catch a glimpse of the small screen on the back and—

Am utterly arrested.

The detail even on that little viewfinder is immense. It's just a tree amongst a hundred, a thousand other trees, but...

It's more.

Fingers wrap around mine, pulling the camera from my grip, snatching away that beauty, slamming me right back into reality.

I want to take it back, to hold it close and stare at it.

Ferret out every tiny detail.

She's supremely talented. I'm not an artist, not even well-versed in the world of art, but I *am* successful in what I do because I have a natural ability, because I work hard, and... because I used to get lost in practice, in the love of the game, in the movement of my hands and feet and body. Kind of like Nova had been doing when I stormed up to her, interrupting her with her head back, face tilted up to the sky, eyes closed.

In the moment.

Damn.

I ruined that. One glimpse of that photograph and I know.

She's got talent.

"Nova," I begin again, stepping a little closer, hating that she steps back, that Steve stands between us, teeth bared.

Clearly, I've ruined any progress previously made with the tiny demon.

"We'll be out of here as soon as I can manage," she says, sliding back another few feet, turning for her bags that are still sitting on the counter. She sets her camera on the granite, furtively looks back over her shoulder before carefully tucking the camera inside.

Then she folds her jacket, shoves it into the bag as well.

And pauses, head dropping forward, shoulders stiff.

I open my mouth, intending to tell her to hang her coat on the hooks in the hall, but that's just more stupidity talking—better that she pack up her shit so she's ready to go, ready to get the fuck out of my house—so I clamp my teeth together, walk to the cabinet next to the fridge, the only one that's completely full.

Of my quote-unquote shit-tasting vodka.

I personally think that my vodka is fucking delicious, mostly because it *doesn't* taste like much, because it goes down smooth with minimal burn but gives maximum buzz.

My asshole teammates, though—

"That's..." A pause as I glance over my shoulder, surprised she's talking to me, surprised that she doesn't seem pissed any longer. "A lot of vodka."

"Yup," I say, opening another cabinet, grabbing two glasses and sloshing a couple of fingers into each glass before capping the bottle then passing one over to her. She surprises me again by taking it, throwing it back.

No comment on it being before five.

Nothing about neither of us having eaten anything.

"Ugh," she says, shuddering. "That's awful."

"It's my vodka," I tell her, downing my own glass and just as quickly refilling it.

"Yeeeah," she says, drawing out the word. "I kinda figured that considering I watched you pull it out of your cabinet."

"No," I tell her, picking up the bottle and showing her the label. "It's *my* vodka."

Brows furrowing, she glances down then up to me. Then back down. "What do you mean, it's your vodka?"

"I mean"—I set the bottle down on the countertop, pick up my glass and drain it a second time—"I'm paid to represent it."

She pauses, head tilting to the side, studying me as though I'm a bug. "So you're not just a hockey player, you're also the face of a vodka company?"

I narrow my eyes at her, ask suspiciously, "How do you know I'm a hockey player?"

"I talked to Ella."

My brows lift in question.

"Knox's sister who so kindly arranged for me to stay at his—at your—house."

Oh. Right. "I thought her name was Daniela."

A short laugh, nothing like the beauty of those giggles earlier. "She hates being called that."

I frown, but don't comment further as I throw back the second glass. Probably because I'm about to be stupid by saying, "You're not pissed about..." I wave a hand at the counter, knowing I'm an idiot to bring up my assholeness, to give her a chance for hysterics and to pick a fight.

She shrugs. "It's your house."

My frown deepens. "I'm aware of that."

But she doesn't seem to hear me. "You know," she says, going to the fridge, pulling open the door. She pulls out a lemon, a ginger beer, one of those clear herb containers—all of which I didn't buy, all of which must have been in her belongings. Those go on the counter and she pauses. "I think I saw..." But I don't hear the rest as she disappears into the pantry, comes back with a jar of honey. "Cool if I use this?" she asks dismissively, as though she expects me to say no but that it wouldn't be big deal if I did.

As if she expects me to be an asshole, but that, also, wouldn't be a big deal.

"Yeah," I say gruffly, ignoring the pinch in my chest.

Easy to do because it's a familiar feeling.

Easy to do because I'm curious to what in the fuck-all she's doing.

She takes her glass to the counter next to the sink, snags mines and opens a cabinet, pulling out a cutting board, snagging a knife out of the rack. And that's as much as I see as she gets to work. I can't discern much as her back is to me—just her arms moving and then I can smell the lemon along with something earthly, can hear the clink of a spoon, the pop of the can of ginger beer opening, a soft grunt, and then the metal-against-glass sound of the jar of honey opening.

A handful of ice snagged from the freezer, *plinking* as she drops some into each of the cups.

More movement.

More spoon clinking.

Then she's turning around, lifting a glass in my direction. "There," she says. "Try this."

I frown.

She's smiling, but her eyes aren't warm.

"Here," she says, jiggling the glass a bit, the ice cubes tinkling.

"What is it?" I ask warily.

Another jiggle. "Just drink it."

"Is it poisoned?"

She laughs and for a moment, I sit in that sound. A pretty, pretty laugh. From a pretty, pretty woman. With just a hint of sadness in her eyes.

I frown.

She moves toward me, presses the glass into my hand.

"It's just a honey rosemary mule."

TWENTY-THREE

Nova

HE LOOKS at me like I'm a bug under the microscope.

Or like how Steve stares up at me when I pull out the jar of peanut butter but don't give him a special treat.

"It's a honey rosemary Moscow mule," I semi-repeat, handing it to him. "*Not* poisoned," I add after he just stares at it suspiciously.

His eyes flick up, the golden flecks sparkling in the bright lights of the kitchen.

There's the barest hint of pink on his cheeks from the cold, also maybe from the two shots of vodka he took in short succession.

Or maybe because he was furious at me.

Yelling at me.

I don't care. I'm *done* caring. I'm biding my time, going to get along and then get the fuck out of here as soon as humanly possible.

Plus, if he drinks enough, he'll pass out and I won't have to deal with him.

Win-win.

And, frankly, I can use a little more alcohol.

Maybe then his cold eyes, his sharp words won't sting quite so much.

Ugh. I turn back to the counter, grab my own glass, and take a big glug, remind myself of the mantra I have been repeating in my head for the last five minutes.

Ever since he caught my camera.

Ever since my heart gave a little flutter at the quick movements. Because he saved my life catching that—or at least my future employment options—

It doesn't matter.

He doesn't matter.

Everyone say it with me—

He. Doesn't. *Matter.*

He shifts on his feet, passing the glass to his other hand as he lifts it to his nose, inhales deeply. "Rosemary in a drink?"

I shrug. "It's good." Smiling, I'm determined to hang on to my good mood as I add, "Something you would know if you tried it."

He holds my stare as he slowly brings the glass to his lips, tips it up, throat working, Adam's apple bobbing, the strong cords in his neck mimicking those in his forearms.

Strong.

Muscled.

Man.

My pussy throbs, remembering those thick fingers inside me, fucking me steadily to orgasm.

I lift my own glass, start chugging, barely tasting my careful mix of honey and lemon, ginger beer and vodka, the hint of earthiness from the rosemary. It would be better if I made a simple syrup with the honey and a few sprigs of the herb, letting that freshness resound brightly in the drink.

But...that whole needing-alcohol-in-my-system thing.

Only when a cube of ice hits my front teeth, the sprig of rosemary I put as garnish inside falling forward to hit my face, sending droplets of the concoction scattering along my cheek, do I realize I chugged so quickly that I've drank it all.

Perfect.

I have a reason to ignore him again.

And maybe this time I'll make that simple syrup, if only to pass the time.

And to get away from those piercing hazel eyes.

I start rotating toward the sink—

"This is good."

I lift my brows. "No kidding." I move back to the counter, to the sink and the remaining half of a lemon, the rosemary and honey, the ginger beer bubbling in its can, the bottle with the pretty etching in its neck—conifers and the outline of a mountain—its label blue with silver writing declaring it Lake Vodka.

I thought that it was referring to Lake Tahoe, to the deep blue water, to the huge body of water hidden in the mountains.

But it's referring to Lake.

As in, *Lake's* brand.

And it bites just as hard as he does, the fire of the alcohol burning in my belly, crawling up my throat, making my head fuzzy and—

A hand on either side of me, gripping the edge of the counter, boxing me in, chest pressing to my back, his body close and burning nearly as hot as the fire from the alcohol inside me. "Why aren't you pissed?" he asks.

It takes me a minute to process his question.

I blame the vodka.

I *blame* that hard, hot body boxing me in.

I shrug, attempting to feign indifference to his closeness. "You saved my camera."

Silence. Then a hand coming to my shoulder. He shifts back—barely—as he turns me to face him. Which means my body brushes along the full length of his and—ho, mama—but that *branch* of his is...

Impressive.

He's still an asshole.

Just also an impressive one.

"That's not it," he says, hand still on my arm, crouching down a little to meet my eyes.

I hold them, even though it's hard, and shrug again. "What else could it be?"

Fingers tightening, body not moving away. "It's something."

I lift my chin. "Why do you care?"

His jaw flexes. "I don't."

Pointedly, I let my gaze slide to where he's holding my arm. "Then why are you pushing this?"

Silence. For long enough that I'm certain he's not going to answer me.

"Because you're calm," he says.

"Uhhh..." I frown. Is this a bad thing?

He shocks me by going on. "You should be hysterical. Throwing plates—or knives at my head, or something."

I freeze. "I should be throwing knives at you?"

His face immediately closes down, hand dropping away. He grabs my glass and his own, filling them both with another shot. He tosses his back, fills it again, then tosses that back too.

Okaaay.

Maybe that passing out is going to commence sooner than planned.

"Lake," I say.

He thrusts my glass in my direction. "Shot time."

The apples of his cheeks are reddened from the alcohol.

"Someone threw knives at you?"

He reaches for the lemon. "Need some of this in that?"

I bat his hand away, snatch his glass back, setting it on the counter next to mine. "Maybe you should slow down."

"Maybe I'll—"

He reaches for my glass now, and I have to bat him away a second time. I take the shot, make a face, then snag the vodka, shoving it out of his way. "Did you like the drink I made you?"

His eyes hit mine, holding for a long moment. "Yeah," he mutters, trying to reach past me for the bottle.

"I'll make you another one." With lots of lemon and ginger beer and not any vodka.

"I don't need the fancy stuff with my alcohol," he mutters, stretching out a hand for the bottle.

"Well, *I* do," I say. "And I need some food with this."

Not a lie.

But why am I stopping him from drinking more? If he finishes the bottle, he'll pass out and leave me alone, and then I can just—

Who am I kidding?

If he finishes the bottle, he'll probably get alcohol poisoning and then I'll be stuck trying to keep him alive through Snowmageddon.

Food certainly.

Then passing out.

"I'll cook something," he says.

"Do you have enough faculties left to maneuver open flames?" I ask, eyes narrowed.

"Nova."

His voice is so steady and serious that I find my gaze drawn back to his. "Yeah?"

"I'm not drunk."

"So says the man who's consumed half a bottle of vodka in the last ten minutes."

His mouth curves up. "I'm two hundred and twenty pounds and hock vodka as part of my part-time gig. It's going to take more than a couple of shots to get me drunk."

I would believe that...

Except, he's holding himself in that careful way I do when I'm feeling a little tipsy.

Like, if I'm super-duper focused, I can pull off a relatively decent approximation of sober.

So, I don't think it's a good idea for this man to be wielding knives and getting close to the open flames of that huge gas stove.

But it's not like I can stop him.

It's not like he gives two shits about my opinions—he's made that exceptionally clear.

I nibble at my bottom lip, trying to think fast while ignoring the way his eyes heat when I do that.

It's the vodka talking, that's all.

Or his *branch* anyway.

Food. More alcohol.

Then figuring out what in the fuck-all I'm going to do with my life while a certain hockey player sleeps it off.

A certain hockey player who's pulling out ingredients and walking toward the stove.

Shit.

"I—"

His head whips toward me and the question just flies off my tongue.

"Do you want to look at my pictures?"

TWENTY-FOUR

I SCROLL through the camera like she taught me, clicking through picture after picture.

Seeing confirmation of what I already knew.

She's supremely talented.

And someone was stupid enough to fire her.

I set the camera to the side, looking at her at the stove, watching the way she mouths the lines to the cheesy Christmas movie she put on a few minutes ago, whatever she's cooking making my mouth water.

Spicy and rich.

Bright and tart.

I don't know what she's making. I'm just ready to eat it.

"Santa! Oh, my God!" she fake screams as she stirs the pot. "I know him. I know him!"

My mouth curves, thinking of my last Christmas. We had a team party and though most of the guys hadn't shown, enough had been around to see Knox dressed up in an adult-sized elf costume.

He hadn't managed to get any of us to sing Christmas carols with him, though.

I set the camera on the counter, round the island, and move to Nova's side, drawn like an idiotic moth to the flames, ready to burn up, happy so long as I'm in the light.

"Why did you get fired?"

She startles, spoon jerking, hot liquid from the pot splashing up and hitting her hand. "Shit," she hisses, but I'm already moving, taking the wooden spoon from her hand, drawing her over to the sink, turning on the cold water.

"Sorry," I say, running my thumb over the reddened spot on the inside of her wrist.

A shrug. "Not the first time or the last I've been involved in a kitchen emergency."

"Yeah, I remember the butter."

Her mouth screws up. "That was Steve's fault. The only thing I usually burn is the bread."

I pick up one of the freshly washed dish towels and carefully pat her hand dry, inspecting the burn, trying to decide if it needs some antibiotic cream and a bandage.

"It's fine," she says softly, drawing away, going back to the pot and spoon and stirring what I now saw was some sort of thick, creamy soup. "But, speaking of bread"—she moves to the oven, opens the door—"it's time for it to come out."

She snags the towel, grabs the sheet pan, and my mouth waters when I see the loaf of bread has been sliced and slathered with butter and herbs and is now toasted to golden brownness.

Food time.

I go to the cabinet, get down a couple of bowls, snag a ladle from the drawer.

"How is it that you don't have furniture, but you have a ladle?"

I shrug as I start scooping up soup and distributing it into the bowls. "I canceled the furniture order when I saw the designer wanted to spend over six figures on it."

She sets the tray onto one side of the stove with a clatter. "S-six figures?"

"Yup." I go to a drawer, open it, grab out two spoons. "Including twenty-five grand for a couch."

Her mouth falls open.

"I like to cook," I say, latching onto the safe conversational topic, "so when I brought my shit over from my apartment, I already have most everything I need. Same goes for my bedroom set. But my couch was old and I trashed it before I found the invoices, fired her, and canceled the orders."

That's the first and last time I tell anyone to do what they want when it comes to something that costs me money.

"And we've been on the road, so I haven't had a chance to go to a store and pick out anything."

"Twenty-five *thousand* for the couch?"

"Yup."

"Not twenty-five hundred?"

"Nope."

Wide eyes. "Oh, my God."

My mouth curved. "And it was white."

Her eyes go wider.

I want to kiss her, and the urge is so strong that it, thankfully, snaps me out of myself. I grab a piece of garlic bread—instead of her—take a huge bite out of it—also, instead of her. "Your pictures are good," I say after I chewed and swallowed, the garlic and butter and herb combination fucking delicious. "*Really* good."

Surprise in those green eyes, as though she's not used to compliments.

And considering what her sister did, what her ex did...

"So, why did you get fired?"

Her eyes slide away.

"Nova."

She looks back. "An ex threw knives at you?"

Touché.

I grab the bowls from the counter. "If we eat in front of the TV, will Steve be a tiny demon and try to get into our food?"

"He sure will."

I sigh, but she just laughs, fills a plate with the garlic bread and carries it over to the pile of blankets. "Don't worry," she says, settling down into them. "I can corral the beast."

❄ ❄ ❄ ❄

Turns out, corralling the beast is not her strong suit.

But, luckily, there's extra soup.

❄ ❄ ❄ ❄

They're singing Christmas carols on the TV when I hear snoring.

I glance over, expecting it to be Steve.

Instead, it's Nova, who's curled up into a ball in that mess of blankets and towels and clothes and pillows. Steve is sprawled out on her chest.

But he's not sleeping.

He's watching me warily, one beady eye open.

Probably expecting me to go asshole again.

And, frankly, he's not wrong to be cautious. It's going to happen.

Just not right now. I take the bowls—which number three because the only way to tame the tiny demon was with his own dish of soup—to the sink and wash up, loading everything into the dishwasher, drying the pot and tucking it back into the drawer beneath the cooktop.

By the time Christmas is saved on TV, the kitchen is clean and I'm feeling drowsy myself.

Only, as I start to walk past the troublesome duo on my way to the bedroom, I stop.

Study them.

The pillow is half under Nova's head, the blankets askew and bunched up.

She's going to wake up with a crick in her neck and a sore back.

Not my problem.

I keep walking down the hall.

But I haven't built a fire yet.

Not my problem.

Only, the power might go out and—

"Fuck," I mutter on a sigh, knowing I'm being an idiot, but still moving quietly toward the woman sleeping in the pile of blankets. I stare down at her, warring, but then I bend and scoop her up into my arms. Steve grumbles, rolls over, tiny legs in the air.

Nova slumps against my chest, breathing slow and steady as I carry her to bed, not moving as I tuck her beneath the comforter.

I tug the blanket up and over her then go back for the dog.

Who also doesn't move when I scoop *him* up and cradle him against my chest and carry him down the hall.

I tuck him in next to her, but when I go to turn away, to leave them to their nap in my bed, exhaustion washes over me.

Exhaustion and alcohol and—

No. Just exhaustion and alcohol.
And because there's only one bed...
I crawl in next to them.

TWENTY-FIVE

Nova

I SIGH and burrow my face into my pillow, feeling more rested than I have in ages.

I don't remember my mattress being this comfortable, but exhaustion will do that to a girl.

Steve's warm, steady weight is settled at my hip, his soft snoring filling the air.

My little guy, always at my side.

"Mmm," I murmur, stretching my arms over my head.

Or try to.

Because they're stuck, and for a second, I think they're tangled in the blankets. But then I come more fully awake, realize there's also a warm weight at my back—

No. A *hot* one.

And it's not the blankets.

It's much heavier than a blanket.

It's—

"Sweet fucking Christ," I whisper, my eyes flying open, head jerking on the pillow that's full of an intoxicating male scent, all spicy and warm, with notes of cedar and sage. I suck in a breath and turn toward...

Him.

Lake is lying on his side, his hand that had been resting on my hip now a solid weight on my belly.

If it slid down a couple of inches—

I shiver, remembering him on the counter, remembering the confident way he stroked me to completion, those thick, blunt fingers spearing into me.

Steve snorts and I realize my little pup is sprawled on his back between us, his puppy paws in the air, jowls hanging open, breathing loudly as always.

Me. My dog. Lake.

In bed together.

I need to get the fuck out of here.

Because *this*—the butterflies in my stomach when I see his face relaxed in sleep, see him passed out next to Steve—screams important.

This screams: Lake. *Does.* Matter.

And he doesn't. *This* doesn't. We're not in a romance novel. We're not snowed in together and suddenly going to fall head over heels in love with each other and tramp off through the white fluffy stuff to our happy ending. This is a series of shitty circumstances and a mischievous friend and her brother over-stepping that have all coalesced into a weird couple of days.

With one bed.

And one orgasm—for me.

And one hot hockey player sleeping next to me.

I exhale long and slow and quietly, mostly because if I don't do that, then I might scream. And if I scream, I might wake Lake. And if I wake Lake, then I'll have to deal with this knot in my stomach, this sense that everything's changing, this reality that I'm unfamiliar with.

I don't want to.

And...I have things to do.

So says the woman who just got fired and has found herself single and—

Fine.

I have a life to figure out.

Plans to make.

Except...that's not me. I can make a to-do list for the next few hours, but making a plan for life and sticking to it? No. That's freaking torture. I want to jump into life with both feet so I can keep moving forward—forward!—toward the next great thing.

I *want* to jump on top of Lake and experience that branch of his.

Which is the moment I realize insanity is creeping in.

I carefully pull the blankets back, slip out of the bed, out from under Lake's hand, away from my snoring pup and attempting not to wake him.

To wake *Steve.*

I pad away from the bed, out of the room, but something has me stopping in the open door, glancing back, feeling...

Something I never had with George.

Something I've never felt at all.

Like I want to turn around and crawl back in beside them.

It's so intense that I actually take a step toward the bed before I remember myself.

Down that path lies madness.

I spin around, walk down the hall, grab my boots, my coat, my camera, and...I step outside into the siren's call of Snow-mageddon.

❄ ❄ ❄ ❄

THE SNOW IS COMING DOWN RAPIDLY, the soft hiss and hum dulling the rest of my senses, encapsulating the world to just me in Lake's back yard, walking through the trees, looking up at the gray sky.

It's late afternoon, so I didn't sleep all that long, but I'm energized, ready, wanting to get lost in these woods, to go off on an adventure.

To look forward and move forward and not think about—

To not think. Period.

If I wouldn't freeze to death and leave Steve to fend for himself, I would just tromp off and not look back.

Never look back.

But Steve is inside, and I'm not loving the idea of turning into a human popsicle, so I stay within eyeshot of the house as I shoot. It's not the same out-of-body experience I had with the trees on the road, but I still get some good stuff. The flakes sweeping sideways across the landscape, falling so thickly it's almost creating an opaque curtain. The sheer amount of snow that's gathered, making everything look like it's covered in fluffy vanilla frosting—clumped onto the branches, sloping between the trees and through the back yard, gathering in drifts near the fence line, sticking to my gloved hands, the top of my camera.

It's quiet in that there's no car noise or kids running around playing and screaming. There are no airplanes flying overhead or phones ringing or neighbors gossiping.

But it's also noisy.

The snow falling isn't silent.

The wind pushing it to the side isn't either.

It's like my ears are filled with cotton, insulated from the rest of the world, like I'm alone on this alien planet and it's just me and my camera.

Up until the last couple of years when I moved in with George and began working for the magazine, when I thought I was settling down enough to get a dog, make a future, I made my living shooting nature shots, traveling the world and living through my camera lens.

I've shot in extremely isolated places in foreign countries, national parks that take days to hike to under dangerous conditions (animals or terrain or locals who may not want me there). I've shot in a volcano, underwater with scuba equipment I barely knew how to use. I've shot on mountaintops and in historic locations.

But my favorites are spots like these.

A random road. A quiet back yard. An unexpected slice of beauty found, not miles out in an isolated location, not at an Instagram-worthy beach.

Just here.

Just around the corner.

Discovered by continuing to move forward.

I sigh and take that bit of advice, walking toward the tree line, my camera at the ready, snapping shots almost at random and definitely just as the moment strikes me, not trying to frame anything too fancy, not trying for the perfect photograph.

Just *feeling*.

But I'm so into feeling what I'm *feeling* that I don't notice the prickling at my nape at first.

The sensation that someone's watching me.

That I'm not alone.

I freeze and listen, half-convinced that I'm about to have my own bear moment like Leo in *The Revenant,* but there's nothing except for the shushing of the snow, the hiss of the wind, and when I turn around, the snow is falling so thickly that I can't make out anything aside from the shadows of the tree trunks, the basic outline of the house in the distance.

Which is a pretty shot, so I pick up my camera, snap off a couple photos then turn back around and keep moving.

Only...

I don't realize the past is coming up behind me.

TWENTY-SIX

Lake

IT'S the snoring that wakes me.

Louder than a damn locomotive, roaring through the room, and rattling me out of sleep.

I groan as I open my eyes, seeing the tiny demon passed out on his back, all four paws up in the air, lips hanging away from his teeth.

He looks and sounds full demon.

And he's drooling on my mattress.

I scowl, and my scowl deepens when I lift my head, see that Nova's gone.

My phone is still in my pocket, jabbing at my hip, and I dig it out, see that barely an hour's passed between me sliding into bed and the tiny demon waking me up.

And in that time, Nova is gone.

"Woof! Woof!" Quiet, high-pitched barks, his little feet bouncing, mouth tightening and relaxing. "Woof! Woof! Woof!"

Dreaming.

It's...dare I say cute.

And that word running through my mind is enough for me to get up, to get out of bed. I toss the blankets back, inadvertently waking the beast as I get up.

He woofs again, does an insane amount of movement to get all of his limbs beneath him and then shakes violently, lips flopping, drool flying.

"Ew, man," I mutter, wiping my arm. "Jesus. Get it together."

Steve looks up at me with those wide, buggy eyes for a moment then his head cocks to the side, whine escaping.

"She's not here," I answer before I realize I'm talking to a dog. "Jesus."

I go to the bedroom door.

"Woof!"

I glance back.

The tiny demon is sitting at the foot of the bed, gaze trained on me, expression concerned.

Anthropomorphizing at its finest.

"Well," I say, impatient with myself, with him. "Let's go already."

Another woof as he jumps down and bounds over to me.

We walk down the hall and out into the family room together, finding it empty with the exception of that pile of blankets and clothes. I move over to them, take two minutes and fold the clothes and towels, setting them on the counter, leaving the blankets where they are because I don't have a fucking couch, worth twenty-five thousand dollars or otherwise.

By the time I finish with that, I've clocked that her camera and coat are gone, and Steve is sniffing at the door. I snag his leash, trust that the tiny demon is going to be capable of leading me to his master as I strap him into the contraption, something that's not easy because he's dancing around and sniffing at my face and he seems to have grown five more legs. Finally, though, I get him in the harness, snap the leash on, and grab my coat, shove my feet into my boots.

Then we're out the door, following her footprints. I pause to put the spare key back beneath the pot before moving around to the back deck that overlooks the couple of acres that come along with this property.

I can see the river that's lined with ice winding through my yard, the clusters of trees dotted throughout, the fence along one side of my neighbor put up years before.

The rest of it is vast and open, several acres of nature and forest and peace and privacy.

I pause at the top of the stairs that lead down the slope.

There are a lot of them, one of the few things I hate about this house, but flat lots are a commodity in this area and I wanted a kickass view from the back side of the house.

So...stairs.

Lots of them.

I'm not hating them so much now, not hating the view they give me of the yard, the way I can easily spot Nova in the distance, even with the snow falling fast.

She moves slowly, carefully, arms moving, lifting her camera.

She hasn't gone far, hasn't even made it to the river yet, to the pond beyond that has to be frozen over by now.

But she's photographing the trees again, and I wonder what the shots will look like.

If they'll be as beautiful as what I saw earlier.

"Woof!" Steve says as he tugs at the leash, clearly wanting

to get to his master. Giving in to that obvious need—and not whatever in the fuck I'm feeling—I start walking down the stairs.

Before I get halfway down, I'm thinking that I need to shovel these off before I break my neck.

Or before this damn dog gets hurt.

Or Nova.

Or her camera gets damaged.

I ignore the pinch in my chest and keep descending.

"Woof!" Steve pulls so hard at the leash that I almost eat shit, almost end up with a broken ass to go along with my broken neck. I throw my free hand out, grab the railing, fingers plowing through the snow gathered on the top of the banister, the cold a shock, but luckily, I manage to snag it so I don't die or allow Steve to plummet down to his snowy death.

"What the fuck, man?" I mutter.

Yes, to a dog.

No, I've not lost my mind.

Or more of it, anyway.

But, swear to fuck, Steve looks up at me then turns his gaze forward and woofs again like he's telling me to get my shit together.

Like he's telling me to fucking pay attention.

I focus ahead of us, eyes squinting through the falling snow.

It's harder to see Nova from down here, but I'm able to at least make out her silhouette in the trees.

"What?" I ask Steve as we reach the bottom of the stairs and he lurches to the end of the leash, a growl rumbling through his little body.

I squint again, letting Steve draw me forward through the snow.

Toward Nova.

Toward—

I falter for a step. "What the fuck?" I whisper as Steve's growl increases in volume, as he all but drags me forward.

Drags me toward—

A man.

A man towering over Nova as she stands amongst those trees.

TWENTY-SEVEN

Nova

ONE SECOND, I'm in the moment.

The next, I'm staring at a man I never wanted to see again.

And he's gripping my arms far too tight.

"What the fuck, Nova?" George shouts over the storm. "What are you doing?"

He starts dragging me forward, dragging me away from the peace I found, away from the sliver of happiness I regained, dragging me backward when I only want to move into the future.

"Let me go," I snap, my camera jerking painfully on my neck as he yanks me toward him. I clutch at it, knowing that I barely managed to reattach the strap, that it could break again, my camera could fall and—

George's eyes flash and he shakes me roughly. "No fucking way."

A tendril of fear curls through me.

Because I've never seen him like this.

Because this is scary.

"Do you know how much of a pain in the ass it was to find you?" he snaps. "Do you have any fucking idea? One day you're staying with Ella and the next, I come home and all your shit is gone."

"Why would you want to find me?" I ask, trying again to slip out of his hold, trying to inch away so I can get away from him, get back to the house. To...Lake.

His hands tighten. "You're my girlfriend."

I laugh. I can't help it. I see that my reaction pisses him off more, know that it's the wrong move, but...I can't stop it. Because, "I saw you and Ashley."

His face changes then, colder, harder, scarier than before. "You didn't see what you think you did."

"I didn't see your penis thrusting into my sister's vagina? Really? I just imagined it?"

"I knew you would be back here," he says instead of answering me. "I just fucking knew that you wouldn't be in the house like a sane person. You'd be out here with that damn camera and taking pictures instead of doing what you should be doing."

"And what am I supposed to be doing?"

"Taking care of me and Ashley," he snaps. "Instead, you just...flit off, living your own life, too fucking obstinate and headstrong for your own good."

Was this man my boyfriend—*ex*—or my parent, or my child?

Because those words were a mishmash of them all...and yet none of them.

"You're both adults," I say. "And, not that it matters anymore, but I think I showed you plenty of care the last time you were sick. I think I showed it when I did your laundry and cleaned the apartment and made your doctor's and dentist appointments. I think I showed it when I learned how to make your favorite meals even though I can't stand meatloaf *or* stew." I tug against him again but can't slip free of his hold. "And not that it's any of your business, but I also think I showed Ashley plenty of care growing up and throughout the years since, and she repaid that energy by fucking my boyfriend."

He sniffs.

"So," I ask. "Why are you really here?"

And really, *how* is he here? Had the roads been plowed?

"I was worried and..."

My brows shoot up. "And what?"

"And when I saw your car on the side of the road, I hiked up here."

To Lake's house. Specifically to his back yard?

I frown.

Speaking of that, where *is* Lake?

Still sleeping?

Or did he sic this asshole on me?

Probably the second one.

Although, the man who carried me to nap in his bed, who tucked blankets around me, wouldn't—

George shakes me again, hard enough that my teeth rattle together, that my head wobbles on my neck, that pain shoots down my spine.

"Stop," I say, squirming against him, trying to get out of his hold.

But all that succeeds in doing is making him tighten his grip on my arms. "You stop," he snaps, shaking me again, this time so hard that my eyes start watering. "You're going to walk your ass down the hill and get in my fucking car and you're going to apologize to your sister and make things right with both of us."

"Fuck that," I say. "I'm not going to—"

He talks over me. "And then we're going home, and things will go back to nor—"

All of a sudden, I'm thrown forward, nearly colliding with a tree, but I don't hit it because there's an arm wrapping around my middle, drawing me back against a strong chest.

But that arm isn't rough.

It holds me gently for a beat before I'm behind Lake's broad body.

"Woof!" Steve barks, a couple steps ahead of us, and I lean around to watch, wide-eyed, as my tiny pup launches himself at George, getting some serious air as he leaps up and latches onto my ex's hand.

"Ow! Fuck," George says, trying to shake him off.

But my dog has demon blood.

He's not easy to dislodge.

Only then George rears back and—

"Don't!" Lake snaps.

Too late.

Steve squeals as George's fist connects with his side and lets go, landing in the snow in a heap.

"Steve!" I gasp, lurching forward.

George lifts his leg, preparing to kick, but before I can get to him, Lake is there, shoving George back into a tree, his elbow pressed into George's throat. A glance over his shoulder. "Check on Steve, butterfly."

I inhale, broken from my stasis with that order, dropping to my knees in front of my baby, who stares up at me with pain in his eyes. He tries to get up, tongue out, panting heavily despite the cold air whipping around us, but collapses with a pained sound.

"Shit," I whisper, eyes tearing up.

That's the worst sound I've ever heard.

I carefully scoop him up.

"Let's get him inside the house," Lake says, whipping George around, taking my ex's arm and bending it behind his back, frog-marching him forward.

We move slowly up the snow-filled stairs, having to proceed carefully because of the accumulating snow, because some of that snow is turning to ice. Steve whimpers a few times, but doesn't otherwise make a sound, doesn't try to launch himself out of my arms in order to chase an errant snowflake, to pee on a deck post.

He just lays limply in my hold.

Worry digs its claws in deeper.

"Breathe, butterfly," Lake murmurs as he draws George to the side at the top of the stairs. "And walk carefully, yeah?"

I inhale.

Exhale.

"Yeah," I whisper with a nod and start moving forward again, rounding the corner of the house, moving around to the front of the house, to the front door—

Then skid to a halt so quickly I nearly fall.

Focused on getting away from him, I hadn't really heard the final words that George said in the woods, hadn't really *processed* them.

But turning the corner and seeing who's standing on the porch has them whipping back through my mind, slamming home, nearly sending me to my knees.

Steve stiffens in my arms, growls softly.

"Shh," I whisper, kissing the top of his furry head. "It's okay."

Footsteps behind me.

A scuffle.

The woman in front of me straightens from where she was bending toward the green pot on the porch and cries out, starting toward us. "What are you doing to him?"

"Don't fucking move," Lake snaps. He comes close, bends forward over my shoulder and I glance up at him. "Your sister?" he asks softly.

"Yeah."

"Jesus Christ," he mutters.

"It's fine," I say. "I can handle—"

A hand on my hip. "Right by me, butterfly."

Then he nudges me forward and we walk side by side to the door.

She opens her mouth. "Nova—"

"Shut up," Lake growls, cutting off my sister.

George starts in. "Don't—"

"You shut up too," Lake says, still growling, still holding George tightly by the arm. Then he moves to the door, punches a few buttons on the automatic lock near the knob, and pushes the wooden panel wide, standing to the side.

A glance down at me.

A nod to go in before him.

I carry Steve to the pile of blankets, carefully maneuver him onto them. He whimpers again but immediately tries to stand up. Only, he's not bearing weight on all of his legs, his back right one hangs limply. "Stay there, honey," I whisper, coaxing him back down, knowing that I'll have to get him seen by a vet somehow.

Knowing that if George and Ashley made it to Lake's house, there has to be a way out for us.

My stomach convulses at that thought, but I ignore it, resume carefully tucking the blankets around my poor pup.

"I know it's shit timing"—my head flies up, eyes going to Lake, seeing George on the floor by the door, Ashley pale-skinned and standing next to him—"but I need you to come out to my place." A pause. "I know the roads are shit and ours hasn't been plowed yet, but you have the snowmobile, Mack, and I need you to pick up Jer on the way." Another pause before he curses softly. "Yeah, man, you know there are tickets in it for you."

Tickets?

I frown, start to stand up.

"They'll even be on the glass if you can be here within the hour."

TWENTY-EIGHT

THE PROPER MOTIVATION IN PLACE, and Mack's assurances that he'll be here as soon as possible, I glare at Nova's sister.

"If I were you, I'd sit your ass down and shut up."

She scoffs, but clambers down next to the asshole whose head I want to rip off.

He hurt Nova.

He put hands on her, shook her like a rag doll.

He hurt Steve.

The urge to commit murder rises again, and I exhale slowly, trying to let it go, trying to release the anger.

Knives thrown my direction.

Shrieking and shouting and weaponized tears.

Stories sold to the press.

Olivia doing—

It doesn't matter.

All of the bad shit—through all of that bullshit, all of the dysfunction and drama and the fucking theatrics, I never once put my hands on a woman.

Fucking. *Never.*

The asshole opens his mouth, probably to spout off about his treatment, but I just shoot him a glare and turn toward Nova. She's crouching next to Steve, her expression set in deep lines, the worry clear even from fifteen feet away.

I want to go to her, but I can't.

I need to stay here, and…

Fuck. It doesn't matter.

I just can't go there.

But my feet start carrying me over anyway, and then I'm squatting down next to her. "Help is coming," I say. "For Steve and to get these assholes out of here."

She glances up at me with glimmering emerald eyes. "What do you mean?"

There's a scuffle back by the front door, so I don't have the chance to explain. Mostly because my next minutes are taken up by tackling the asshole to the floor, ripping his car keys from his pocket, and then, pulse pounding, adrenaline ramping, hands fisting, desperate to plow into the asshole's face, I shove him down to the floor.

"You can go," I say and hold up the keys, "but you'll be going without these."

"Fuck you," he snaps.

"Right back at you," I mutter, pocketing the set before turning to Nova's sister. "And you're welcome to fuck off right out of here too."

"I-I'm just trying to talk to my sister." Her lip quivers, and I don't buy the innocent act at all.

"That's not happening."

She crosses her arms, innocent falling away right on cue.

Drama and bullshit coming out, as is typical of women. "You can't tell me what to do."

Just not *all* women.

Or maybe...just not Nova.

"Sure can," I say, narrowing my eyes at her. "Especially when you're trespassing."

A blip of something crosses her face—guilt, calculation. But it's gone a second later. "I don't even know who you are," she snaps.

"And I don't give a fuck," I tell her. "Brave the storm or shut the fuck up."

"Brave it in an empty house?" she sneers.

"An empty house with heat, or a blizzard that's going to get worse in the next hour." I shrug. "Your choice." Not giving her a chance to reply to that, I go to the kitchen, fill up a couple of bags of ice, and bring them to Nova.

"Coat off," I order, carefully removing her camera, setting it on the floor.

"What?" she whispers, pausing in her gentle stroking of Steve's forehead, skin pale, eyes damp. No drama here. Just care and concern...and a woman who's taken more than a few hits in life.

"Butterfly," I say more firmly. "Coat. Off."

Her throat works. "I'm fine—"

I tug the tab of her jacket down, peel it from her arms. Then I undo the zip of her hooded sweatshirt, tug up the sleeves of her T-shirt beneath.

Then have to bite back the urge to slam my fist into her ex's face again.

There are fingerprints on her arms, dark bruises already forming.

She winces and I release the fabric. "Ice," I grunt, setting the bags gently over those short sleeves, knowing it probably won't make a difference, but needing to do something.

No hysterics.

No tears—or at least none for herself.

She's calm, but I hate the vacant look in her eyes, hate how rocked to the core she looks, hate how it reminds me of how she was when I yelled at her on the side of the road.

But she rebounded then.

She can do it now too.

"Snap out of it, butterfly," I say. "That asshole cheated on you, remember?"

A flash of fury in deep green eyes. "Yeah," she hisses. "I remember, considering I walked in on him balls deep in my sister."

Good.

Fire. Rage. Not lost and hurt and scared.

"Then act like it, yeah?" I say, reaching for her hands, gently lifting them, crossing her arms over her chest and settling her palms over those bags of ice so she can hold them in place. "Instead of mooning over a shitty man and your bitch of a sister."

Her chin juts out. "You really are an asshole, you know that, right?"

"Maybe," I agree. "But when a woman's mine, she's mine. I don't look anywhere else, I don't want anyone else, and I will *never* be balls deep in a cunt that isn't mine."

She sucks in a breath.

But I don't stick around to watch her face, don't stay near her and allow myself to feel what that look in her eyes does to me. I don't do anything but stand up, move to the door and watch out the windows for Mack and Jer.

❋ ❋ ❋ ❋

I HEAR the motor of the snowmobile before I catch a glimpse of it coming up the road, the nose visible through the trees first.

Squinting, I crane my neck, relief sliding through me when I see two bodies on the back of it as Mack navigates into my driveway.

I have the door open the next instant, wanting to meet the sheriff, to brief him on the shitshow, the extra assholes I have in my house. But I'm not leaving Nova.

Or Steve.

So, I just wait for them in the doorway, impatience in every cell, fury blooming in my stomach.

Finally, they grab their shit and come up to the door.

"These have better be the best tickets of my life," Mack calls, clomping up to my front door.

The snow has slowed, but the temperature has dropped.

Which means we're going to be contending with an ass-ton of ice in the morning.

Now, though, we have bigger shit to deal with.

"Did Jer bring his stuff?"

Mack cocks his head to the side, but, no doubt taking in my tone, he just nods and picks up the pace. "Want to break it down for me?"

"Have a friend staying at my house. Her—"

Mack's brows shoot up, probably because I don't have female friends and I sure as shit don't have female friends staying at my house, but I ignore him.

"Her," I say again, "asshole ex decided to show up and assault her."

"I did not!" George says, exactly like the asshole he is.

Mack barely glances at him, flashing his badge. "I'll be with you in a minute, sir," he says calmly, but I know just from my one statement and the outburst from George that he's already lost whatever little amount of patience he would have had with the other man. Mack doesn't tolerate violence toward anyone, but he sure as shit doesn't tolerate it against women.

"Then he kicked her dog," I say.

"That little shit bit me—"

"The dog is all of fifteen pounds and was determined to protect his owner," I interject.

Mack's jaw hardens.

I also know him well enough to understand this is the kiss of death for George.

Violence against animals is another trigger point for the local sheriff.

"That dog *bit* me!" George shouts, pushing to his feet, moving toward us aggressively.

"I wouldn't," I warn.

George puffs up his chest. "Fuck you!"

"Sit down," Mack snaps.

"And fuck you too!" George yells at Mack.

This is the wrong move.

This makes me smile for the first time since I looked out in the back yard and saw what was happening.

Because approximately three seconds after George tells Mack to fuck off, Nova's ex is face down on the hardwood floor, his hands cuffed behind him.

"You rang?"

My smile is wiped away when I see Jer on the threshold. The vet had a big bag in one hand, another tossed over his shoulder.

"Yeah," I say, tilting my head toward the pile of blankets.

He starts toward Nova and Steve, glances back over his shoulder. "I get tickets too, right?"

I sigh.

"Yeah, Jer. On the glass."

TWENTY-NINE

Nova

"I DON'T THINK this is broken," the kindly old vet says long minutes later, stethoscope draped around his shoulders. He's given Steve an extremely gentle and thorough exam. "But I'll splint it anyway, and you should make sure he takes it easy."

Steve huffs out a sigh, slumping into the blankets, much more comfortable now that Jer—the kindly vet with the shock of white hair—had given him an injection for his pain.

"I don't think that will be a problem," I say softly, as the snores start to come.

Jer smiles. "Not for today, anyway. I'll leave you some oral pain medicine and small supply of tranquilizers, just in case, but have Lake call me if anything seems off with him and I'll come right back out." He pulls out some supplies, starts expertly wrapping up Steve's leg, and doing it in such a way that my little pupper doesn't so much as miss a snore. "And then," he says, "once we're dug out a little bit, come into the clinic for an X-ray."

"Okay," I say softly, eyes stinging.

Because Steve is okay.

Because this man dropped everything to come help me.

Because Lake made the call in the first place.

And because...my sister is still sitting inside the front door, her gaze on me.

Pleading, even from a distance. Calculating, even from a distance.

My stomach churns, and not in a good way. I've always known she was selfish—it's hard not to be when we grew up as we did. The urge to hoard anything that feels good, any love and care and kindness shown to us. It's...a ravenous beast that's never satisfied, always wanting more and more and more.

She always wants more.

I...I just find my *more* by hitting the road and searching out—

Snore!

Something I haven't figured out yet.

I tear my gaze from my sister, turn back to my pup and the vet, and help Jer pack up, thanking him as we move toward the door.

He smiles, nods toward the brooding hockey player shooting arrows from his eyes toward my ex and my sister. "Thank Lake," he says. "I'll never turn down free tickets to the Sierra. In fact"—he looks around—"you don't have a cat I can help? Or a guinea pig? A bearded dragon?" He waggles his brows. "Then I can *really* turn the screws on Lake."

For the first time since George showed up, I feel like smiling. "No," I say. "I just have the one pet."

"Thank God," Ashley mutters and I glare at her then focus on the scene outside the large window behind my sister, see George standing by a large black SUV with flashing lights on top.

George, who hurt my pet.

George, who hurt *me*.

"Damn," Jer says lightly.

I focus back on him, try to think of something to say, and settle on, "I think you might be able to trade tickets for a couch."

Jer's mouth twitches and he taps his temple. "I like the way you think."

"Can I help you carry your stuff out?"

He shakes his head. "I'm fine. Stay in here where it's warm."

I force a smile, one he sees right through if his eyes gentling as he reaches in and squeezes my hand is any indication. His next words confirm it. "Your pup is okay, and I think with Lake at your side, you will be okay too."

"Thanks," I whisper.

But he's wrong.

Lake isn't at my side.

He's made that quite clear.

Another squeeze and Jer's gone, walking out the door, pausing next to the heavy-duty SUV that has made it through the snow, its bright headlights illuminating the scene. There's also a gathering of snowmobiles, several other members of the sheriff's department having congregated in Lake's driveway.

They're all standing around and talking while George is handcuffed and forced to stand out in the cold.

I don't feel bad.

He hurt my baby. He can be left to go full human popsicle, for all I care. I turn away from the windows—

"Sissy."

My insides clench, but I force myself to look at my sister.

At another person who doesn't matter because she's shown that I don't matter to her over and over and *over* again.

I lift a brow as I turn to face her.

"I didn't mean to hurt you."

Laughter bubbles up in me. "So you were fucking my boyfriend as what? A favor to me?"

Her bottom lip immediately slides out into a pout.

Same shit. Different day.

Only...I'm tired. "Look," I say. "You hurt me. A lot, but"—I sigh—"you did me a favor. George is clearly a jerk and—"

"Yes." She nods rapidly, playing bobblehead. "George is *totally* a jerk and—"

"And you are too."

Ashley rocks back, shock on her face.

"This surprises you?" I ask.

"It's always been the two of us," she says.

"No." I shake my head and bite back another sigh. "It's always been you, Ash. What you want and need. I haven't let myself factor into our relationship in years, maybe not ever."

"Mom and Dad left—"

"Yeah," I say. "They left. But they left *me* too, and that also hurt me. And, Christ, it's not just about you and your feelings all the time, Ash. I—" I sigh. "*You* hurt me, not just a couple of times, not just a few days ago, but *too* many times over the years." I shove a hand through my hair, strive to stay calm. "I'm done, babe."

"I didn't *mean* to hurt you."

I study her closely. "Didn't you?"

She flinches, but there's something in her expression, in the way she lifts her chin. She's sorry, yeah, but mostly, I think she's sorry she got caught.

She's sorry I'm distancing myself so I'm not an easy target.

She's sorry—

I sigh. It doesn't matter. I can barely look at her, let alone think about having her in my life at this moment. "You've never cared when you hurt me before," I say, hating the cynicism that's filled me, but knowing it's there for a reason.

Because I've allowed her to treat me like this.

Let it go. Look forward. It doesn't matter.

Only...sometimes it does.

I shake those thoughts from my mind. "Why did you really light a fire under George's butt to get him to bring you up here?"

Ashley doesn't have a car.

She usually borrows mine because I rarely need it. I can —*could*—walk to work, the grocery store, my favorite restaurants.

Guilt slides across her face, and my gut clenches.

"You didn't," I whisper.

She looks away.

And that's answer enough.

My eyes sting again, but this time it's because I'm furious, because I cannot believe my sister would do this to me, would hurt me this way...and that she doesn't even care enough to fix it. She only allowed herself to come along because—

I go ramrod stiff, gape at her.

My words are a hiss. "Tell me you didn't."

Her eyes, a familiar green I see in the mirror every day, darken with guilt. A sad sight, if only it wasn't complete bullshit.

"I—" She licks her lips, presses them together. "They're not just yours."

Betrayal slices through me, but the fury slices deeper, exposing...

How done I am.

How stupid I was for dating someone like George.

A user. Just like my sister.

Selfish. Just like my sister.

Pathetic—no, that's just me.

"You've really burned through everything I gave you?" I ask.

She flinches again. "But—"

"No buts," I say. "No excuses. No...*more.* I don't want to see your face or hear your voice and I-I—" My voice cracks and it takes everything in me to inhale, exhale, and have my words come out steady. "I don't think I can ever forgive you."

"George—"

"Is a fucking jerk," I say. "But you're worse."

She shrinks back.

I move to the kitchen, to my duffle, to my hastily packed belongings, my memories of my parents, of my grandmother who stepped in and cared for us when good old Mom and Dad skipped town, leaving us alone in an apartment without food, without rent paid, all when Ash was six and I was eight years old.

Kids abandoned.

Alone.

Then not...because our grandma stepped in.

She died, though. Died and left us and we were stuck fending for ourselves again—I was stuck taking care of my sister and then, as an afterthought, myself.

Probably why we are here at this juncture.

I reach into the bag, pull out the black velvet box, and move back to my sister.

"Here," I say. "Just take them and go."

She snatches them from my hold, flips open the lid, all business, solely focused on herself.

That's a familiar feeling.

"Where's the butterfly pendant?"

My fingers itch to reach into my pocket, to feel the familiar rough texture of the stones from our grandmother's necklace, all that I'll have left of her now that I've handed over that small jewelry box to my sister. "Steve chewed it up and broke it."

Truth.

But also not.

A disdainful look toward my pup. "Clearly, he deserved that kick George gave him."

It feels like *I've* been kicked with that comment, but I just lift my chin. "I'm going to need you to go."

"But—"

"Go, Ash," I say, yanking the door open.

She closes the jewelry box, walks outside, doesn't look back.

I close it behind her.

Then I go to the kitchen.

And I get out the vodka.

Forward. Just keep crawling fucking forward.

THIRTY

"THANKS, MACK," I say, shaking his hand as one of his deputies shoves George into the back of the SUV, not being all that careful of the asshole's head.

Hit it a few more times and maybe then we'll be equal.

No, we won't be.

But I would feel better, at least.

"No thanks required." Mack grins and rubs his hands together. "I've gotten all the payment I need."

The sheriff doesn't get that my tickets often go unused or donated. My family has seen enough of me playing hockey. They're not going to travel halfway across the continent, sleep in a bed that's not their own, disrupt their regularly-scheduled routine.

Definitely not my mom—she does best in her own home with all of her familiar things.

Certainly not my dad—he would have to give two fucks about me for that to happen.

My siblings have their own lives—and, anyway, it's not their job to support me.

The SUV pulls out, taking the asshole with it, leaving room for Nova's car, which is idling on the street, dug out of the snowbank thanks to a break in the storm and another pair of tickets to the local tow company.

They pull it into my garage, pass over the keys as the metal door rolls down.

Mack lifts his brows. "I'm sensing a story here."

"No story," I say.

The look he shoots me tells me he knows that's bullshit, but the wind's picking up again, and we're all ready to go the fuck to sleep.

So, he lets that go.

Jer claps a hand on my shoulder. "Keep an eye on that one, yeah?" He nods toward the house. "There's something special about her."

I'm seeing that too.

I've *seen* it too.

Which is why I sacrifice another pair of my tickets before I let him go.

"About that," I say. "Do you still have that contact at the gallery?"

❄ ❄ ❄ ❄

WITH A PROMISE from Jer that he'll follow up with me after he makes a few calls, I wait until I'm sure everyone gets off safely— the engine noise of the snowmobiles reverberating through the trees as they pull away.

Nova's car keys are in my pocket, but George's are long gone because I gave those to Mack to deal with.

I *was* slightly annoyed that when Ashley came out of the

house, he merely passed them over to her, though the petty in me loved that no one offered her a ride down the hill to where she and George left the vehicle, unable to make it all the way up to my driveway.

Watching her slip and slide her way down the street was perfection.

And it was definitely worth gifting those tickets to the tow company for whatever magic they pulled to get Nova's car to my house.

Now, though, my driveway is clear and my peace is restored, and I have nothing keeping me out here except for...

The knot in my gut that's telling me if I *do* go inside, everything will keep changing.

Slippery fucking slope.

And not just out here.

Sighing, I embrace the inevitable and make my way into my house. Nova's cooking something that smells delicious, but it's not her at the stove that has my stomach knotting.

It's the bottle of vodka on the counter.

The smell of lemon in the air.

Damn.

I move to her, taking a peek at her face, seeing the slightly reddened eyes, the puffiness around them. Crying, but not any longer.

Christ, she's strong.

"Just grilled cheeses and tomato soup," she says. "Nothing fancy."

I want to pull her close, to bend my head and inhale the scent of her, to get that tingle of cinnamon in my nose. "You didn't have to cook. I could—"

She smiles brightly. "You got my car out of the snowbank. It's the least I can do."

"It's nothing." I shake my head. "There was a break in the storm, and the tow company—"

"You asked."

I couldn't fudge that over. "Yeah," I admit.

She sighs, that bright smile dimming.

"What?"

A little of her this-is-fine, everything-is-fine veneer shatters. "Why would you do that?" she whispers. "I—you don't even like me."

"It doesn't matter if I like you." I shrug. "Because, like I said, it's nothing."

Her shoulders go stiff and her eyes study mine. "Right." She stirs the pot. "Just so I'm not confused where I stand. It's nothing. I'm nothing. This is all"—she waves the spoon, sending splatters of red soup onto the counter—"nothing."

It's not nothing.

But I don't tell her that.

"Yup. Nothing special."

"Exactly," she mutters, ripping off a paper towel from the roll and using it to wipe up the droplets. "I'm nothing special to you, but you helped me—more than once." A breath. "So, dinner is the least I can do. Then," she says, flipping one of the sandwiches, revealing a perfectly crisp, golden-brown toasting, "I'll eat, gather my stuff and Steve, and get out of your hair so you can get back to your life."

My brows drag together. "What the fuck are you talking about?"

"Like we've established." She lifts one shoulder, drops it. "This is all nothing, and since my car's back, and George and Ash made it up here, clearly, the time to get out is now." A beat. "While I still can."

The smart thing would be to let her go. Hell, the smart

thing would be to help her pack her shit so she leaves all that much sooner.

But...some part of me can't.

"That's a terrible idea," I blurt instead.

She drops some sprigs of rosemary into a pan then frowns up at me. "I'm sure you're ready to have your house back."

I should be. But...it would feel empty. Too quiet without the tiny demon's snoring, without Nova's presence.

She starts juicing a lemon, catching the seeds in her palm.

"Stay tonight," I murmur.

Her shoulders hitch up again. "Lake, I—" She shakes her head. "This is a dumb conversation. It's pointless to have me stay here when you just want me to go. When *I* want to go. When I want to be anywhere else, with *anyone* else."

I should let her leave.

She doesn't want to be here.

But my palms settle on those shoulders drawn up so high and tight, my fingers gently rubbing at the taut muscles. "Maybe," I admit. "But it's not safe for you to drive home. The roads are still dangerous."

She cranes her neck to look up at me, her hand tight around the lemon, juice dripping slowly over her fingers. "They made it up here."

"Butterfly."

A blink. Slow.

Her cheeks red.

Her body wavering the slightest bit and giving me the only excuse I have.

"They also didn't have half a bottle of vodka."

She frowns then sighs. "I—"

Reaching by her, I bring the bottle close, point at it's almost empty contents.

"Oh." A beat. "Right."

I slide my hands down the outsides of her arms, turn her, and cup her jaw. "Stay tonight," I order softly.

Her shoulders rise and fall on a slow exhale. "I would be fine."

"I know," I say, still soft. "Stay anyway."

Silence, her gaze drifting from mine, focusing on the counter.

I hold my breath.

Until she nods. "Okay."

I exhale silently. "Good, butterfly," I say, taking the lemon from her hand and ignoring the warning sirens blaring in my mind. "Now, teach me how to make this magical drink of yours."

Now she smiles. It's bright but isn't fake, and that does something to my heart—those fingers squeezing again, my pulse picking up.

"I did make my rosemary simple syrup," she says, nodding at the pot with the sprigs of herbs in it.

I squeeze the lemon into the bowl. "Does that make it better?"

She huffs out a laugh. "Does it make it better?" She tosses her hair over one shoulder, rubs her hands together. "My rosemary simple syrup is *everything.*"

"Well," I say, moving closer and sniffing at the concoction in the pot. "It doesn't smell like much."

Outrage now, but it's good-natured.

And it distracts her enough that she stops talking about leaving.

Instead, she teaches me how to make the drink.

And then supervises me as I match the next batch.

Then the next.

And eventually, we find ourselves back on the pile of blankets, bellies full of soup and grilled cheese sandwiches and

Twix bars for dessert, glasses topped off with mules that are definitely better with that simple syrup, and a snoring Steve between us, watching another classic movie—this one *Die Hard* (the original, because that's clearly the best one).

And eventually, I have two mammals snoring next to me while gunshots sound on the TV.

That's when I stop fighting it.

This urge to get closer.

This urge to push her away.

I'm probably leaping from a plane without a parachute, plummeting to my demise.

But...I don't care.

I scoop them up one by one and carry them to my bed. Then I stand there, just for a moment, before I slide in next to them, the pleasant fuzziness in my mind from all those honey rosemary mules making the battle to resist all that much shorter.

I just...wave my white flag again, get under the covers, and wrap my arms around them.

Then I let sleep come.

But when I wake up the next morning, it's to find Nova not in bed beside me.

THIRTY-ONE

Nova

IT LOOKS CHEAP.

Probably because of the bite marks.

And, truthfully, it's not all that expensive, just some gemstones, maybe even a few crystals, but there's also a pair of minuscule diamonds at the center.

I know they're real diamonds.

Because I bought this for my grandma.

Saved up for ages to afford it.

Now the pup I love has chewed it and there are missing stones in the wings, and one of those diamonds has disappeared into the ether—

That is Steve's digestive system.

My heart pulses as I run my finger over the rough surface, feeling the bumps of each stone against my pads.

"It's just stuff," I whisper, shoving it back into my pocket.

But it doesn't feel like just stuff.

It feels like more.

My head is pounding and I want to say it's because I drank too much, it's because I'm nursing a hangover.

That's a lie.

The aches in my heart and head are because my sister just...took the jewelry and left without a backward glance. She didn't drive up in the middle of a snowstorm to make things right with me, to apologize.

She wanted something.

And George, what? Was mad I left without a word? Wanted his maid and laundry girl back? Really needed my recipe for meatloaf? It *is* kickass, but...I don't think it's any of those. I think he was seriously shocked that I *would* leave.

I hadn't before.

I put up with everything, took it. Because that's what I do.

Run off my back. I don't care if you hurt me. It doesn't matter because I'm fine—I'm *always* fine.

Or maybe Ashley just wanted the jewelry.

I rub at my forehead, find I don't have any more space in my brain for George.

He's gone, hopefully forever, and I don't have to look too closely at the reasons we were together, at why I picked someone like him to be with in the first place, to be with for so long.

"It doesn't matter," I say out loud.

"I find that usually the more I say that, the more it *does* matter."

Gasping, I turn around and see Lake standing there shirtless and beautiful, Steve tucked under one arm, looking much more alert this morning.

"It's time for his medicine," Lake says, moving toward me and passing my pup over. "Why don't you get that for him, and then I'll take him out to the bathroom and make us all breakfast."

Drawing my brows together, I shake my head. "You don't have to—"

But he's already turning away, disappearing back down the hall.

By the time I wrap a pill in a piece of cheese and feed Steve his breakfast, Lake is back, socks on his feet and tugging a shirt over his torso.

Sad, that.

Covering all that muscled gloriousness.

He stops next to me, eyes on the floor—thus, thankfully missing my drooling. He glances up, head shaking, mouth curved. "I still cannot believe a creature that small can make that much noise."

My lips twitch. "Steve's just making sure he gets every last crumb."

A snort that's very much like my starving pup's. "It doesn't look like he's ever missed a crumb."

Gasping, I bend and cover Steve's ears. "Don't listen to him, baby. You're perfect, just the way you are."

For what it's worth, Steve *doesn't* listen to Lake, and he doesn't listen to me either. He's fully focused on food, on licking up every last morsel from his bowl—even with my hands over his ears. I look up at Lake, and it's to see something on his face that has my hands dropping away, my heart squeezing again.

I straighten, brush my palms on the front of my sweats. "I'll get his leash."

Lake opens his mouth, and I hesitate, but he just says, "I'll get my boots."

And then when Steve finishes licking his bowl—read, I finally pick it up and bring it to the sink so I can wash it—Lake carries my dog outside.

❄ ❄ ❄ ❄

MORE SNOW HAS BEEN DUMPED and I have the feeling that I missed my window to drive out.

To keep moving forward.

I *should* be upset.

But instead, I'm standing in the window, watching Lake trying to get my pup to focus enough to use the bathroom.

He's put the leash on, which I don't think is strictly necessary, since Steve's leg is still in the splint, but one never knows with my pup, so I can't really fault Lake. But even with my pup down a leg, he's pulling his typical walk shenanigans.

Sniffing.

Barking.

Not focusing.

Not using the facilities.

I keep expecting Lake to be impatient, and almost went outside to interject. But...he's patient, just walking Steve slowly back and forth, letting my dog choose the path, letting him sniff to his heart's content. And when my troublesome pupper finally does deign to make use of his outside bathroom, Lake lets out a whoop I hear through the glass, bending to rub my pup behind the ears.

Steve's tongue lolls out, a puppy smile on his face.

And there my heart goes again.

Stupid, huh?

❄ ❄ ❄ ❄

"I THINK the snow's going to keep falling like this for a while yet."

I look up from my plate of blueberry pancakes—something that might be the most delicious thing I've ever eaten—and meet Lake's gorgeous hazel eyes. "Yeah," I say, when he seems to be waiting for an answer.

"Are you going to go out and take more pictures?"

I inhale, heart doing that thing again.

But then I shake my head. "No," I whisper. "I don't think so."

He frowns. "Why not?"

"I have enough shots to choose from," I lie.

Hazel eyes on mine, studying the very depths of my soul. "I don't think that's it."

I shrug. "You don't have to think anything about my life."

His head tilts the other way, still studying me closely. "You know your pictures are uncommonly good," he says softly.

I shove another bite into my mouth, shrug. "If they were so good, I wouldn't have gotten fired, would I?"

"Bullshit."

I narrow my eyes.

"You don't believe that."

No, I don't believe it, even though it's a convenient excuse.

I'm good at what I do, and I enjoy it.

"You're freaked after what happened yesterday."

I freeze, a bite of pancake hanging off the tines of my fork.

Shadows coalescing into a person.

George's angry face.

Pain shooting down my arms.

"Easy to solve," he says, scooping the last of his pancake off his plate and into his mouth. "Just a matter of getting right back out there before the fear sets in."

"Why do you sound like you're familiar with that?" I ask softly.

He shocks me by actually answering. "I had a bad injury right after I made it into the league, nearly ended my career, and it fucked with my head during my recovery. The best thing my asshole of a coach ever did for me was sending me right back out there, letting my instincts take over, getting me right back into my groove." He fixes me with a look. "So that's what we're going to do."

Heart fluttering then squeezing hard.

"Why do you care if I get back into my groove?" I whisper.

He looks away from me for a long moment, long enough that I'm not sure I want to know the answer. So, when he looks back, I blurt out, "Steve can't walk far."

A pause.

Then, "You've got the crate"—something I retrieved from my car the night before—"But"—a nod behind me—"I think he's happy where he is."

I follow his stare, see that my pup is passed out in the nest of blankets.

My pulse speeds up.

I search for another excuse, another reason to not do this.

Lake doesn't give me the chance.

He pushes up, takes my plate that I've somehow scraped clean without really noticing. "Get your shit, butterfly. We're going to take some pictures."

THIRTY-TWO

Lake

SHE'S SELF-CONSCIOUS AT FIRST, glancing back at me over and over again.

Until I ask her to explain what she's doing.

Then something unlocks in her, a brightness.

A lightness.

A woman I've only had glimpses of before then.

She talks about aperture and shutter speed and something called ISO. She mentions the importance of white exposure and shows me how she frames a shot, what catches her eye.

"You see?" she says, holding up the camera so I can look at the back of it. "That's not quite right, but if I angle it like this and pull back here—"

I hear the rapid clicking of the shutter opening and closing before she holds it up again.

"This is better, right?"

I blink, actually seeing that it *is* better. "Yeah, butterfly. That's really good."

She smiles up at me and swear to fuck, my heart skips a beat before I manage to rein that in. Luckily, she's focused on the camera, on powering it down and putting on the lens cap. "I think that's enough for now. Should we go back?"

"Nah," I say. "Let's go a little further." I lift my chin. "There's a lake on the corner of my property you'll like."

She blinks, cheeks pink from the cold, nose kissable as she looks up at me. "Planning on drowning me?"

"Nah," I say, glad she's relaxed enough out here that she's able to snark at me again. "I would have done that in the river. The lake is frozen over."

"Considering all your options," she says with a quick grin. "I do like a man who plans ahead."

"Nah, baby," I say, "I think you like to fly by the seat of your pants."

She misses a step and I reach out, snag her arm, steadying her. My bag hits her arm and she winces. "Planning to brain me with your backpack instead?" she teases.

"Sorry, butterfly."

Another missed step, but this time I manage to steady her without attempted murder.

"Why do you keep calling me that?"

Yeah.

Why?

Because I'm an idiot and I can't seem to stop.

"The butterfly pushpins," I lie. Because it started that way.

It just...feels like more now.

Watching her come out of her cocoon, seeing the beauty beneath as her wings unfurl, ready to take flight.

Something that both brings relief and...

The urge to get a net ready.

"Oh," she says, throat working, eyes not meeting mine.

Then she's looking away again. "How far is the lake?" A beat, the half of her mouth I can see curving. "Lake."

"Funny," I say dryly, holding a branch back so it doesn't smack her in the face.

She steps through, follows me along the winding path that I've traversed so often by now, I have it memorized.

"What do you have in the backpack?" she asks after a moment.

"You'll see."

"How ominous," she says lightly.

I don't snark back only because we're taking the last turn and the lake—well, really, it's more *pond* than lake, otherwise it wouldn't be cold enough to freeze over—is right in front of us.

"*Oh,*" she whispers.

Out from beneath the cover of the trees, I see the snow is still falling, but not as rapidly as before. It's like a romantic movie spewed to life as the picture-perfect sprinkling floats through the air, clinging to her beanie, her coat, the ends of her hair as she moves forward and lifts her camera.

It's beautiful, one of my favorite places.

The reason I bought this property in the first place, even though it's risky to set down roots when my career can send me anywhere.

I was visiting Mack, whose property backs up to mine, and he conned me into helping him clear some trees. A wrong turn, stumbling onto this piece of land...

Now I have roots.

And a place to settle when all the rest of it is over.

Nova moves forward, camera clicking, putting all those skills of hers to work, and knowing I have some time, I move over to my typical boulder.

Empty the backpack.

And wait.

❄ ❄ ❄ ❄

"I'm sorry," she says about ten minutes later, whipping around, eyes wide, mouth pulled into a grimace. "*Shit.* I totally forgot you were there."

"What a compliment," I quip.

She glares at me, plunks her hands on her hips. "Seriously?"

"Come here, butterfly," I say instead of engaging, patting the boulder next to me.

"Why?" she asks suspiciously, even as she clomps over, kicking up snow with each step.

And it's fucking stupid, but I won't ever forget the look on her face when she sees the skates in my hands.

Not calculated. Shocked. And then her expression goes gentle.

For me.

My heart does that thing again.

"What did you do?" she whispers.

"Nothing," I say, taking her hand and nudging her down onto the boulder. "Sit down."

"I don't know how to skate."

I grin at her. "Luckily, I'm a hockey player." Her face goes soft again, and I hold up the skates. "So, you game?"

That soft surprise again but she stays sitting on the rock as I tug off her boots, as I pull on one of the spare set skates I keep at the house, tighten them. They're a little big, but not by much, especially when I tie off the laces.

"Am I going to end up under the ice?" she asks as I start pulling on my own skates.

My lips twitch. "The pond is solid," I tell her. "It's been frozen through for weeks now."

"Still," she says. "Just out of curiosity, how deep is this lake-slash-pond?"

"Come on," I say instead of answering, holding out my hand and helping her up, guiding her to the edge of the pond.

I step on before her, bounce a few times. "Solid, see?"

She nibbles at the corner of her mouth.

But then she takes my hand and I guide her out onto the ice.

Immediately her legs slide out from under her and I have to react quickly, drawing her flush against me, preventing her from going full Bambi.

She shrieks, clings to my body to stay upright even though I have my arms securely wrapped around her, even though I'm not going to let her fall.

"Bend your knees," I say, coaxing her a little lower. "Good. Like that." Slowly, I adjust my grip so I can spin her around, so that her back is pressed to my front. "Stay bent, yeah?"

I wrap my arm around her. "Yeah."

"Now like this."

She carefully mirrors my movements as I take one stride then another.

"Good. Just like that."

Her nails dig into my arm, but she nods and keeps moving slowly forward.

"Keep going."

She does, and picks it up remarkably quick, gaining her balance, that lush ass of hers rubbing against me, distracting me as we make several slow loops around the pond.

My dick twitches and I nudge her forward a little bit, trying to get the cold ass air to do me a favor.

"Lake!" she shrieks, clinging to my arm again, bringing our bodies flush. "Don't let me go."

"You've got this." But I stay with her for a little bit longer before pulling away again.

This time she doesn't freak out and clutch at me.

She lets go, takes a few strides on her own. "I'm doing it!" she says picking up speed.

I rotate as she makes a loop on her own, coming back around to me, now skating at a decent clip.

I'm transfixed.

By her and the soft whistle of the wind whispering through her hair. The *shush* of the snowflakes landing on the ice as she makes her circle. The *crunch* of her skates on the surface of the pond with each stride she takes. The beautiful smile on her face.

Nothing exists aside from her.

Not the past. Not the future.

Just Nova.

I move closer, intending to take her in my arms again.

Her words carry toward me. "I'm freaking doing—!"

I realize my miscalculation about a millisecond too late.

Because while I was lost in the music of the moment, the beauty of her excitement, I neglected to teach her something important.

How to stop.

"—it!"

THIRTY-THREE

Nova

THE WIND IS on my cheeks.

The ice is bumpy below my skates.

But—"I'm doing it!" I navigate the turn, the little dip that's almost taken me out a few times. "I'm freaking doing it!"

The last word leaves my mouth at the same time I look up...

And see Lake right in front of me.

Right in front of me.

I see his mouth move in a curse, see him try to get out of my way.

Too late.

We collide.

Or more like, I bounce off his hard chest, fall backward—

"*Oof,*" I grunt as his arm bands around me, dragging me against him, stopping me from falling straight over and cracking my head on the ice.

But not stopping himself.

"Shit," he mutters, feet sliding out from beneath him. He

tries to release me, but ends up taking me down too, and I land on top of him, making *him* grunt this time.

"Sorry," I say, trying to push on his chest, trying to get off him.

"*Fuck,*" he groans.

Damn. I know it can't be comfortable with all my limbs jabbing him in the stomach. I scramble to get my feet beneath me. "Shit, I'm sorry, honey, I—"

"Fuck," he says again, but this time it's paired with his hand diving into my hair, knocking my beanie from my head, tugging me more fully over him. "As in *fuck,* you are so goddamned beautiful."

And then he kisses me.

And then...it's like what happened in the kitchen.

One spark...and flames.

I don't feel the cold ice seeping into my knees. I don't feel the wind whipping at my hair. I don't feel anything but this man beneath me and touching me and kissing me.

The ice can give way.

Snow can bury us.

And I will still be kissing this man.

He rolls us, pressing me into the surface of the pond, our hips aligning, grinding together, all while his tongue is fucking my mouth.

No mercy. No quarter.

This man can kiss.

This man can *fuck.*

I know it instinctually.

In the way his lips guide mine, taking the kiss hot and wet and deep, in the rhythm of his pelvis, the weight of his body, the sureness of his hands as he dips them under my clothes and—

I squeak.

Because one of those big, warm, *sure* hands has shoved my shirt up and my back is on the ice.

"Shit," he mutters, dragging me up, just hefting me like I weigh nothing, carrying me over to the boulder, bending like he's going to take off my skates, but I stop him, fingers digging into his shoulders, drawing him toward me.

Needing another taste of him like I need my next breath.

I won't survive without it.

His hands dig into my hips, drawing me flush against him, ass teetering on the edge of the boulder.

"Fuck, you taste good," he mutters, hand fisting in my hair, tilting my head back, flicking out his tongue and tasting me under my jaw.

I shiver, not from the cold this time, but he pulls away, eyes hot as he kneels in front of me, dragging off my skates, his own, hands shaking as he puts on the guards and shoves them into the backpack.

But when he picks up my boots and says, "Let's get you back to the house," I say, "No."

He freezes and I take advantage, pushing him backward, sending us both toppling to the snow. It's so cold it takes my breath away, but only for a second. Because then I'm clambering on top of him again. Then I'm kissing him.

Then I'm *riding* him.

And that branch.

And—

"Fuck," he groans.

"Yes, that," I say, shoving my hands between us, running them over the hard planes of his chest, squeezing his pecs, grinding against him, feeling pleasure rise up in me.

"Come here," he orders, fingers diving into my hair again, drawing my mouth down to his for a long, searing kiss.

Then he's releasing me, batting my hands away, and

flicking open the button on his jeans, unzipping and freeing the hard length of his cock.

"And it's cold," I breathe reverently, reaching for it, wrapping my fingers around the velvet-covered steel, stroking once, twice—

"You either sit on that or find your ass cold in the snow."

I freeze, the rough words like fingers running through my wet pussy, but they're effective, sending me to my feet so I can wrestle my pants down and off one ankle. They bunch up around the other in an incredibly unsexy way, but I don't care and Lake doesn't seem too either. He just unzips his jacket, spreading it open so I can kneel on it as I straddle his hips, rubbing myself over him, the slickness of my desire allowing me to glide easily forward and back, forward and back.

"Nova," he urges.

The wind is cold, the snow is still falling.

This is absolute insanity to be here with my ass hanging out, about to fuck a man I barely know.

But something in me pauses, tightens, tells me this is a time to go slowly forward instead of careening into the future like normal, barely noticing the present because I'm so focused on moving to the next thing.

Enjoy this.

Remember this.

I rock forward again, loving the way his hands come to my hips, gripping tight, freezing me when I would have slid back once more.

"Nova," he growls. "This is your last warning before your ass is in the snow and I'm pounding into you."

I shiver, arch just the slightest bit, notching the head of his cock at my entrance, sinking down the barest amount, feeling the burn of him stretching me, the ache in my pussy to take him all, the shakiness of my legs and the way my head spins and—

One hand on my hip pushes me down.

The other slides up to dive under my bra, cupping my breast, rolling my nipple.

Both beams of pleasure—north and south—collide and then I've got him inside me, filling me to the brim, making me cry out as his cock bumps against my womb, as his fingers tighten just on the right side of rough.

"Move," he orders, but he's already doing that, already thrusting against me, fucking me even though *I'm* supposed to be the one riding *him*. He's taking over, and—

And I don't give a fuck.

It's glorious, especially when I drop my hands to his chest, slide them to his abdomen, feeling all of the strong muscles of his torso working as we grind together, as he thrusts his cock into me.

Again.

And again.

And *again*.

"Oh God," I groan, head falling back. "That's good. That's—"

He sits up, going deeper, and—*oh fucking yes*—that's better.

"So. Fucking. Beautiful," he grunts, fucking me slow and deep and sure. "So. Fucking. Perfect."

I shiver, my pussy convulsing, pleasure gathering between my thighs and—

He presses his thumb to my clit.

I jerk, eyes going wide. "Lake," I whisper.

His hazel eyes spark with heat, burn into me, pin me in place. Then his mouth curves up into a sexy smile. "I'm going to need you to come now, butterfly."

"I—"

That thumb presses harder.

Pleasure spirals through me, tightening in my belly, between my legs, a storm gathering before—

He thrusts up harder, the fingers around my nipple squeezing, and his mouth latches onto mine.

Rough. Slow. Deep.

Sure.

And...explosion.

I feel my pussy convulsing around him as that taut pleasure bursts out from my middle, spreading like wildfire through each of my nerves. It increases as his thrusts speed, as he somehow fucks me harder, as he stills, cock buried deep, mouth breaking away from mine, my name in the air.

Fucking beautiful.

Fucking *perfect*.

THIRTY-FOUR

Lake

BY THE TIME I pull my head out of my ass and focus enough to get us dressed, Nova and I are half frozen.

I get her pants up, her boots on, shrug my backpack over my shoulders, mindful of the camera I zipped carefully inside.

She's shivering now, so I don't take her hand, just scoop her up and make our way back to the house.

Steve's still sleeping fifteen minutes later as I carry her in through the front door, but he wakes as I try to walk quietly by him, probably clocking that his owner isn't one hundred percent and that I'm responsible. "Stay," I order him before adding like he can understand me—and hell, at this point, I'm half convinced he can, "I'll be back to get you and you don't want to hurt your leg more."

Beady eyes narrow.

But he settles back down onto the blankets with a huff.

My ankles thank me as I move to the bathroom and set

Nova on the counter. I crank on the water in the tub, putting it as hot as I think she can stand. Then I shove down the plug and turn back to the shivering woman. "Arms up."

She complies, teeth chattering. "Th-that w-was st-stupid."

"Maybe," I say, "but I think your pussy is worth a little frostbite."

Her mouth falls open and I take advantage of her befuddlement to tug off her sweatshirt, tee, and bra, to guide her off the counter, to take off her pants, her underwear, her boots and socks.

The musk of her cunt as I'm kneeling in front of her—lifting one leg and then the other—is tempting, but she's still cold, her pert pink nipples proof of that, even if they're just as mouth-watering as her pussy.

I lean in. Inhale. Flick out my tongue—

Focus.

Because she has goose bumps all over too.

Deal with hypothermia first.

Fuck her exactly as I want to second.

Plus, Steve is bound to lose patience soon.

I scoop her up, bring her to the tub.

She dips a toe in, hisses.

"Okay?" I ask.

"It feels good."

Once she's beneath the water, I go back for the mutt, grabbing one of his beds from Nova's duffle and setting him up in the corner of the bathroom.

Then I turn away, intending to go change.

I *want* to strip down and crawl into the tub behind her.

But...I've crossed a lot of lines today. I've pushed and—

"Lake."

My name on her tongue is a fucking siren's call. I turn

around, dick going hard when I see all of that glorious woman on display for me.

"Where are you going?" she asks.

"To change," I say gruffly—too fucking gruffly considering I was just inside her.

Those pine needle green eyes change, head tilting to the side, the ends of her hair dipping into the water. "You can do that if you want, but"—here she takes a breath, as though shoring herself up—"if you want to join me, I"—she nibbles at her bottom lip—"I would like that."

Women bring nothing but complications.

Women bring nothing but pain and drama and bullshit that I don't want to deal with.

But Nova's invitation...

Is one I can't resist.

So, I ignore all of that and I just...give in to what I want with her.

Again.

And the first touch of that hot water is nothing like the brand this woman has burned into my heart.

❄ ❄ ❄ ❄

"You know," she says as she lies in bed next to me, another Christmas movie playing in the background—this one featuring a kid besting a pair of burglars through all manner of mischief and pranks, "you don't have to spend twenty-five thousand dollars on a couch."

I tilt my head so I can look down at her.

She's uploaded the photographs from her memory card onto her laptop and is carefully scrutinizing each one.

"I know that," I say, ignoring Steve's panting and puppy

breath far too close to my face. "Hence, the reason I canceled that order for the twenty-five-thousand-dollar couch." I nudge the pup away again, reach over him and sip at the honey rosemary mule I've become seriously addicted to.

The guys will give me a hard time for drinking something so prissy.

But I know they're going to be addicted to it as much as I am once they take that first sip.

I have the secret weapon now—rosemary simple syrup.

It's the shit, one hundred percent, and makes the already tasty drink even better.

I bet the marketing company for the vodka brand would want to share the recipe on their socials—because branding and shit—and I wonder if Nova would care if her secret drink concoction was out there.

But first, couches—twenty-five thousand or otherwise— because she glances up at me, mouth curving. "I ask that because I'm not sure if you're aware, but there are also online stores where you can order said *not* twenty-five-thousand-dollar couches." She taps a finger to her chin. "And other things you might need, like a table or barstools or—*eek!*"

Steve grunts unhappily as I snatch her laptop from her, tossing it to the side and pinning her beneath me. "Does this sass mean I need to give you orgasms?"

"No," she says, trying to reach past me for her laptop. I just nudge it a little further, moving it out of her reach. "It means that I'm going to help you find an awesome couch that's not twenty—"

She squeaks again, but this time it's because I'm tugging off her pants, tossing them to the side, and—

Pinpricks of pain, this time on my wrist.

I glance at Steve, lift a brow. "This is becoming a problem, dude."

He lets me go, bares his teeth, but I just get up, lift him from the bed, tuck him onto the bed in the bathroom and shut the door behind me.

Saving my limbs from the killer attack pug one wooden panel at a time.

He woofs once, but doesn't otherwise complain, and by the time I make it to the bed, Nova's naked, sprawled back against the pillows, hand skating down her belly.

"Getting started on those orgasms, butterfly?" I ask, my voice like sandpaper.

Pink cheeks. Deep green eyes.

"Yeah," she says silkily. "Want to watch?"

My cock is instantly hard.

Because fuck yes, I do. I drop my mouth to hers, taste her deeply, then kiss my way down her throat, her chest, laving her nipples, sucking them hard, teasing her as she teases herself. I spend a long time there, listening to her moans, her breath catching, feeling the way her body rocks and tightens and relaxes as she draws herself up the edge. I need to see it, see her fingers in her pussy, see her face as she comes part, so I drag my tongue down, tracing the path of her arm across her belly, down between her thighs, pausing to inhale the musk of her desire.

Fuck, she's hot.

Fuck, I want to be inside her again.

I grunt when she slips a finger into her pussy, watching her thumb work, adding my tongue to aid her when I can't keep my distance.

She hisses out a breath, widens her legs. "Do that again," she orders, the slick sounds of her finger fucking herself loud as she moves faster.

I suck at her clit, press the flat of my tongue to the bundle of nerves.

She jerks then moans, fingers sliding in and out. "Oh fuck," she whispers.

"Keep going," I order. "Don't you fucking stop."

Her eyes hit mine. "Don't you stop either."

I grin, drop my head, work her clit, and get to see, get to feel, and, best of all...

I get to hear her come apart.

THIRTY-FIVE

Nova

I'M limp and exhaustion is pulling at my limbs, but I want him inside me.

I *need* him to fill me, need him to fuck me hard and fast.

He starts to pull away, crawling back up my body, giving no indication that he's going to get undressed, that he's going to take what's freely on offer.

Butterflies in my belly again.

Because I'm learning that's Lake.

He and his branch may have a reputation, he might be gruff and a bit of an asshole (all the better to keep people away from him), but he's also nice and considerate and—

Has a supremely talented tongue.

A finger traces along the perimeter of my mouth, the edges of my smile. "What?" he asks.

"You're a good guy."

I feel him still, manage to peel open my eyes to see his face. "What?"

A shake of his head. "Why are you smiling?"

"Because I like your tongue," I say lightly, sensing he needs the light, needing that lightness for myself.

Because of the squeeze in my heart, the butterflies in my belly.

Because of this man.

His mouth curves. "I think I got that."

"And," I say, bending my leg and rubbing it along his side, "I know that you promised me orgasms—as in *plural*—so you're not about to go back to watching the movie."

He dances his fingers along my side. "I'm not?"

"No." I lean up, press my lips to the hinge of his jaw. "You're not."

His mouth curves into a wicked smile. "No," he says, hand diving between my legs, a thick finger sliding deep without warning.

I gasp.

"I'm not."

And then he's fully on top of me, his mouth dropping to mine, his tongue in my mouth, his hand working me. I just came. My limbs are heavy and aftershocks of pleasure are coursing through my body.

But he has no mercy.

He plunders my mouth and fucks me with his fingers and just when I think I can't go another second without breath, he breaks the kiss, contorts his body and uses his lips and teeth and tongue on one breast and then the other and—

"Fuck," I gasp, pussy clamping around his fingers, the orgasm coming so quickly that I'm flying apart before I even realize I've ascended the peak.

Even then, though, he doesn't give me a break.

He just spreads my legs, slowly pulls his fingers free, and

then his hips are poised over mine and he's notched the head of his cock in my pussy and—

I groan, dropping my head back as pleasure fires through me in tiny bursts of sensation as he strokes home—a long, persistent thrust this time, no mercy again as he impales me until he's balls deep.

That sends a blip of something through my mind, a worry, some distant thought my brain says I should pay attention to.

But I'm in too deep.

The sensation is overwhelming, but in the best possible way.

"God, you feel good," he rasps with a nip to my throat.

And it's that little press of his teeth that pulls the pin.

Everything unfurls, explodes open, reality screeches to a halt and...

Then disappears as I break apart again.

I slide back to life with him fucking me hard and fast, his gold and green and brown eyes burning into mine, his muscles taut and standing out in sharp relief.

"Fuck," he grunts, hips pistoning. "So *fucking* beautiful."

And then I get to watch him come.

And it might be the most beautiful thing I've ever seen.

Butterflies take flight in my belly.

In my heart.

Because the most beautiful part is what comes next.

He collapses on top of me, his heavy weight almost too much, something I know he's thinking about because he immediately rolls us to our sides.

And then he takes me in his arms.

And I think that perhaps rushing to move forward isn't always best.

Because in this moment, with Lake's arms around me, my

body lax with pleasure, smelling his spicy scent, feeling warm and safe and...

Wanted.

I can't imagine ever wanting anything else.

❄ ❄ ❄ ❄

"What do you think of this one?" I ask, mischief coursing through me late the next day.

We didn't do any online shopping the night before.

We fucked and saved Steve from his prison in the bathroom then watched crappy television until we both passed out. I slept clear through to the morning, helped by those multiple orgasms and the many honey rosemary mules I made.

The recipe for which, apparently, was going to be on Lake's social media. And the vodka company's.

Something that was Lake's idea. He asked me and then mentioned it to his publicist and the marketing department for Lake Vodka.

Everyone loved it.

Now my drink was going to be Instagram—and TikTok, I suppose, since we also made a video of us creating a couple of the cocktails earlier today—famous.

Go me.

Nothing was posted yet, so my fame awaited, and aside from the making the video and drinking copious mules and alternating between Christmas movies and looking through the shots I took over the last few days, I spent the hours eating the delicious food Lake made in between fucking on the relatively few flat surfaces in this house.

A busy day.

But it also sort of feels like a vacation.

No fighting. No angst. No asshole.

Just me. My dog. And Lake.

Who glances up, already having lost any enthusiasm for shopping online after about five whole minutes. The last couple of hours as we've trolled the interwebs for deals on barstools and a guest bedroom set and a couch (and a coffee table!), he's alternated between focusing intently on the string of movies playing and looking out the windows, the snow still falling but much less steady than it had been even earlier in the day.

Snowmageddon winding down.

Soon we would be plowed out.

I would go back to my life.

Go back to looking forward.

Steve huffs out a sigh, leaning more heavily against Lake's strong thigh.

"What the fuck is that?" he asks.

I start giggling.

I can't help it.

His expression is just too good.

"It's only the perfect piece of artwork for your family room," I say, chortling at the portrait of a reality star sitting on a throne, a lion perched at his side. "It's five feet by eight feet and—"

He plucks my computer out of my lap. "I see you can't be trusted for any more furniture shopping, butterfly," he says, disturbing Steve, who groans, as he sets the laptop on the night-stand, well out of my reach.

"Why do you really call me butterfly?"

He stills. "I told you," he says edgily.

I still.

Then...forward.

"You spun some nonsense about the pushpins."

"Considering I plucked them out of your body, I would say

they made an impression."

I shiver and he notices—something I'm realizing is normal for him. He pulls the blanket up over me, tucking me in, covering me in warmth. It's a distraction and a good one, and if this was any other day, any other man, I would just let my question go.

But it's Lake.

And...I want to know.

So, I take a breath—convince myself this is me moving forward—and I say, "That's not the only reason."

THIRTY-SIX

Lake

STUPID.

This conversation, plunging headfirst into this pool of delusion.

And...yet, I'm standing at the end of the diving board, ready and willing to launch myself off.

I look over at Nova, at those pine needle green eyes, at the wariness in those emerald depths, at the casual smile that does nothing to belie the tension in her frame.

She's expecting me to shut her down.

I expect it too.

So when the opposite comes out of my mouth, I almost don't know what to do with myself.

"It's the pins," I say. "But it's also you."

Her head tilts to the side, brows drawing together.

"There's something about you, something that's hidden below the surface, and it's like if I just wait long enough, it'll emerge and"—God, I sound like an idiot—"I just know it will be beautiful."

She inhales so sharply I'm surprised she doesn't choke. "Lake," she whispers, lips quivering before she turns her head away. "I-I—" A breath before she turns back, eyes glimmering with tears. "I don't think anyone has ever said anything so nice to me."

I hate that for her.

I hate that I've taken away the mischievous side, made her go serious.

I hate that she has fucking tears in her eyes.

"Don't cry," I say gruffly, because my heart is doing that thing again, and my throat is tight and I fucking *hate* that she has tears in her eyes. "I'm sorry. I shouldn't have—"

"It's not you," she whispers. "It's also"—she reaches into the front pocket of her hoodie, pulls out something blue and black —the same something blue and black she retrieved from Steve (literally from Steve) a few days ago—"this."

She opens her palm and I get my first full glimpse of that quarter-sized item.

"I bought this for my grandmother." A deep breath. "She's the one who found my sister and I in foster care, who brought us to California after our parents left us. They'd cut contact and she didn't know my parents abandoned us until—" A shake of her head. "It doesn't matter, really. She didn't know at first and when she found out, she got us out. We had *nothing*, fucking *nothing* during the years we lived with her. Just love and food and a safe place to sleep. I—" She closes her eyes, exhales. "She loved butterflies, and I worked one summer to be able to buy this for her. She—"

A tear slides down her cheek and I wipe it away.

"She," Nova says again, "wore it every day until she passed away. That's why I was so upset when Steve tried to eat it." She touches the center of the butterfly. "It's a little worse for wear and it's missing one of the diamonds, but it's my memory of the one person in my life who was always there for me."

I wrap my arms around her as she closes her fingers around the charm.

"It's silly," she says, "just a necklace a kid bought for her grandma. But when she left it for me, she wrote in her will that she wanted me to emerge from my cocoon like a butterfly, that she wanted the world to see me as the beautiful person I am."

"And have you?"

Her eyes slide away. "When she died, I left. I followed the wind, traveled all over the world taking pictures. I did so many things I never dreamed were possible, met people, visited places I never could have imagined. I lived a big and exciting life doing what I love."

That's a lot.

And I want to know every detail of those exciting times. Later. Because I feel like there's more to the story.

"But did you let the world see you?"

She looks away. "I don't know."

"Bullshit."

She looks back, eyes flashing. "It's not," she snaps.

I just lift my brows.

A long, tense silence before she exhales. "Fine. You're smart enough to get that I didn't. I lived big and did exciting things, but I spent most of the time thinking about what was next instead of enjoying where I was. I want to do better. I want to be different. Especially because I left, was gone for so long that my sister became..." She trails off, eyes skating away.

I cup her jaw, force her to meet my gaze. "You are *not* responsible for the person your sister has become."

Nova stills. "Why do you sound like you have personal experience with that?"

I inhale, know this is put up or shut up time.

Know that if I pull back now, I might as well keep doing it. Because this woman has cracked open a door into her heart and mind and if I don't push through, she'll shut it, lock it tight.

And she might never open it again.

"My mom is...difficult," I say.

Nova shifts a little closer, rests her palm on my thigh. "How so?"

"She had a...mental break—or that's how they described it to me when I got old enough to ask why she is the way she is," I say. "She was excited about being pregnant, but the reality of it, of labor and delivery and all the things that came after." I shake my head, bite back a sigh. "She didn't take it well, was hospitalized for a while, and she's always been...fragile and prone to hysterics and she's so focused on herself and her problems that she forgets she's a mom sometimes."

Most of the time.

All of the time.

She's a mess.

A complication that brings too much drama into my life.

And, worse, she's an emotional vampire because unless I engage with her bullshit, talk her down from the edge, she spirals.

And then I'm left picking up the pieces.

"That must be really hard."

"She does her best," I hedge.

"I wasn't insinuating she doesn't, but"—Nova squeezes my thigh—"it still must be hard for you."

I think of the yelling. The throwing things. The accusations of me never seeing her.

I think of the way she tore my room apart looking for the girl I was supposedly hiding there when I was in high school.

I think of the broken plates and my dad getting fed up, working longer hours, staying away as much as possible.

Because he couldn't handle it.

Leaving it for *me* to deal with because I wasn't going to leave it to my siblings—who, smartly, moved out at their first opportunity and cut contact to almost nil.

"Yeah," I say. "It was difficult."

"Was? Or is?"

I think of the calls I've been ignoring, the texts that have been sending my cell vibrating on the regular, the voicemails she's left often enough that I know I'll just have to clear the entire inbox without listening to any of them. "Is," I mutter.

Her fingers tighten around my thigh again, and then she's moving closer, crawling over me, wrapping me in a sort of spider monkey type hug. "I'm sorry," she murmurs.

"Don't apologize."

She just squeezes me again, kisses my throat. "I'm still sorry."

"Butterfly," I rasp, winding my fingers into her hair.

"Shh," she orders softly. "I'm being nice for once."

She's nice—*more* than nice—but I like her where she is, so I just shut up, wrap my arms around her, and inhale her spicy cinnamon scent.

"Was she—" Nova breaks off, shakes her head.

"What?" I ask, stroking a hand down her back.

"I was going to ask..." She hesitates, voice dropping. "If she was the one who threw the knives."

My heart pulses and I bury my face in her hair. "No, butterfly. She wasn't. I'm...good at picking women who act like her, unfortunately."

She tenses.

I stroke my palm up and down her back. "Not you," I reassure her. "You're...peaceful, I guess. Easy. It's relaxing being with you."

She pushes up and I watch as her face does that thing again, goes soft and warm, which means that my heart does its thing again, convulsing in my chest—or maybe, it rolls over, exposes its vulnerable underbelly, especially when she deliberately lightens the conversation after we've shared all this heavy.

"I mean," she says. "I may not be the type to throw a knife, but I *did* drive my car into a snowbank and stab myself with pushpins, so..."

I tug a strand of her hair. "So long as you're not stabbing *me*."

A gasp. "Rude."

I grin, steal a kiss, sliding my hand down, dipping it beneath the waistband of her sweats, cupping that lush ass. "I think you like it when I'm rude."

I stroke a finger lower.

Dip it inside.

A gasp, her head falling back. "This is you rude?" she teases, but it's more than a little breathless.

"Yup," I say, stroking slowly through her slick heat. "It sure is."

"Okay." She rolls to her back, dislodging my hand, but she also shoves her pants down and spreads her legs, allowing me full access. A wave of her hand as she orders, "Commence with the being rude."

I chuckle.

But I follow that order.

To the letter.

THIRTY-SEVEN

Nova

I STAND at the kitchen window, cup of coffee in my hand, watching the plows making their way up and down the street.

It's not snowing.

In fact, it's been almost twenty-four hours without the fluffy white stuff falling from the sky.

Which is why the plows are out, I suppose.

And why I need to get back to my life.

Lake's in the shower, which I think is a little weird considering he's going to the gym and then practice—why shower when he's going to get hot and sweaty?

But I'm not the professional hockey player, and he says it's part of his routine.

Plus, I need coffee.

And maybe a little distance.

Because I'm leaving today.

Because...Snowmageddon is coming to an end and the roads are being cleared and I have no reason to stay.

We've had our fun.

Now I need to get on with my life.

Figure out what I want to do for work. Figure out where I want to live—because it's definitely not going to be that apartment in San Francisco.

Luckily, I never signed a lease with George and I have all of my stuff.

No lie, that hurts—I picked him. He betrayed me with Ashley—who got the jewelry she wanted, and...

I haven't heard a word from either of them.

Done with me as I am with them.

Perfect.

It's better than going backward.

It still stings, I just don't have the energy to focus on it. Maybe I'll find some place to rent here in the Sierras, some place with snow and trees and maybe a frozen pond. Maybe I'll find this same sense of peace there.

Maybe I'll learn how to skate and—

No, it's better I move on.

This time has been...perfect. Better than I ever expected. Peaceful and lovely and filled with plenty of orgasms and enough camaraderie that I know I'll look back at Lake fondly.

But...it's time.

Sighing, I glance down at Steve, his brace clunky and heavy, but he's been leaving it alone for the most part, and since he's moving around better, he's been getting up to his old mischief again.

None the worse for wear.

Thank God.

I do think he'll miss Lake though.

"It'll be fun," I tell him. "Just me and you, bud," I say. "Like always." On the road, finding where we fit, a new place to shoot. That bright, shiny future.

I reach into my pocket, the bumpy wings of the butterfly charm beneath my fingertips.

And…breaking out of my cocoon.

But is it if I'm just blindly moving forward again?

I push that thought away. I'll get there, one step at a time. And anyway, Lake and I had our fun. We made our peace and I enjoyed hanging here with him. I owe him a couple dozen honey rosemary mules (which is why I'm making a new batch of the rosemary simple syrup to leave with him). But he needs to have his house back.

Which is why I finish folding the load of laundry I threw in the night before and start tucking it into my duffle, along with my camera and my laptop and my phone charger.

I'm corralling Steve's copious amounts of toys when Lake pads down the hall, hair still wet from his shower.

He stops next to the island, and I see that he's frowning when I finally get my fingers around the stuffed bunny and crawl out from beneath the countertop.

"Packing up," I say in response to that scowl, shoving it into Steve's tote bag before rounding the island and heading back to the stove, stirring the simple syrup. Most of the water has boiled off and the room is filled with the earthy scent of rosemary.

It's all but done.

I flick the knob, turn off the heat.

"Do you want a cup of coffee?" I snag a mug and rotate back to face him, brows drawing together when I see he hasn't moved from the island, and that…

His expression has become thunderous.

"No?" I ask, setting the mug I grabbed back down on the counter. "Is no caffeine another pre hockey ritual?"

He scowls. "What the fuck are you talking about?"

I slide my eyes from side to side. "Umm...pre hockey rituals?"

Lightning and thunder in his hazel eyes, and I freeze when I find him suddenly in my face. "*Packing*, butterfly. What the fuck?"

I exhale. "I mean...the roads are open and you need to get back to your life, your routine."

Flashing hazel eyes. "You got a place?"

"What do you mean?"

"Do. You. Have. A. Place. To. Go?"

My lungs inflate on a rush. "I mean, not yet," I say after I exhale, after I summon a smile. "But I'm good at figuring that out as I move. And I'm really good at landing on my feet no matter what."

"So everything you said last night really *was* bullshit." He shakes his head, reaches past me for the mug and fills it with coffee.

"What—?" I rock back on my heels, rubbing a hand over my chest, my heart convulsing beneath. "I don't know what you're insinuating."

"I'm not *insinuating* anything," he snaps. "Last night you said you run off without enjoying the present." I freeze. "You said that you want to do better. But here you are, running forward again, no plan in place."

"Don't tell me you don't want your house back."

Something crosses his face, an emotion I can't identify, there and gone before I can process it. "I'm not even here half the time," he grits out. "I don't need my house back. But if you're too fucking scared to stay, or in such a hurry to leave, or, hell, too proud to accept a hand up, then just go. Flit off, fly around, keep doing the same shit over and over again." He turns away, mug in hand. "I need to get to practice. Tell the demon dog bye from me."

"Why are you being such an asshole?" I snap.

He turns back, lifts his brows. "Why are you such a coward?"

Those butterflies in my belly take flight, whirling around and making me feel sick. "Fuck you."

He salutes me with his mug. "Drive safe. Try not to end up in another snowbank."

Irritation bubbles over and I march up to him, taking the mug right out of his hand and dumping it down the drain. "That coffee is mine. This"—I go to the stove, point at the pot— "rosemary simple syrup I was making for you is mine. Those cookies I made for you last night are *mine*. The—"

All of a sudden, he's in my space again, his face mere millimeters from mine. "I don't want the cookies or the coffee or the simple syrup." He kisses me, deeply, intensely, and with lots and lots of tongue. So much that I waver when he finally lets me go, lungs heavy and struggling to draw in enough air. "I just want you here," he says, fingers in my hair, palm pressed to the hinge of my jaw. " I want you to stay and enjoy the present. I want you to be right here in my house when that couch I bought comes, so I can fuck you on it. I want you here until Steve is better." His thumb presses to my bottom lip. "I want you to stay until you're ready to go."

My heart is pounding.

Those butterflies flutter in my belly, wings creating a ruckus. "You do?"

His forehead drops to mine, and he seems to be warring with himself.

But then he sighs, fingers tightening in my hair.

"Yeah, butterfly, I do."

THIRTY-EIGHT

Lake

THE SNOW IS PILED up ridiculously high on the sides of the road.

The wind is still flying and there's ice everywhere.

In other words, it's sketchy as shit.

But I have practice. I have to get back out into the real world, have to do my real job, even though I want to be back at my house, watching crappy movies—

Or watching *Nova* watch crappy movies.

When I left, she was sitting in my bed, Steve at her hip, laptop open, editing photos.

I want to be right next to her.

Not pulling into the rink, my shoulders already getting tight. Not grabbing my shit and walking into the practice facility, moving by the offices and through the kitchen, the player's lounge, trying to avoid talking with anyone because even though I love playing hockey, love living in Tahoe, I don't love the roster, don't love my coaches.

And I sure as shit don't love walking into a room that's tense and frustrated.

So palpable, I can cut it with a knife.

I'm the captain. I lead by example.

But examples don't matter with these guys—or most of them, anyway. Knox is a good guy—with the exception of him orchestrating Nova's arrival at my house. Leo and Riggs are solid too, and I'm lucky to have them on the team.

The only bright spots.

Our goalie is weird. I mean, goalies are strange in general, but this guy takes the cake—as in, literally, he can't play well unless he has a slice of cake before a game.

And it's vanilla cake with vanilla icing, no less.

Eating the cake pregame is weird enough—but I could shrug it off because hockey players *are* weird with our rituals— but the man has his choice of a hundred varieties of cake and he chooses *vanilla?* What the actual fuck?

So, asshole coaches, a group of older guys who are lazy, settled in their routines, and not interested in pushing forward, an owner who may or may not be a criminal—the investigation into that was inconclusive, so it's business as usual, apparently—and a weird fucking goalie. And then the icing—vanilla or otherwise—on top is that the young guys are so fucking young they can't even name three characters from Harry Potter—and in fact, half of them couldn't even name Harry Potter himself when asked by the team's social media crew.

Yup. My team's awesome.

I grind my teeth together, ignore the tension, and drop my shit in my locker.

We made it to the playoffs last year before crapping out, and I'm not saying that we deserved to win just because our roster is talented—*everyone* at this level is talented. But we didn't do all we should have, all we *could* have to take the Cup home.

It was an uninspired battle.

One that left me feeling like shit.

Though, I did get to officiate a wedding.

What I wouldn't give to have what the Gold do—my officiating skills were put to use because those guys are a family that's made up of more than just blood, and I'm just lucky enough to exist on the very edges of the periphery.

But that kind of trust and closeness isn't something that just happens. It takes time to build that, especially when I haven't been all that open to well...openness.

Damn.

I sigh and rub at my forehead then shove it out of my mind to deal with later.

Mostly because I've spotted the exact person I want to confront—er, *talk to.*

Knox.

The bastard smirks as he strolls across the room and sits down in his spot next to mine. He's in workout gear, clearly planning to do the same as I am—hit the gym before the ice.

"I should fucking blast you," I mutter.

"Would *Nova* get mad at you if you do?" he drawls, fishing for information, *and* still smirking as he shoves his feet into his sneakers.

"Nova's too nice to get mad." I glare at him, not that it does any good. What I say next will, though. "She won't get mad even though you and your sister's shenanigans meant that I came across her and her car stuck in a snowbank instead of her snagging my spare key"—something I need to relocate from beneath that damn pot, since everyone, apparently, knows where it is—"and just showing up at my house."

That grin fades. "What?"

"Yeah, asshole," I snap. "She doesn't have experience driving in the snow and nearly killed herself and that fucking dog."

Another reason I don't want her leaving my place—anything might happen on the road.

Which is true.

But also...I know I'm lying to myself.

I just...don't care.

"Who almost died?" Leo asks, sitting down next to me, Riggs on his other side. Those two are my wingers, and along with Knox, are the only guys on this team who seem happy to put in hard work on the regular.

Case in point?

We're the only ones in the locker room early, ready for our workout, ready to put in the extra effort.

Yeah, Coach made it optional.

But where the fuck is the drive to do more?

Lost in fucking Never Never Land.

Sighing, I yank off my jacket, change from boots and jeans to sneakers and shorts. "It doesn't matter."

Knox's brows lift. "Lake has a woman staying with him."

Leo and Riggs stare at me, mouths agape.

"And she's hot."

"Knox," I warn.

"Really fucking hot," he goes on, ignoring me. "Greenest eyes you've ever seen, man. And an ass that should be worshipped. If my sister wouldn't kill me for fucking her best friend, I would totally hit that—"

I react without thinking, spinning toward him, grabbing his neck and slamming him back into the lockers. "Don't fucking talk about Nova's ass."

The fucker clearly has a death wish because he just smirks again, wider this time, before he glances over at Leo and Riggs.

"And apparently, our captain likes Nova's ass so much, he's feeling possessive."

I squeeze my hand.

He coughs.

Then because it won't be great for our season to kill one of the few decent guys on the team, I let him go.

"He saved her and her dog from a snowbank," Knox rasps, rubbing his throat, his snark and bullshit not tempered in the least. "Now he's gone full caveman and claimed her. Should I get you a stick to bang her over the head with too?"

I retie my shoes—only so I won't throttle him again. "Dead. Fucking. Man."

Knox laughs.

Leo leans back, crosses his arms, studies me. "You like her." Not giving me shit. Not pushing my buttons. Just an observation.

Riggs nods in agreement.

Fuck, this is why I don't do this shit.

But...I opened up to Nova and she didn't run away screaming. She opened up to me and—

Normally, I would have told them all to fuck off then hauled ass to the gym. Today...I want something different.

Something more.

I ignore how fucking stupid that sounds—even in my own head—and mutter, "Yeah. She's cool."

Knox snorts. "Cool?"

"Dude," Leo says. "Do you *want* him to murder you?"

Another nod from Riggs.

"Cool, though?" he says. "That's seriously how Lake Jordan, sexiest athlete around, glistening cover model, vodka slinger, and big, tough hockey player is going to describe the first woman he actually *likes* since I've known him."

Murder.

M.U.R.D.E.R.

"Baby steps, man." Leo yanks off his sweatshirt, shoves it in his locker. "Take the win, take that he's not still choking you, and let's move the fuck on."

One more nod from Riggs.

But not from Knox. He just opens his mouth—

And I lose it, the words exploding out of me. "She's beautiful and cool—really fucking cool—and I'm going to keep her, okay? So fuck off and let's go work out."

Silence.

I backtrack through my words.

Realize what the fuck I just said out loud.

Fucking. *Stupid.*

"Dude," Knox says.

"Fuck off," I mutter.

"*Dude*," Knox says again.

"If you know," Riggs interjects, "then you know. So just shut up, leave the man alone, and don't do anything to fuck with his woman, yeah?"

More silence.

This time because...

"That's the most words I've heard you say at once," Knox says, eyes wide.

I agree, albeit not out loud. Riggs is one of the quietest players on the team—very much of the head down, keep skating mentality. And he's a good guy. Solid, dependable, and fiercely loyal once someone has gained his trust.

Hence him putting the quiet aside to interject on my behalf.

"What other opinions is he hiding?" Leo asks, tapping his chin.

"Jesus Christ," Riggs mutters, pushing up from the bench. "Are we ready?"

"For Lake to kick our asses?" Knox asks. "That's a no."

Riggs rolls his eyes.

Leo reaches for his workout clothes, glances at me. "So, what are we doing today?"

I grin. Is it evil? Sure as fuck is. "I'm thinking A to Z."

All three of them groan, which makes me feel significantly better.

Because A to Z is a series of twenty-six exercises, each corresponding to a movement, starting with Archer pushups and ending with Zercher squats. It's brutal. It's something I do when I want my body to hurt so much that my brain shuts down.

And thinking about what I just declared—and the possibility of Nova leaving anyway—thinking about that shit happening inside my heart, thinking about what I want deep down and how it goes against everything I've been holding tight the last couple of years...

Well, I would really like for my brain to chill the fuck out.

"No, man," Knox begs.

"It's good for us," I say, grabbing my towel because shit is about to get sweaty.

And...it's payback, muahaha.

Leo shakes his head. "No man. It's fucking torture." He yanks on a Sierra-branded tee and bends to tie his shoes. "I mean, I'm going to do it because I'm not going to bitch out on our agreement"—that we would push ourselves on days like this, push ourselves to be better—"but, just saying, you don't have to punish us all when Knox is the asshole."

Riggs nods in agreement. "Word."

Which almost—*almost*—makes me laugh.

Because, as Knox pointed out, he uses so few of those.

But I don't comment, don't argue, and I sure as shit don't give them an out. I just go into the kitchen, grab some bottled waters from the fridge, and come back, tossing one to each of them. "Hydrate, boys. We've got to get to Z."

They groan again.

But they follow me to the gym.

And all the way down to Z.

And Leo's right.

It *is* torture.

Especially when we have to get on the ice right afterward.

But I'm right too.

It's good for us.

And for those couple of hours, I stop thinking about Nova and the complicated feelings in my head and heart.

I stop thinking about everything.

At least until I walk into the house and she's lying in my bed, a movie on the TV, the smell of something delicious in the air, her expression relaxed and her face warm.

She smiles at me.

And the punch to my heart almost sends me to my knees.

"Woof!" Steve barks, tongue lolling happily as he tries to get up and greet me.

I move toward him, scoop him up, and get a kiss on my cheek.

And another punch to the heart.

Christ.

My mind is working—too much and too fast, erasing everything I thought I knew and wanted and reducing it down to this woman in front of me.

I want her.

But how do I let go enough to actually keep her?

Forever.

THIRTY-NINE

Nova

"I STILL DON'T UNDERSTAND how George knew where you were?"

I rub my forehead, toes digging into the mattress, phone on speaker as I talk to Ella. "I don't know, either. I just...I asked and he didn't answer, and it was chaos for a couple of hours before he was hauled off by the sheriff, and..."

"What?" she asks when I don't say anything else.

"Ashley," I supply on a sigh.

"Babe." A beat. "I know *you* know that I think you shouldn't have given her the jewelry." My heart pulses, hand going to my jacket pocket, running my fingers over the butterfly charm. "But I get why you did it. Some part of you loves her and always will. She's your sister, and you went through a lot together."

"Yeah," I whisper.

"So, I get it. I wish you didn't feel that you had to do that. I wish that she saw you for how wonderful you are, but she's...not good, babe. And I don't think she will."

"I told her I don't want to see her again."

An inhale rattling through the speakers. "I think that's a good boundary, but also..."

"What?"

"Just don't beat yourself up if that changes. Family is complicated."

I think of what Lake told me about his mom.

I think of Ashley and our tangled world—the hurts and betrayals and the way I still clung to something that wasn't healthy.

I think of Ella and Knox and *their* very complicated family.

"Yeah," I agree softly. "It is."

We're quiet for a blip.

"And, for the record," she says. "I'm glad that George is out of the picture. He's an asshole."

"I haven't seen him since that, and I hope I don't."

"He's probably on his way to Vegas to con some poor, innocent woman out of her time and energy and money."

I wrinkle my nose. "Maybe."

"And you wouldn't see him, anyway." A beat. "Considering you're stowed away in Lake's shag mansion."

Those wrinkles deepen because...ew.

I mean, she's not wrong.

But still...*ew.*

She giggles into my disgusted silence. "Too far?"

"Uh, yeah," I say, picking up my mug—now filled with hot cocoa because today, while Lake is at practice, I'm watching Hallmark movies to go alongside my cheesy action flicks.

And scrolling through my photographs.

And catching up with Ella.

Read: giving my friend the riot act.

Then catching her up.

Now, though, the sun is setting outside and I'm snug in Lake's fluffy blankies and hot cocoa is the best cozy, comfy, snuggly-in-fuzzy-blankets drink around.

"You went too far when you started in about his *branch*," I tell her. "You went too far when you sent me on a collision course with a grumpy hockey player and an empty house. You went *infinitely* too far just now by referring to this beautiful house as a shag mansion."

Even though we *have* been fucking like jackrabbits.

Ella feigns seriousness, but I read right through her. My best friend doesn't do serious. At all. "First," she says. "Don't yuck my yum. Second"—I can picture her ticking these off on her fingers—"I didn't know the house was empty."

I sigh. "Meanwhile, she doesn't mention the grumpy hockey player,"

"*Third*," she says over me. "Lake knows how to use that *branch*, if what you've told me is the truth"—because, yes, I spilled everything to my friend—"so really, you should be thankful."

"*Or* the snowbank."

Ella huffs out a laugh. "Considering the orgasms he gave you, I would brave the snowbank *and* take a little, or I guess, *big*"—she cackles—"grumpy."

I narrow my eyes even though she can't see me. "It wasn't little."

The grumpy *or* the penis.

"Okay," she says. "How about this? I would take a lot of grumpy from a man who looks like Lake Jordan. I mean, have you *seen* his underwear ads?"

No. In fact, I have not.

My fingers start moving on the keyboard.

"You're looking them up right now, aren't you?" she asks, chortling.

"Damn right, I am." I click and the picture pops up and—

I shiver.

Because I've seen that broody look directed my way. I've seen those six-pack abs and those strong thighs up close and personal.

But I haven't seen them all oiled up, glistening, and—

"Jesus Christ," I mutter.

"I hope you've licked every inch of him," Ella says dreamily.

I haven't yet. But I'm *going* to, just as homage to this photograph.

And maybe I was going to two-day ship in some body oil, just for good measure.

"I'll definitely stick around long enough to do at least that," I say, so focused on the pictures that it takes me a moment to realize Ella isn't snarking back. "What?" I ask.

"You're leaving again?"

Her question is taut, unhappy.

"Ells," I begin. "I don't have a job. I'm single because my boyfriend—who, yes, I've come to realize is a major asshole—cheated on me with my sister. I'm not talking to either of them. My parents are...wherever. My grandmother is dead." I lean back against the headboard and sigh. "So, really, what's holding me here?"

"Me," she snaps. "You're my best friend. I should actually be able to see you."

"Honey, I always visit, you know that. But this is a good thing. Steve and I can go explore, and—"

"Hide because you don't want to actually live your life."

I still, but her words keep coming.

"Be too proud to actually accept some help from a person

who's willing to freely give it," she all but yells. "That person is me, by the way. Or Knox. Or, I think, given what you've told me, Lake."

That's so close to what he said before he left for the rink this morning that I freeze, fingers clenching into fists. "Ells," I warn.

"And I'm *here*. I want to see you and talk to you regularly. When you disappear for months at a time, that doesn't happen."

Guilt curls through me. "Ella—"

"And you said Lake told you that you can stay as long as you want."

I shake my head. "That's just him being nice."

"The grumpy hockey player being nice," she says dryly.

I hate that she makes a point, hate the way that sends the butterflies in my belly soaring.

"Honey," I say gently. "Please don't be mad."

Silence that's so tense, I hold my breath.

But then she blows out a breath, and I do too. "I'll always be here for you, you know that right?"

My heart squeezes. "Yeah. And I'm here too."

"Just not in person."

Another squeeze, almost violent now. "Honey—"

"Sorry," she says, exhaling again. "That was bitchy." Another breath. "I love you, and I'll do that wherever you are."

"I love you too."

"Good, good." A quick acknowledgment of my feelings that might make *her* feel something she's uncomfortable with before pressing forward, moving on to something less tetchy—and seriously, it's no wonder she and I are close. We're flip sides of the same coin. "Anyway," she says. "Knox told me that while Lake's been extra grumpy lately, he's a good guy." A beat. "Maybe you just stumbled upon him at the apex of that and he's swinging back to his normal self."

That, I don't know.

I just...also don't want to look at *any* of this too closely.

I don't want to think about what there is about me that might make him be less grumpy—

It doesn't matter.

I'm staying here until I've got things in place, a plan to move forward, and in exchange for that—and copious orgasms—I'll make him as many honey rosemary mules as he wants.

And help him order more furniture online.

And cook a meal without burning it...hopefully.

Then we'll move forward and each go our own way and everything will be great.

It'll be *perfect*.

There's noise in the hall, and Steve perks up his ears. "I've got to go," I tell Ella.

"Okay, Nov," she says, and then like the emotional ninja she is, pushing me to be better when she, herself, is stuck on the sidelines, she slips in some wisdom I *know* she doesn't accept into her own heart. "Remember that it's okay to want something more than you think you deserve."

My stomach flutters—fucking butterflies.

But I just say, "Yeah," and hang up, trying to get them to settle, to pretend her words don't land somewhere deep inside.

Because my parents left, my grandma died, my boss didn't value my work, and my sister...well—

A sigh.

Sometimes I think I've already gotten what I deserve.

FORTY

SHE SMILES UP AT ME, butterfly piercing in her nose twinkling from the lights overhead.

Steve's body is a wriggly, furry mass in my arms.

"Hey," she says. "How was practice?"

Shit.

Coach was in a fucking mood, not satisfied with anything we were doing, pissed off in general, and so he worked us hard.

Which meant our A to Z beforehand was dumb because Leo, Riggs, Knox, and I were slower than normal.

Did the rest of the team pick it up to compensate for that?

Nope.

They matched us—only it wasn't because they were maxed out. It was because they are lazy as fuck.

Which meant we got our asses handed to us and then a dressing down afterward for our trouble.

Fun times as a pro hockey player.

But all of that tension disappears when I walk into my bedroom, when I see Nova in my bed.

When I see the tiny demon, get that kiss on my cheek.

Nova's brows pull together as she tosses back the blankets, her laptop and the movie on the TV forgotten. Then she's moving toward me, stepping close—albeit careful of squashing Steve between us. Her hand comes to my jaw, and she runs her fingers through the stubble on my cheeks. "Practice was that bad, huh?"

My heart does that thing—the squeezing, the pulsing, the perking up and paying attention to this woman. "It was fine," I say, brushing it off, brushing off her concern. "It's not all rainbows and puppy dogs—"

"Woof!"

I grin, and pat Steve on the head, then look back at her. "Sometimes it's not rainbows and sunshine. Sometimes it sucks."

Her face gentles. "I'm sorry today sucked."

I didn't say that—at least not explicitly. But she gets it anyway.

My heart.

Fuck, I like her.

Fear coils along my spine, but I push it down. I'm not a fucking coward. I strap blades to my feet and hit people for a living. I can take a chance with a beautiful woman who looks at me like that, who's not like my mom, not like Olivia, not—

Enough.

Running my finger along her bottom lip, I say, "I know something that will make it better."

Her mouth curves as her hand slides down between us. "Oh? What might that be?"

Exactly where her hand is heading.

I steal a kiss—make it hot and wet and short because then

I'm turning for the bathroom, setting Steve inside. He huffs out a sigh and immediately goes to his bed, even before I reach for the doorknob, having been in this position enough times over the last days to know his place.

Good pooch.

I grin, turn back.

And immediately, my cock goes hard.

Nova has pushed down her pants, tugged off her loose sweatshirt, leaving her in a flimsy bra and barely-there panties.

Her breasts—fuck, they're my favorite thing in the whole world.

Or maybe that's her ass, I think as she turns around, scooping up her clothes.

Okay, fine. It's all of her—tits to ass to thighs to hair cascading down her naked back.

Her eyes. Her lips. Her gentle expression when she apologized for my shit day.

The scorching look she gives me right now.

I take a step toward her—

My cell rings.

"Fuck," I mutter, digging into my pocket, rejecting the call.

Taking another step toward her.

It immediately starts ringing again.

I yank it out, glance at the screen. My fucking mother—and I seriously don't have patience for this shit. I reject it a second time.

Take one more step.

Ring!

Nova is watching me, her teeth pressing into her bottom lip. "Maybe you should take that?"

I reject it a third time.

Ring! Ring!

"Fuck," I mutter. "Sorry, butterfly. I'll just be a few minutes."

"Take your time," she whispers.

But I don't miss the wide eyes, the concerned expression—concerned for *me*. Then I'm walking from the room, swiping at the screen, lifting my phone to my ear.

"Why didn't you tell me?" my mother shrieks, practically loud enough to blow out my eardrums.

Jesus.

I pull my cell away. "Tell you what?"

"That you almost died!" she wails.

Did I miss something?

"What are you talking about?" I say. "I'm fine. I didn't even play tonight." No hits for her to worry about. No sticks or skates flying for my face.

"You were *snowed in!*"

My temples are throbbing, and I close my eyes, hang my head. She's calling about Snowmaggedon...after Snowmaggedon is over. Why is that so fucking typical?

I inhale, shake my head, and let it out. "The roads are clear and we got dumped on, but it was just a little snow—"

"A *little!* I just saw a report on the news and they said you got a full season's snowfall over a few days! That's not a little! Oh my God, did your power go out?"

"No—"

"What *if* your power went out? You could have frozen to death. My baby boy, freezing to death in that empty house of his, all the way across the country from me."

"I have a generator—"

"And what if your generator broke?" she moans. "Then you could have *died!*"

Fucking hell.

"I'm fine. I had practice today—"

"You drove on those roads?" Another wail that has me sighing, leaning back against the wall. "That's so dangerous. My baby…"

I slowly sink down to the floor, head coming to my knees, and sigh as I let her ramble on about avalanches and dangerous tree limbs and downed powerlines and my well-being.

While not actually asking about my well-being.

Because that's not her way.

She just keeps going and continues dropping the mantle of her emotions onto my shoulders, and I keep sitting there, accepting it, accepting the drama and hormones and her drawing on my emotional well until it's empty.

Accepting that this is reality.

Knowing that what I told the guys about wanting to keep Nova was insanity. Or orgasms talking. Or gangrene from the tiny demon's bite.

Yeah, I like Nova.

She's a cool chick.

She's a great lay.

But that's all it'll be.

That's all it will *ever* be.

FORTY-ONE

Nova

THE HALL HAD GROWN SILENT, and I don't know if I should stay in the bedroom, give Lake his privacy, or if I should go find him and make sure he's okay.

Maybe make him a mule and present it as a peace offering? A balm for an otherwise shitty day?

Steve whines from the bathroom, but I don't let him out, just pull on my clothes, quietly pad to the bedroom door, and peek out into the hall.

My gut clenches.

Lake is sitting there, head on his knees, phone a couple of inches away from his ear, not saying anything even though I can hear the faint din of the voice on the other end.

I move closer, settle at his side.

He stiffens, but doesn't look up, doesn't acknowledge me.

This is my first clue—unfortunately, I don't pay attention to it.

His voice startles me when it finally comes several minutes

later, the shrill voice on the other end of the call showing no sign of calming. "I know you're concerned—"

But he doesn't get the full sentence out before the voice increases in volume.

I can't make out much aside from noise—and maybe a *"My baby!"*—but Lake seems to be hearing just fine because he just sighs again, settling in, though this time it's by lifting his head and plunking it back against the wall behind him.

His lids are closed.

His hair's a mess.

His jaw is tense—along with his shoulders and torso, his legs, even his fingers have formed taut fists, and his toes are curled tightly in his socks.

I nibble at my bottom lip, debating.

But...he asked me to stay.

So, I reach for his free hand.

He startles, eyes flying open, locking with mine, his cell still an inch away from his ear, the voice going on and on, a la *Charlie Brown.*

But he allows me to gently unfurl his fist, to lace my fingers through his.

Relief in my belly, settling the butterflies when he doesn't pull away.

"I'm going to need you to listen to me," he finally says several minutes later. "Nope. Not to yell at me. But to take a breath and really *listen.*"

He waits again, almost an interminable amount of time before he's able to speak. "Right. There was a snowstorm. I never lost power or was in any danger. I stayed home, ate and drank and slept. It was like a vacation—"

He breaks off again, the voice on the other end of the call going a mile a minute.

"But tonight," he says loudly, after waiting less time. "I just got home from practice and I'm tired. I'm going to hang up—"

The voice increases in volume.

"I'm going to hang up, and I'll call you tomorrow."

A wail that almost hurts my ears.

I wince, clutch at his hand.

"Goodbye, Mom."

He jabs at the screen with his free hand, drops it to the floor, sending it skittering along the hardwood.

After the noise on the other end of the line—and his mom not even on speaker phone—the quiet that falls between us seems exceptionally...*quiet*.

I nibble at my lip again, still holding tightly to his hand.

"Well," I eventually say. "Um...that happened."

His big chest rises and falls on an exhale before he rotates his head to the side, gold and green and brown eyes locking with mine.

Not warm.

Not soft.

Not...Lake.

He pulls his hand from mine.

Looks away.

My nostrils flare, but I manage to rest my palm on my thigh, to not clutch it to my chest, to not reach out to him and cling to him.

"Want to talk about it?" I ask, long moments later, the silence getting to me.

"No," he mutters, rotating his head back so our gazes meet. A sigh as he pushes to his feet. "You should go to bed."

My stomach convulses, but it's not from the butterflies this time.

It's...

Wrong. This is wrong.

"Lake," I begin.

He turns away, starts for the family room.

I struggle to my feet, trail after him. "I made some soup," I say, watching his back go stiff, his shoulders hitch up. I go to the fridge, pull out the container. "If you want any..." I finish, trailing off when he brushes by me, heading toward...

The vodka cabinet.

"Or not," I whisper as he opens a bottle and drinks straight from the open top. "Um...how about a grilled cheese? At least that's small and will soak up"—he takes another long guzzle—"some of that alcohol."

He drops the bottle to the counter, sending it sloshing out the top. "Why are you still here?"

I freeze, more stomach churning, less butterflies.

No butterflies.

"Lake," I say carefully. "It sounds like the call upset you—"

"Wow," he drawls. "Did you come up with that all on your own?"

I inhale sharply. "Don't do that," I murmur.

He takes another sip. "I'm not doing anything."

Except pushing me away.

"Honey," I say. "Let's either talk about it, or find a way to take your mind off—"

He smirks. "What are you offering?"

I go statue-still then blow out a breath. "I know you're upset."

"You don't know anything."

Frustration dancing off the tip of my tongue. "Then clue me in, honey. Talk to me. Or, fuck"—I toss up my hands—"let's put it aside and do something else."

He shoves the bottle back then strides over to me, face an inch from mine, his eyes...yeah, I don't like his eyes. "You don't get it."

"Get what?" I whisper.

"That I don't want anything to do with you."

Those words...

They cut.

Because—

First my parents. Then my sister. George. And...now Lake.

Still, I try. "That's not fair. Honey, I"—swallowing hard, I gird my loins—"I really think it would help if we talked."

"What do you care?" he asks coldly. "You were ready to hit the road this morning."

I suck in a breath, skitter back a step. "Fuck you," I whisper.

He picks up the bottle, salutes me with it. "Right back at ya. You're just like all the rest of them, shoving into a space where you're not welcome."

Pain in my middle.

Another shaky step backward.

But I manage to lift my chin, for my words to be frosty. "Cool," I tell him, waving a hand at the bottle. "I'll just let you get drunk like an idiot."

He shoos me away disdainfully. "Finally."

I turn on my heel, hurry to the bedroom, thinking that as soon as it's morning, I'm getting the fuck out of here.

Because if he's like *this*...

Like this not even one goddamn day after asking me to stay—

Then fuck him.

The open road is a hundred times better.

FORTY-TWO

Lake

TAP. *Tap. Tap.*

I jerk, lifting my head from my steering wheel, glancing out the window.

Mack's standing there in his sheriff's uniform, flashlight out, expression furrowed in concern.

I hit the button to roll down the window.

He looks at me for a long moment.

Then turns on his heel. "Get your ass inside my house."

I scowl, open my mouth to snap out—

"I can make that an order—and one with handcuffs—if you don't get your head out of your ass."

"Fucking hell," I growl, jabbing at the button to turn off my car, snatching up my phone, and getting out of the SUV. "I haven't been drinking."

Or not since I shoved the bottle away and got the fuck out of my house so I wasn't tempted to go down the hall and find Nova.

To apologize.

Or to get rip-roaring drunk and do something worse—like tell her what I'm feeling deep inside—

Mack slams my car door, and I snap out of it.

This shit needs to end now.

Before it gets worse.

Before I become more attached and she becomes—

Someone I can't look at or talk to or stand to be in the same room with.

"I can smell the vodka on your breath, idiot. But I'm not worried about you being drunk—I know it takes more than what I can smell on you." He hitches his head to the right—to his house.

Which, apparently, I parked in front of.

I'm an asshole...*and* a fucking idiot.

"It's below freezing," he mutters. "So, get your ass inside." He starts up his driveway, clomps onto his porch, then opens and holds the door wide for me.

I tromp in behind him, stomach sinking, immediately looking for an escape route when I see Jer is sitting at the table, along with John, a detective for the sheriff's department, and Ronnie, the owner of the bar in town the guys and I like to frequent called...Ronnie's.

Does the moniker lack creativity?

Maybe.

But we all know who it belongs to, don't we?

The men turn and stare at me, Ronnie and John curious, Jer suspicious and more than a little pissed.

"You fucked up," he says without preamble as he shuffles the deck of cards in front of him.

I think about lying.

But since a similar sentiment has been running through my mind over that last hour, ever since I watched Nova walk down the hall, looking like I socked her in the stomach, I can't even summon a denial.

"I fucked up," I admit.

He sighs, shakes his head, and starts dealing the cards. "Get the man a beer," he orders Mack before nodding at me to take one of the chairs. "Sit the fuck down and tell us about it."

I sit, but I don't spill my guts.

These guys...

They won't get it.

A punch to my arm. "Don't look like that," Jer says tersely. "*We're* the happily married ones. You're the single idiot who keeps picking women who either want to cut off your dick and gild it, spend all of your money, or who make so much drama in your life that you're fucking miserable."

"Don't tell me your wife isn't dramatic," I mutter. "I remember the fuss she threw up about curtains."

"I'll take curtains with ugly ass flowers on them over knives being launched in my direction any day of the week."

Since he has a point, I don't argue, just look down at my cards and start organizing them. "It's easier to just not have a woman at all."

They freeze—no cards shuffling, no beers being consumed.

Then they start laughing.

"Oh God," Mack mutters, taking a swig from his bottle. "He's still in the Idiot Stage."

I inhale, narrow my eyes.

Jer shoves a stack of chips in my direction. "If you really wanted to be alone, you wouldn't be sitting there looking like that."

"I'm not *looking* like anything."

They all laugh again.

Then Mack tosses a chip in the center, and that moves around the table, everyone anteing up.

"Fucking liar," Jer says, "and not even a good one."

I throw my own chip in, ignoring him...because, again, he's right.

Which is fucking annoying.

I discard then draw another card.

"What'd she do?" Ronnie asks, cigarette hanging out of his mouth.

I eye the door, wonder at my chances of escaping this fucking conversation.

"I'm old but have an explosive start," Mack says quietly. "You won't make it outside."

Reading my mind. And not bullshitting me—one look, and I know he won't hesitate to take me down.

Which is even *more* annoying.

"So?" John presses, just as much of a nosy fuck as the rest of them.

I throw in a few more chips, draw another card. "My mom called"—they still, all knowing me well enough to understand that my mother is a pain in the fucking ass—"Nova was there for the conversation...which didn't go well."

"What did Nova do?" Jer asked.

I glare down at my cards. "She tried to comfort me."

Silence again—albeit this time it's tinged with confusion.

Then Jer tosses down his cards, folding. "Tell me you're not *that* much of an idiot."

I inhale, fold myself. "I barely know her, man, and she's trying to interject herself into my life."

Which is bullshit I don't believe, even as it's coming off my tongue.

She's had one foot out the door the entire time she's been staying at my house.

"By comforting you after a tough conversation," he says dryly.

I take a swig of my beer in answer.

Mack curses.

Jer turns to me.

And...I snap. This day has been fucking ridiculous—Knox and his remorseless bullshit, the hard-ass workout in the gym, Coach and the practice from hell, my mom cock-blocking me and pulling her usual drama, the...

Look in Nova's eyes.

Christ, I can't fucking think about that.

I set my bottle on the table with a *plunk*, foam bubbling up and spilling down the sides. "Look," I growl. "I'm happy to walk the fuck out that door and leave you interfering assholes to your game. *You*"—I glare at Mack—"brought me inside. *You*"— at Jer—"dealt me in. You two—"

Ronnie lifts his hands. "I'm just here for the poker, man."

"Same," John mutters, throwing another chip in the pot.

I sigh.

"You're a fucking moron," Jer says, shaking his head.

Done with this shit, I start to stand up.

Mack shoves me back down. "We'll be done with this conversation after I say this." His fingers tighten on my shoulder, voice going gruff with grief, and I still because—

Fuck.

Because Mack lost his wife last year.

"Mack—" I begin.

He talks over me. "I would give anything to fight with her over curtains. I would give anything to have her there trying to comfort me after a shit day or a phone call with an annoying ass relative, to have to clean her hair out of the goddamned drain." His chin drops to his chest. "I would give any-fucking-*thing* to hold her, talk with her, hug her. Give anything to just have one more moment with her."

My throat goes tight. "Mack," I rasp.

He releases me, obviously seeing that his words struck home.

And they have. Deeply.

Because...Steve's tiny teeth in my ankle.

Nova's honey rosemary mules.

The soft way she looks at me.

The beauty of her photographs.

The butterfly charm and the pain in her eyes when she told me about her childhood.

Her wanting to leave, *so* scared to stay...and yet taking a chance that morning in my kitchen.

And meanwhile...

"I fucked up," I whisper.

Jer starts dealing the next hand. "Of course you did, you idiot."

"That's not what's important," Mack says, words still pained.

"What is?" I ask, pushing the question through my tight throat.

He glares at me. "How you're going to fix it so she doesn't leave your dumb ass."

Then he's true to his word—none of them talk about women or Nova or me being an idiot as we continue the game.

But I don't think I would have heard them if they had.

Because I *am* a fucking idiot.

And I have no clue how to fix it.

FORTY-THREE

Nova

I TOSS the blankets back when the sun starts peeking in through the window, and exhale deeply.

The treetops are lined with glittering snow.

There's a sliver of blue in the sky.

It's...time to go.

My stomach twists, but...

There's nothing else to be said.

Last night was enough.

And it's not like Lake crawled into bed with me, apologized, and fucked my brains out. Far as I can tell, he didn't come home at all.

Certainly, he didn't sleep next to me.

And not in front of the fireplace either I find when I make my way into the family room.

That's enough of a message.

Not only does he think I'm just like every other woman who's used him, he also wants me gone.

Well...*that* I can do.

I move to the coffee pot, flick the switch, starting it up, then glance at my bags on the counter. At least I don't have much to pack up.

Just my whole life...that fits into a few bags.

"Pathetic," I whisper, turning away, reaching for a mug—

Freezing.

Because there's a pad on the counter, and it's filled with equal parts masculine scrawl and crossed-out words.

"What—" I whisper.

But then my brain actually begins to process the words there.

~~Dear Nova,~~
~~I let my past affect the way I treated you—~~

~~Dear Nova,~~
~~I don't want you to leave. My mom makes my brain stop working—~~

~~Dear Nova,~~
~~I've never dated a woman like you. I shouldn't have said—~~

Dear Nova,

I was an asshole. Please give me another chance.
-Lake

"I'M NOT DONE WITH IT."

That soft statement has me looking up over my shoulder... into Lake's beautiful—and remorseful—gold and green and brown eyes.

"It seems like you covered it all," I say lightly, pushing the pad away.

He moves toward me in a rush, and I shrink back, the wounds from his sharp words the night before barely healed.

Head up. Move forward.

This is all fine.

"I didn't," he says. "I have plans for serious groveling and—"

"Right," I whisper, heart pounding as I turn my back on him, as I fill my mug with freshly brewed coffee.

When I rotate around again, intending to go to the fridge for cream, he's already there, reaching inside and pulling out the carton, carrying it over to me, setting it on the counter next to the steaming mug. A second later, the canister of sugar settles beside it.

"I have to leave soon," he whispers and my heart convulses, even though I know it's for the best. "I have to meet the bus to the airport for our away game tomorrow, but I need you to know this first."

It's early, and I barely slept.

My insides feel shredded and raw.

I should just leave.

But I still ask, "What do I need to know?"

His throat works, the words a rasp. "I know I fucked up. I

know *why* I fucked up. I just"—more remorse in those eyes—
"don't know how to fix it."

I shrug. "There's nothing to fix. You had a bad moment. I
happened to be there for it—"

"Bullshit," he says. "I took it out on you because you're *not*
like the other women I've had in my life."

My brows drag together.

"And that's fucking scary."

I inhale sharply, feel my head go a little fuzzy.

"So, instead of coming back here and groveling like I should
have, I had to have Jer and Mack set me straight, and then I sat
in my car all night and tried to get my fucking head together.
Only...I didn't," he says. "Because underneath all the bullshit
excuses I tried to weave about my behavior, there's only one
thing that's actually true."

I let out that breath.

"I'm a fucking coward."

"What?" I frown. "No, Lake. That's—"

His hand comes to my jaw, tilting my head up. "You got too
close, saw too much, and then you didn't react like any woman
in my life ever has, and...fuck, but that made me like you even
more, butterfly, and that's fucking scary, and *that's* what makes
me a coward. Because instead of talking to you, I pushed you
away."

My heart is in my throat. My stomach is awash with
butterflies.

"I mean," I whisper. "We barely know each other, so it
makes sense why—"

"Bullshit," he says. "You know me better than anyone else
in my life."

I freeze.

Because...he's right.

Because I've told him things that not even Ella knows. Because he's let me in deep too.

"And," he says, "because you deserve to be treated better."

My stomach fills with butterflies. "Lake," I breathe.

His fingers trail over my cheek, along my jaw, dip into my hair, forehead settling against mine, golden green eyes holding mine. "I'm so fucking sorry," he murmurs. "And I'm begging you to please give me another chance to prove that I see how fucking wonderful you are."

My knees wobble, and I exhale shakily.

I'm not sure I'm that person.

"I don't want you to leave." His eyes slide closed, forehead pressing closer. "I'm not sure I *ever* want you to leave."

I go stiff, inhalation sharp. "Lake."

"Shh," he murmurs. "Just..." His eyes open and he straightens slightly. "Just promise me you'll stay here, promise me you and Steve will be safe while I'm gone. Promise me you'll fill another memory card with photos, and drink my vodka, and watch crappy movies on my TV. Promise me you won't run off without showing me all of the beauty of you."

Tears sting the backs of my eyes and I close them, leaving them that way for a long time.

"Promise me you'll stay long enough for me to prove to you how fucking magnificent you are."

This is insanity.

This is...*perfect.*

This is nothing I want...and yet, it's everything I've hoped for.

I want to pull away, to grab my stuff and Steve, and run.

I want to stay forever and fill this house with our memories.

But beneath it all is the *need* to run—

Remember that it's okay to want something more than you think you deserve.

Ella's words whip through my mind and I pause, eyes flying open and locking with Lake's—reading the depths of his emotions, feeling them, knowing how much it cost this big, strong man to make himself vulnerable to me.

And...

I exhale.

I leap.

And I decide that—for once—moving forward might mean staying right here.

FORTY-FOUR

Lake

"TELL me something about yourself that no one else knows."

My heart does that Nova thing, pulsing, squeezing, reminding me it belongs to her, and I roll to my side, fussing with my phone in order to get it positioned correctly, to keep the camera on my face as I rub discreetly at the ache in my chest.

She's at home in my bed, Steve at her side, her hair piled on top of her head, cheeks pink from the spiked hot cocoa she's drinking and also probably from her excitement of showing me some of the photographs she took that day.

So far, our conversation had been carefully light, both of us aware of the events of the day before last.

Or maybe that's just me.

She's as bright and beautiful as normal.

Only...she's also holding herself carefully.

Expecting me to push her away.

So, I know this question is a test—though I don't think she

realizes it. There's nothing calculating about her tone or expression.

Nothing but that cautious way she's holding herself, and how she's clinging to Steve.

As though her pup will keep her safe from me.

Fucking *hate* that.

"I like Twix," I say, going for easy-breezy.

Her mouth curves and the tightness in her eases slightly, shoulders dropping, grip on Steve gentling. The pup huffs out a breath and, swear to fuck, he glances into the camera with thanks before settling down to snore away in her lap. "I think I got that from the size of your stash in your pantry."

I grin, waggle my brows. "I think you like the size of my stash."

She giggles, but I don't push us onto another conversation, don't use light and breezy to keep her out.

Not again.

Not *ever* again.

"I never wanted to be a hockey player," I admit.

A gasp that disturbs Steve, if his groan is any indication. "Really?" she asks.

I nod. "I mean, I love the sport, love what I do, and I'm fucking thankful that I'm able to do it for my job, I just..." I sigh and sit up, bringing the camera with me, shoving a hand through my hair, bracing myself as I admit, "For a long time, I loved it because it was my only escape. My mom didn't like coming to the rink, and if she did, she couldn't get to me. I could hide out in the locker room or the gym or on the ice, could leave her bullshit behind."

"Did your dad—" She breaks off with a shake of her head.

"He didn't come to my games."

"At all?"

"No," I say gently. "He basically abandoned my siblings

and me. Yeah, he lived at home, paid the bills, but he wasn't there, and he sure as fuck didn't intervene on our behalf with my mom. He just let me and my siblings take care of her." I shake my head. "I know it's nothing like what you went through, butterfly."

"Don't," she whispers.

I focus on her through the screen on my phone.

"Don't discount your pain," she whispers.

My lungs loosen, air I didn't know I was holding inside sliding out on an exhale.

Her next question is soft. "Where are your siblings?"

"My brother is married and moved to Canada," I tell her. "My sister lives in Arizona."

"And your parents?"

"Connecticut."

She presses her lips together, releases them. "So, you've all gotten as far as possible away from them."

I take another breath, let it out. "Them by choice. Me by chance."

"Are you guys close?"

"No." I exhale, rub at my chest again. "I think...well, I think it's better that we've all gone our own way."

"And are they still together?"

"My parents?"

She nods.

"Yup," I say, rolling my eyes. "For God knows what reason, since they hardly ever spend time together." I huff out a laugh that's nowhere close to amused. "My dad works more than ever, so my mom tries to find ways to fill her days—and that's usually by creating chaos and drama, and spending money. I love her despite all of her shit, but swear to fuck, what I wouldn't *give* for her to find a charity or something that would dominate her life. Instead, it's all about shopping and filling the house with shit and redoing the rooms over and over again, and then, when she remembers me, it's about driving me fucking insane for short bursts of time before she forgets and goes back to her life."

"And your dad?"

I sigh, unable to hold her eyes through the camera. "Same shit, different day. He doesn't come to my games, missed my brother's wedding, never met my nephews."

"Asshole."

"Yeah," I say. "I come by it naturally, apparently."

She narrows her eyes at me. "Hush, you."

A lightness slides through me—and somehow despite the conversational topic, I'm amused. "I could maybe forgive him for the shit growing up—"

"I can't," she mutters, causing my eyes to shoot back to hers, seeing they're filled with fury.

That amusement fades. My heart squeezes hard. "It's not just forgiveness, though, and I'm not delusional. He's shown us all who he is over and over again, and I can't absolve him of the shit he pulled. But, after all this time, any good opinion I've had of him is shattered forever."

"Honey," she whispers.

I swallow hard.

She sighs. "I wish I was there with you."

I force a smile. "It's all good, butterfly."

She falls quiet for a long moment. "Thanks for sharing that with me."

"Got any other skeletons you want to disclose?" I ask with false lightness. "Or interrogation questions you need to ask?"

"Now's the time to press you?" Her voice is gentle. "Is that what you're saying?"

"Yup."

Her head tilts to the side, expression soft and hitting me

hard in the heart. "Considering that, I think this is the time for me to admit that I ate the last Twix."

I still.

Then I throw back my head and laugh.

This woman...

She's fucking perfect.

***

"Are you going to help?" she asks testily a few days later, standing on a stool and lifting the curtain rod toward the brackets I just finished installing.

The Sierra are off today.

Tomorrow, I have to get back to the rink.

Today, though, I can spend time with Nova, with my woman who hasn't held my idiocy against me, who's slowly unfurling and showing me the beauty of her.

Today, I can eye the tight jeans covering her from ankle to waist, the tee that's risen to give me a glimpse of silken skin I licked my way across earlier this morning, after I returned from the away game, and shake my head. "Naw, butterfly, I can admire you much better from here."

Her head whips around, eyes coming to mine, voice husky and clearly reading my intent when she asks, "Are we *not* putting up curtains?"

"We can put up curtains," I say softly, prowling toward her. "But I also would be fine with breaking in the console table."

I now know what a console table is.

A pointlessly skinny piece of furniture that's supposed to hold China that I don't own.

Nova showed it to me on that website, and her eyes lit up, and...I understood exactly why Jer had given in about the floral curtains.

Now that table has a place in my house.

Now—

"Oof," I grunt in surprise as Nova launches herself off the stool and into my arms, somehow having secured the rod—okay, not *somehow*. As I was staring at her ass, she hung the curtains, and now—

"Let's break in the console," she says.

I have my woman in my arms, those curtains framing my window, and a table I don't understand the point of.

And I can't help but think that life is pretty fucking perfect.

Especially, when she shoves her hands between us and flicks open the button on my jeans.

Perfect...

So long as I don't do anything to fuck it up.

FORTY-FIVE

Nova

A WEEK LATER, Steve and I are waltzing into Jeremy Blevins, DVM's clinic.

It's a bright and cheerful place, full of pictures of animals and an office kitty sitting on a bed behind the reception desk.

I've successfully driven—without ending up in any snowbanks—from Lake's house down into town.

Go me.

"Woof!" Steve barks, tail uncurling and hanging low like it does any time he's scared—and vet offices might be number one on that very short list. But we need to get his leg X-rayed so the splint can—hopefully—come off.

"Hello, welcome in," the receptionist says. "Who do we have here?"

I make introductions, do my check-in, and sit down for a bit before we're called back and follow the tech to a room. Jer is coming in just as we walk through the door. "Nova," he says, his eyes narrowing slightly. "Lake treating you well?"

I think back over the last couple of weeks.

Movies in bed together. FaceTime calls when he's on the road. Delicious food in my belly when he's home. A pair of butterfly-printed fuzzy socks left on my nightstand. Another skating session that didn't end with me taking him out, or having an orgasm in the snow—

Though, it did end up with me *having* an orgasm, this one just inside the front door.

My cheeks heat.

But my belly is full of butterflies.

Because he *has* been treating me well, so well that I'm...

Falling for him.

Those butterflies move faster, fluttering around like they do every time I think of Lake.

It almost takes my breath away because it feels so good.

"Yes," I say softly. "He's treating me well."

Jer studies my face, nods, and I think I see approval in his eyes as he reaches forward and squeezes my arm. "I'm glad, sweetheart." A gentle sentiment before he gets down to business with my pooch. "Steve"—he makes a pit stop at the jar of treats—"it's good to see you!"

He extends his hand toward my pup, revealing a handful of treats sitting in his palm.

Clearly, the man knows the way to Steve's heart.

Who gets over his shyness and starts creeping forward. A sniff. A lick. And then the treats disappear.

That's enough to endear Jer to Steve and the rest of the exam proceeds without much excitement, even when they take him back for the X-ray.

"It's clear," Jer says five minutes later, showing me the digital film on an iPad. "His splint can stay off, and he can return to normal activities, which"—he rubs Steve's ears, turning my pup into a limp puddle of dog as he slumps onto the exam table—"I suspect will consist mostly of snoring and sleeping."

My lips twitch. "And sneezing and grunting."

Jer laughs and the iPad dings, drawing my gaze to the banner notification that appears on the top of the screen.

"Sorry," he says, swiping it away. "Our clinic tablet crapped out and I had to bring in mine from home. I guess it must still be connected to my personal account."

I frown.

Because that sends a niggle through my mind.

"Oh, hey," he says, reaching into his pocket. "Speaking of personal things, I need to give you this." He pulls out his wallet, opens it, and passes me a business card from the depths of it.

I look down at it, expecting it to contain the clinic's information.

Instead, it's for a gallery owner.

"What is this?" I ask softly, feeling strangely choked up.

Because some part of me knows.

Because he's already shown me.

Not Jer, but—

Lake.

"When everything went down at his place with your ex a couple weeks back, Lake asked me to reach out to my sister-in-law." A nod toward the card. "She owns a gallery in town and is always looking for local artists. She's expecting your call."

My heart is pounding really fast.

Really fast.

Those butterflies are whipping around my insides.

Lake did this?

For me?

Weeks ago, back when we were snowed in and barely getting along?

Before the call with his mom. Before we slept together.

Before...the curtains and mules and fucking outside by the frozen pond.

He had pulled some strings to get my photographs in a gallery.

Those butterflies still.

And then rush into motion again.

Because he did it for me, and I don't know what to do with that, with the feelings that gesture send rushing through me. I don't know *what* I'm feeling at all, what—

It's okay to want something more than you think you deserve.

I want Lake.

More than I've ever wanted anything before.

"Oh," I rasp to Jer, throat beyond tight, edges of the card pressing into my fingertips. "Thank you for doing that."

Jer smiles. "Of course. It's not a problem at all." Then he squeezes my arm, scratches Steve's head, waves goodbye, and heads off to his next client.

Leaving me with those butterflies like a tornado in my abdomen as I check out and pay and head to my car.

As I snap Steve into his puppy harness.

Then, once we're both safely inside, I pull out my phone and text Ella.

> I need you.

Thankfully, she's in town, having come up to visit Knox, and responds quickly.

> What's wrong?

I close my eyes, thunk my head against the steering wheel.

I think I'm falling in love with Lake.

The "..." starts and stops.
Starts and stops.
Then she sends,

Meet me at Ronnie's.

The bar is just around the corner.
Fucking perfect.
I need alcohol.

FORTY-SIX

"I DON'T KNOW how I let you talk me into this shit," I mutter.

Riggs grunts in agreement.

Leo just drinks deeply from his beer.

"You're supposed to be the captain," Knox says, slugging back his beer. "Which means that you should get that this is team bonding."

I sigh, roll my shoulders.

I know he's right.

I'm still grumpy about it because I want to be home. With Nova.

Because I'm fucking obsessed.

Because...I've fallen deep and hard, and it's better with her than—

Spending time with these idiots.

And because practice was another shit show.

Not just tough and tense and frustrating—or not because of

the usual reasons, anyway. We were being filmed for a sports show, so now the internet has a video of two of my teammates exchanging blows...

And Coach jumping in to punch them both.

Coach has a black eye and a fat lip for his trouble.

The two idiots are benched.

And my social media is no longer flooded with requests for more of Nova's drink recipes.

I'm tagged in videos from every angle, breaking down exactly what happened (none of which are actually right since the fight was about something so fucking stupid, it doesn't even bear discussing), and listing all the things *I* should be doing to make it better.

I'm the captain.

I'm responsible.

The problem is very few people in that locker room respect what I say.

Because they don't respect each other or themselves or the sport or the fact that we're meant to come together.

It's a team of individuals.

And we're never going to make it all the way to hefting the Cup without working with each other.

It's a fucking miracle we've won as many games as we have.

I lift my brows at Knox. "Since you've got the A"—the assistant captain position—"I'm open to any and all suggestions."

He winces. "Nah, man, I'm just here for the fun times and shit-giving."

"Right," I mutter. Which is exactly the problem. I seem to be the only one who gives a fuck and is trying to change the way the team is working. Sighing, I roll my shoulders then lift the pitcher and refill my glass with beer, deciding that I'll take any type of alcohol at this point, but also wishing I had a honey rosemary mule.

Because I've been thoroughly corrupted by Nova Cassidy.

Who...

Walks in the door, arm in arm with Knox's sister, Daniela—or Ella, as everyone calls her.

Or Trouble Number Two as she *should* be known.

Nova spots me and smiles, but when she starts to head for an empty table, I inwardly shake my head, get up, and move to her.

This woman doesn't get it.

She's staying in my home, even when I'm not there.

She ordered the furniture that's now filling the rooms inside.

But I can't shake the feeling that she still has one foot out the door.

And what are you doing to convince her to stay?

Not running in the other fucking direction, that's what.

Tell her that I want her to stay.

And letting her pick out furniture and stay in my house, and fucking her into oblivion every opportunity I got.

Cooking for her.

Watching crappy movies.

So everything and...nothing.

I rub at the ache in my chest, my heart doing that Nova thing again—squeezing, rolling over—and make my way to her, snagging her hand before she can sit down. "What are you doing?" I growl.

Growling at her.

Probably not the right move when I want her to stay forever.

She frowns up at me. "Ella and I are getting a drink."

"Here?" I ask.

Her frown deepens and she makes a show of looking around. "I mean, is your name on this table?"

"No," I snap. "I'm sitting there." I look over at Ella. "With *your* brother." I look back at Nova. "And you two are going to sit *here?*"

"Have you ever heard of girl talk?" Nova asks sharply.

"Have your girl talk later," I tug her toward me, drawing her away from the table and back to mine.

This makes Ella cackle, but she doesn't argue, just picks up her purse and follows us, slanting a look at Nova. "Sure you need to have that existential crisis?"

Nova glares at her. "Shut up."

I don't know what that's about.

I just know that she lets me nudge her down onto my stool at the table.

❄ ❄ ❄ ❄

"No, no!" Nova says with a laugh, her cheeks flushed, four honey rosemary mules in. "That's too much. The whole thing is going to taste like soap."

"Can't taste any worse than the vodka itself," Knox says, tossing back the drink he'd dumped a shit ton of rosemary simple syrup into.

Then almost immediately gags.

I bust up, Leo alongside me. Riggs shakes his head, and Ella just sighs and shakes her head. "I can't say you didn't warn my idiot brother, Novs."

"God," Knox wheezes, downing a glass of water. "That's foul."

"Yup," Ella says. "Because you're the dumbass who doesn't follow directions."

Knox glares at her. "You're just testy because I broke the doorbell of your Barbie dollhouse fifteen years ago."

"Hey"—she pokes him—"it's more like twenty, old man."

I snort.

Nova giggles and goes back to what she was doing before Knox sent this off the rails, like usual—making more mules.

Knox likes to make trouble.

Leo is quiet, but confident, charming the servers, but always aware of his surroundings.

Riggs is focused, as usual.

But tonight he's focused on Ella, which *isn't* usual, and given the look in his eyes, the *interest* in them, this is going to spell trouble for my already beleaguered locker room.

"And," Ella goes on, "it wasn't *just* a dollhouse. It was my Barbie Dream House and you ruined it." She lays the back of her hand on her forehead. "Oh the humanity."

Riggs's mouth twitches, but he doesn't otherwise speak, his man-of-few-words personality exacerbated in this type of environment. Quiet. Observing...

Ella.

Damn.

"And you"—Ella turns and points a finger at Nova—"I cannot believe that you carry a bottle of that at all times in your purse."

"I don't carry a bottle at *all* times," Nova says from the other side of the bar, mixing up the drinks like the almost pro she is. "I just grabbed this on a whim when I dropped Steve off at the house."

The house.

Not *my* house.

I stare down at my drink, consider the feelings sliding through me.

The. House. That's...good. I like that.

Our house would be better, but—

"Likely story," Ella teases, nearly falling off her stool.

Riggs catches her arm, nudges her back in place.

"Thank you, kind sir," she slurs.

"And I think *that's* the sign for you to be done," Nova says, snagging the still half-full glass back.

"What? No!" Ella reaches for the glass, but Nova just lifts it out of reach and tosses it back.

"Ah, that's good," she says, setting the empty glass on the bar top—where we've relocated because she's teaching Sue, one of the regular bartenders, how to make her drink—"and look at that, I'm all out of rosemary simple syrup. Darn." She winks at me as she rounds the bar and slips out, ignoring Ella's protests.

Protests that result in Riggs having to catch her again.

When Nova walks close enough, I loop an arm around her middle, draw her close.

"I'm jealous," Knox slurs, gaze on my arm.

I glance down at Nova. "Apparently, the Adlers can't hold their alcohol."

Her lips twitch before parting and I lean in to hear her but Knox butts in, as usual. "Hell," he says, wavering slightly, and I don't miss that Riggs doesn't try to catch *him*. "I even made a pass once at all that hotness." A pouty face as Knox waves a hand in my direction. "And he turned me down."

Leo snorts because he knows better.

Riggs brows shoot up as he looks toward me.

I shake my head.

Bullshit. As always.

I narrow my eyes at Knox. "Sit down before you fall down."

"But I waaaant you," he says, arms outstretched, lips pouted into a kiss. "Don't turn me down tall, dark, and broody."

I drop my chin to my chest. "Christ."

Nova giggles.

"I don't know if I should be disgusted or recording this," Riggs mutters.

Same, linemate. Fucking *same*.

"Recording," Leo says, digging in the pocket for his phone. "Definitely recording."

Fucking hell.

I exhale, shove Knox away when he gets close, and for some godawful reason, the next words come out of my mouth.

"You're not handsome enough to tempt me."

FORTY-SEVEN

IT'S a line I would have teased Lake about if not for the fact that I've just looked up and spied George coming toward us.

"Um," I whisper.

"Dude," Knox says loudly, laughter bubbling up in his chest. "You did *not* just quote Mr. Darcy."

Lake had.

Probably because I've had the movie on repeat over the last few days. There is just something about it that sucks me in and—

Not the time.

Just like it's not the time to clarify why Knox knows that quote well enough to immediately remember it's from Mr. Darcy.

Because George is coming closer...and my sister is behind him.

And they're both wearing huge grins on their faces.

What. The. Hell?

"Fuck off," Lake grumbles, shoving Knox back again, "and sit your ass down before you fall down."

"I think he has major Darcy vibes," Ella says conspiratorially, grinning goofily up at me. "All serious and broody and a kickass businessman with a hidden heart of gold." She clamps her hand to her chest and sighs, fluttering her eyelashes up at Lake. "Are you worth ten thousand a year too?"

Knox grins, leans in, and taps his sister on the nose, nearly sending both of them toppling. They right themselves, and Riggs shoves a glass of water in each of their hands.

Smart man.

Because seriously, these two should not be allowed to coexist in the same city. They are Trouble. With that capital T. "How uncouth," Knox says, setting the cup of water on the bar top. "Darcy would never deign to be a businessman. Everyone knows that the truly rich don't *work*."

They are hilarious.

And I read enough Regency-Period romance novels to know that's true—or close enough, anyway.

And I want to hear them continue to banter. I want to watch Lake's scowl deepen.

I want...to kiss the frown lines away, to tease a smile out of him instead.

But my ex is incoming.

"Guys," I say, my fingers tightening on Lake's, trying to get him to focus. "I—"

Too late.

George and Ashley have hit our orbit.

"What the fuck?" Ella says, lurching off her barstool and nearly toppling forward again.

Riggs snakes out a hand, draws her back against him, saving her from face planting, and clearly, I should have cut her off a few honey rosemary mules ago.

But I don't have time to feel guilty about that.

Lake is turning, his fingers tightening on mine, drawing me behind him.

Putting his body between me and my ex and—

Butterflies.

"Are you fucking stupid?" Lake snaps.

I tug against his hold, trying to shift enough to see something that isn't Lake's broad back. He doesn't let me move in front of him, but I do succeed in gaining a couple of inches to the left.

Which is enough to see George's dumb face.

And my sister's smirking one.

My sister who's all but floating, tossing her head, sending the shoulder length—and the petty queen in me says *crispy*, since she's far too fond of the bleach—floating behind her.

God, she's even lifting her hand to—

Lifting her hand.

Her *left* hand.

I frown, lean closer, and—

Go absolutely still.

"You're engaged," I breathe.

Her smirk widens. "No, sissy. We're *married*."

I rock back on my heels. "What?"

George puffs up his chest, and my shock fades. What is their end game here? Do they think, after what they did, that I'll be upset about this news? Does George think I'm going to beg him to give me some scraps of a relationship after he fucked my sister?

After he put his hands on me? After he hurt Steve?

And my sister—she's staring at me just as expectantly. Like she wants to get a reaction out of me, like she wants to hurt me.

And...I suppose she does.

"I don't get you," I say to her.

She smiles coldly.

I shore my spine, straighten my shoulders. "I don't get why you want to hurt me. What did I ever do to you?"

Her chin comes up and she looks away.

And...I want answers, but I have the feeling that I'm not going to get the ones I want.

"This is one of those times when you can just move forward, butterfly."

I jerk, my belly fluttering as I look up, get lost for a moment into Lake's pretty eyes of gold and green and brown.

I exhale, eyes sliding closed, then nod before opening them back up again.

"I sacrificed a lot for you," I tell Ashley. "For *both* of you," I add, flicking my gaze to George. "But what you did is unforgivable." I look back to my sister. "I love you, and some part of me always will, but I can't forgive you for deliberately trying to hurt me."

"Don't try to pretend to be all stoic and unaffected," she snaps. "You hate that I finally got something you want."

My lungs tighten, and I hold my breath for one long moment. Then I release it slowly, the truth dawning on me. "You've already spent the money you got from the jewelry."

Her eyes narrow. "That's none of your business."

But it's confirmation enough.

"Well, I'm not giving you anymore," I say. "I'm done."

Her eyes go to Lake and I can practically see the dollar signs flash to life.

That's why they're here.

To hit up my boyfriend because he has that big house, the sponsorships. I'm here and an in...to his wallet.

I inhale sharply, but Lake has clearly read the situation too. "Don't even try it," he says. "I don't give money to users, and especially not ones who've hurt my woman."

My sister gasps. "That's—"

"Let's go," I murmur and start to turn away, shaking my head, determined to let this just roll off my back. I thought... well, it doesn't matter what I thought.

The proof is right in front of me.

My sister only cares about herself.

My sister only wants to use me.

To hurt me.

I don't want to do the same, don't have the resentment she clearly does, and I don't know that I'll get an explanation from her tonight—or *ever*—that will make this all make sense.

So...I just turn away.

Ella is there, buzz clearly fading—or maybe altogether lost —from the drama. She grabs my shoulders, pulls me into a hug.

I whisper, eyes stinging, "I just...I don't understand how she can do this."

"I don't know, Novs."

I drop my forehead to her shoulder. "I don't know if I want to stick around to find out."

She stiffens.

"I'm not leaving," I say softly, pulling back enough to meet her eyes. "I like it here. I like that I'm going to see you more now that we both have an excuse to be here. I like..." I bite my lip then lean even closer, drop my voice even lower. "No. I *love* Lake."

Her face softens. "I know."

"A lot."

Now her lips curve. "I know."

"So, I'm not going to run," I tell her. "I just...I just don't want to be part of this conversation anymore."

She's still for a beat then her face softens, her lips turn up. "I couldn't agree more," she says, looping her arm through mine. "And I think *that*"—a sniff toward George and Ashley—"calls for more alcohol."

"Definitely. Because—" I lean in as though I'm imparting state secrets, love for my friend, for *Lake* filling me, helping me see what's truly important. It's not the people who want to hurt me, to use me, but the ones who truly show me how much they love me. "—I have a second bottle of simple syrup in my purse."

Her eyes widen, and she opens her mouth—

"Don't."

I freeze then jerk around at Lake's sharp command, seeing that George has taken a huge step toward me, chest somehow puffing up further.

But Lake is still between us, and I find he asks the question I should have, "How did you know she was here?"

George straightens his shoulders...at the same time he tightens his grip on his phone—

His phone that is logged into my iCloud account.

Jer swiping the message up, still signed into his personal account at work.

George not wanting to shell out for an app that I already purchased.

Me logging him into mine so he could download it.

But...I don't think I ever logged him out.

Which means...he can see everything on my cloud—calendar events, emails, and—

Text messages.

Meet me at Ronnie's.

And *that's* how they're here to rub my nose in their marriage, to con me into giving them money, to—

"Let me see your phone," I order quietly.

George scowls, fingers tightening further on his cell as he retreats a step. "What are you talking about?"

Yeah, that's confirmation enough.

Whatever. There has to be a way to log out remotely.

I turn to Lake, see fierce hazel eyes staring down at me.

"I know how he's here," I tell him. "And I can solve it without him." I step closer, pressing my front into his side. "And really, I'm done with this." I glance at my sister, holding her eyes. "You took something I thought I wanted. Congratulations. I hope you have a happy marriage. But I'm not giving you anything else. I'm done."

Then I'm moving forward and—perhaps for the first time in my life—I'm doing it for a healthy reason.

"Fuck, butterfly," Lake murmurs, drawing me close as we turn away from my past. "I'm proud of you."

I inhale so sharply my vision goes unfocused.

How?

How does he know exactly what to say?

How does he know exactly what I need to hear?

That I'm looking forward, but it's fragile. That I'm strong, but I feel like one push might send me skittering backward, might send me back onto that open road.

His encouragement, his gentle pride...it's like stepping into the sun for the first time since...my grandmother.

I can still see the open road and adventures and new experiences...

But for the first time in my life, I'm not alone as I unfurl my wings.

FORTY-EIGHT

Lake

"YOU'RE A BITCH."

That hits Nova hard, even though we're walking away from her sister and that asshole of an ex.

I see it.

The entire bar can see it.

And...I've had enough.

It's vitriol. Bullshit. I knew what bitches—I have plenty of them as exes—act like.

And a big ass one is standing in front of me as I release Nova, spin back around to face her sister.

I lift my brows. "Really?" I say, shifting over to block her when she tries to move past me. "If there's even a small part of you who wants your sister in your life someday, don't spew out whatever bullshit is in your mind right now. Just turn around, go off and live your life, and maybe someday you'll get a clue, get your shit together, and grovel to your sister enough that things will be different."

Her eyes narrow. "Look, asshole—"

"Yup, I'm an asshole. One who's not going to cut a check. Not today or tomorrow or *ever*. One who's not going to stand by and allow Nova to give you anything else."

She scowls.

"So, yeah, I'm an asshole, and I'm the asshole who's going to have your sister's back." I spin away, cutting off whatever retort she might have made, taking Nova with me.

"But—" Nova whispers, eyes shimmering with hurt when she looks up at me.

I start walking. "Don't give her another moment of your time."

"Why is she like that?"

"I don't know, baby." I shake my head, tuck her closer, and draw her further away, thankful when Riggs and Leo stand up and step between us, stopping the idiotic duo from following as I draw Nova away from the bar and out the back door.

She immediately shivers when we step onto the snow-covered patio.

Dumb. But it's not like there's a lot of places in a bar where we can go to have a moment of quiet.

She's shaking, and though I know it's not just from the temperature, I shrug off my hoodie, tug it over her head, and draw her against me. The material and my body aren't enough to keep her warm for long.

But it will be long enough.

I exhale, know this is another of those put up or shut up times. "You know about my mother."

Her body goes very still.

"You know about the ex who threw knives at me."

A breath—hers, mine, I'm not really sure which of us it belongs to because my pulse has started pounding hard in my ears, and the memories—shouting, piercing screams, palms smacking against my cheek, nails digging into my skin—are right *there.*

Fresh.

Painful.

I fucking hate it.

But Nova's wounds are open and fresh too, and—

I need her to know. I need her to understand what I barely do myself.

Her palm settles over my heart, and it's such a gentle touch, so much like what I didn't get growing up, in the relationships with all the women before, that it's jarring.

And it jars the rest of the words out of me.

"But you don't know about the one who stole from me to fuel a drug habit I didn't know about, and you don't know about the one who would punch and kick and hit me if I did something to upset her—and I upset her a lot."

"Lake," she whispers, eyes filling with tears. "I'm so sorry."

"And you don't know about the ex who thought she would convince me to marry her if she was able to get pregnant."

She sucks in a breath.

"I figured out the condoms had holes in them eventually, but not before a pregnancy scare."

I thought then that I didn't want kids, didn't want the life-long tie to a woman who might very well make my life miserable. Now...

I watch a tear slide out from the corner of a pine-green eye, and I *know* I want something different.

Something more.

"I'm so sorry that all happened to you," Nova whispers.

I know she is.

Because she's not them.

"Hey now," I say, brushing the tear away. "I didn't tell you that to make you feel bad, butterfly. It's so you know why I close everyone out, even"—I cup her cheek, tilt her head back so I can stare into her eyes—"a beautiful woman with a beautiful heart."

Soft. Warm. For *me*.

This time I'm expecting my heart to make its roll.

Especially when she nibbles at her bottom lip. "But we didn't—" A wince. "Those first couple of times, we didn't use protection and I'm not on anything—"

I brush my thumb along her mouth, freeing that lip, that truth coming to me too. *God*. I'm so fucking oblivious, a damned ostrich with my head in the sand. I *never* fucked a woman without a condom, but with Nova, I didn't even blink about doing it. Twice. "I know," I tell her gently. "It was stupid on both our parts, but I think, for me, I knew you were different even then or I wouldn't have ever taken the risk."

Her shaking exhale coats the tip of my thumb. "I think"—a breath, her eyes filling with the slightest bit of mischief—"that I wasn't much thinking at all."

My dick twitches even as amusement ripples through me. "And that too," I say lightly. "There wasn't much thinking going on by either of us." I slide my hand back, cover her cheek with my palm, holding her head in place. "I'm sorry."

She covers my hand with her own. "It took two of us." And proving she had those moving forward skills, she squeezes my fingers. "If something comes of it, I'll figure it out."

I drop my forehead to hers. "If something comes of it, *we'll* deal."

Her eyes go warm again, and her body melts against mine.

Fuck.

But this is a woman I can love. A woman I *do* love.

She takes a breath and then curls into me again, arms wrapping around my waist. We stand in the quiet, the waves of the lake lapping against the dark shore behind us, the world quiet and reduced to just the two of us. She's still shivering, but when I'm about to hustle her back inside, she lifts her head and whispers, "You asked Jer to make contact with a gallery."

I freeze.

"He gave me the card at the vet today."

I wind my fingers into her hair at her nape, the silky strands dancing over my skin. "The world deserves to see your photographs."

Her eyes slide closed, forehead dropping to my chest.

Then she exhales. "You really do have that soft side, don't you?"

I kiss the top of her head. "It's nothing. I—"

She presses her palm to my chest, whispers, "Thank you."

"For what?"

"Thank you for the hoodie and the console table and sharing your Twix bars. Thank you for the gallery and letting me stay with you even though I was an unwelcome intrusion. Thank you for standing up for me with my sister and George and..." She takes a breath and I find myself holding mine. "Thank you for giving me the courage to stay right here."

"Butterfly," I whisper, touching her jaw. Her teeth chatter beneath my fingertips, and it's fucking freezing. I need to get her inside, but I don't have the strength to pull away in this moment.

"You have to know," I murmur.

She glances up at me, eyes warm, face soft. "Know what, honey?"

"That everything I've done, that everything I'll do"—I lean close, cup her cheek—"it's all for you."

She exhales, bottom lip quivering, and is quiet for a long moment. Her response, when it finally comes, is barely above a whisper. "I want to run away from this feeling."

Always moving forward.

Toward the future. Away from the terror of the present.

I draw her closer, wind my fingers in her hair again. "I know."

I'm not going to let her go so easily.

I'll follow her if she goes, trail after her to the ends of the earth and back, until she knows that her place is here.

With me.

"But I want to stay here with you more."

Surprise ripples through me, but only for a second. Because courage. That's Nova too. My heart rolls over in my chest. "Fuck, butterfly."

"I know," she whispered, pressing her face to my throat. It's icy cold, but I don't push her away, don't bring her inside, not just yet.

I wrap my arms around her and hold her close.

And I keep her exactly where she needs to be.

FORTY-NINE

Nova

"REALLY?" I ask and immediately clamp my teeth together.

Because that response isn't the least bit professional.

Luckily, Jocelyn just smiles, her brightly painted lips curving upward. "Really *really*," she says lightly, shutting my portfolio and handing it back after having spent a long time flipping through it. "I know the tourists are going to eat your stuff up."

I suspect this statement is good—she likes what she sees.

But I also worry it's bad—not wanting to hurt Jer's feelings, so trying to find something she *did* like.

Such is the life of an artist.

Wrapping my heart up in a bow, presenting it to the world, and expecting everyone to stomp on it.

(And often crawling forward with boot marks on the aching organ after that happens).

Jocelyn glances at her watch. "Let's make an appointment

to sit down next week. We'll figure out the best shots for prints and what size originals we want to carry. Sound good?"

I nod, barely resisting the urge to say *Really?* again.

"Sounds good," I manage instead, grabbing my things and standing up.

We exchange goodbyes, and then I'm walking out of the gallery, my phone buzzing even before I make it to my car. I tug it out of my purse, smile at the screen.

How many are they taking?

My smile grows at Lake's text.

Complete confidence in me.

That settles deep, alongside the words on the patio at Ronnie's, and how he holds my hand while we skate, and the cuddles he gives Steve, and the soup he left for me in the fridge before he headed out for the road game he'll be playing in tonight.

I call him, and he picks up immediately.

And that settles deep too.

So does the conversation and the laughter I coax out of him, even though he's confided in me that the Sierra's locker room has been extremely tense of late.

Infighting.

Rumors flying about their coach being fired and the unsavory things the team's owner has been up to.

And a series of losses.

So, hockey-wise, not the greatest.

The rest of it...*us.* Well, I have full access to his stash of Twix and become very familiar with all of the various uses of his *branch,* and it's been—

Peaceful.

Easy.

Wonderful.

"You still with me, butterfly?" Lake asks softly.

"Yes," I say immediately.

Because it's been peaceful and easy and wonderful and I *want* to be with him.

So why is part of me inching toward the road?

I shove that feeling down, ignore it.

This is perfect. *Lake* is perfect.

"...and I have tickets for you and Ella in your account. You'll just need to scan them the day after tomorrow and..."

I dig my toes into the soles of my shoes hard enough that my bones protest.

But I manage to stop the inching.

I manage to focus in on what Lake is saying.

And I manage to keep myself firmly *off* the road.

Remaining in that peaceful, that easy.

In the love for this man.

❄ ❄ ❄ ❄

I'VE NEVER BEEN to a professional hockey game, even with having a best friend with a professional hockey player for a brother.

Part of that is...moving forward, not stopping long enough to enjoy the spoils of the present.

The rest is something I'm only just beginning to understand.

Fear and hiding, yes. But also...not wanting to impose on Ella. To take her up on her offer of free tickets. To take advantage. Because if I take, if I express what I want, then they—my grandma, my boyfriends, my sister, my parents, my friends—might leave me.

And because of that fear, I sacrificed time and fun with my best friend.

Ugh.

Sighing, I break off a piece of the soft pretzel, shove it into my mouth. It's salty and delicious and takes my mind off the buzzing in my head.

Too much thinking.

Too much time in my own head.

Not enough *branch* time.

And not enough time with Ella, who's been making the trip up regularly, but who also has a life in the Bay Area.

It's almost Christmas.

That's one of the busiest times of year for hairstylists—everyone wants to look good for family get-togethers and work events and holiday parties—so she's been working eight or ten hours a day, six days a week.

Not these next two days, though.

She's *mine*.

And Knox's too, I think with a scowl.

Damn brothers, cramping my style.

"Drinksies!" Ella says, plopping down next to me, carrying two drinks and rosy cheeks.

I frown, taking one of them, thankful that I woke up with my period that morning, that Lake's and my relationship can keep moving forward without becoming supercharged by a baby. Thankful that I can drink because there's something weird going on with Ella. "Where have you been?" I ask her.

She rolls her eyes, but I see her cheeks grow a little pinker. "Knox wanted to do his hair." A shake of her head. "Can you believe that?"

I sip, but there's something about her tone that isn't right.

Something that tells me she's hiding something.

Call it Best Friend Radar.

"No," I say, holding her eyes with my own. "I *can't* believe that."

More pink, but I don't have the chance to prod at that tell because the lights go down and the music goes up and the Sierra's mascot—a giant pine cone skates out on the ice.

The stadium fills with cheers.

The music blasts.

The players come out.

And...the puck drops.

And the night is that perfect mix of peace and easy and *wonderful*.

Right until the game ends, when I drive back to Lake's house, and I walk into his house.

Then that urge to hit the open road ramps up.

And takes over.

FIFTY

Lake

"YEAH!" Leo calls, cutting hard across the ice, stick down and ready to receive a pass.

I grunt as I absorb a hit, the air leaving my lungs, but then I'm pushing off, angling my stick, flicking the puck up to my teammate.

He corrals it without losing speed, carrying over the red line and then chipping it into our offensive zone when the other team bears down on him.

It's been like this all night.

Not a lot of space.

On our asses in a second.

A tight game.

I want it to be a blowout, want to give Nova a show.

Tonight's not that night.

It's a battle, a grind, a fight for every foot of ice, for every shot, for every pass.

Riggs streaks into the zone, almost a blur, he's moving so fast.

Which isn't typical.

Because he plays defense. Because his specialty is blocking shots.

Because he isn't often streaking, hauling ass down toward the goal, stick on the ice—

Scooping up the puck when the other team tries to clear it.

Hell fucking *yeah.*

I'm already moving, having shoved the asshole who tried to pin me off, skating my ass off to get into the zone behind Riggs.

I whistle, something that can't possibly be heard over the crowd noise, over the sounds of the game, over the other team shouting.

But he *does* hear it, and he reacts, shooting the puck over to me when I take the lane on the far side.

Time slows down.

It's like I have all the time in the world—to look, to breathe, to *see.* I cut hard to the left, drawing a player from the other team with me...

And leaving the center open.

For *Riggs.*

Who keeps skating, his big, fast-moving body a distraction that allows Leo to slide in and camp out by the back door, by the opposite side of the net to me.

Fucking perfect.

I lift my stick like I'm going to take a shot, grinning when the goalie scrambles, when he flinches, anticipating the puck to be flying toward him.

But I'm not shooting.

I'm passing...

Through Riggs's feet—

And straight onto Leo's stick.

He doesn't need to make a move, doesn't need to get fancy. He just needs to keep the blade of his stick on the ice, needs to angle it properly—

Just. Like. *That.*

Time starts moving again as the puck ricochets off Leo's stick with a resounding *snick*, changing directions so quickly my mind can't process it.

But then it catches up...

Right as the puck flies into the back of the net.

There's always a moment of quiet when someone scores, as though our brains can't quite accept it, and the crowd is usually several beats behind us.

Then the red light comes on.

The fans react—mostly cheers, a few boos from supporters of the other team.

And...it gets *loud*.

But I only hear my teammates as we collide, nearly taking Leo down at the boards, "Fuck, yeahs!" exchanged, bear hugs given.

Euphoria for one glorious second.

Then it's back to work, skating to the bench, frustration creeping back in because they're mostly assholes, and can't even summon a "Good job" to Leo for putting us up a goal. There's jealousy and indifference and annoyance at listening to Coach blabber about shit that doesn't matter, considering he's likely to be out of here before we make it to the All-Star break.

Tightness in my shoulders.

Anger in how fiercely I grip my stick.

I sneak a look across the ice and see Nova smiling and cheering, her and Ella doing a little dance.

And...everything in me settles.

The irritation. The tightness. The sense of everything going wrong.

Because I have Nova, the rest of it doesn't matter.

* * * *

Since press always takes a ridiculous amount of time, Nova and I made plans to meet back at the house.

Can't have her first taste of pro hockey be tempered by sitting around, twiddling her thumbs, waiting for me to answer an endless amount of dumb questions.

I noticed that you lost the puck on that one play, what are you doing to make sure that doesn't happen again?

You guys struggled on the breakout tonight, how are you going to fix that?

Was Rome Dawson, the newest addition to the Eagles, your toughest competition tonight?

I mean, those weren't the actual questions.

But close enough.

And they all result in useless fucking sound bites.

Especially when everyone knows that Rome is the only reason the Eagles are doing as good as they're doing.

Traded after spending his entire career with the San Francisco Gold, he's now found himself playing for the newest team in the league and his Bay Area rival.

Tricky shit.

Especially when he's still really close with the guys from the Gold.

He's a pain in the ass on the ice, though.

So winning tonight feels good.

Even *if* I have to answer dumb questions.

But press is done, I'm showered and heading for my car. Soon, Nova and I can chill for a few days, and not that I'll admit it to her, but I find that I'm looking forward to some shitty Christmas movies now that we're actually in the month of December.

I start up the engine and head out, thankful the drive home is less than half an hour, the arena situated closer to Reno than South Lake for ease of access. Which means that I'm in a kickass neighborhood that's surrounded by nature, situated in the forest and still has a small-town feel, but also the perks of living close to a decent-sized city.

It's why I was initially excited to play here.

That's changed, clearly.

But it still has the perk of being away from my family—

As if summoned by the devil himself, my phone rings and I look to the dash, see it's my mother calling.

"Jesus," I mutter, jabbing at the screen, rejecting the call.

I want to go home.

I want to enjoy myself.

I want *peace*.

And I want to have all of that with Nova.

I don't want drama and bullshit and...I don't want to deal with my mom right now. I'll call her in the morning, endure the long, frustrating phone call.

Tonight, I just want peace.

Only, the moment I reject the call, my cell rings again, my mom's number coming up again on the screen set into the console.

"Fuck," I say on a hiss, jabbing at the button to accept it.

Just get it over with.

"Hi, Mom."

Her voice is a shriek. "Lake! Oh my God!"

And all that peace I want...

Is shattered.

FIFTY-ONE

Nova

SHE LOOKS LIKE HIM.

Only smaller. More petite. Much, much shorter.

And there's something absolutely fragile about her.

Like the wrong word, the wrong action, the wrong blink of my freaking eyelids, and she would explode or shatter or—

Worse.

"I don't know why my son didn't tell me he was dating someone," she whispers, tears streaking down her cheeks, eyes darting from side to side. "Why wouldn't he tell me?"

"I—" Her head whips toward me so quickly that the words stick in my throat, and I have to force them out. "We just started dating."

"And you're living together?"

I wince.

Steve woofs.

And neither of those two things are helping this situation.

Frankly, this situation probably can't be helped, considering I walked into Lake's house and found his mom sitting on the couch that I ordered weeks ago now, Steve warily watching her from the other side of it.

"Well," I say. "He was nice enough to let me stay for a bit."

Now her face changes.

In a not nice way.

In a—

"So you're using my son."

I freeze, heart suddenly in my throat, and I force a smile. "Can I get you anything? A glass of water? Wine?"

"Offering me hospitality in my *son's* house?" she asks archly.

My head goes a little woozy, but I force a smile. This is fine. It's all fine. Lake has already told me that she's a handful, that she tries to seek out drama—and finding out her son has a live-in girlfriend is perfect fodder for that.

I just have to buy enough time for Lake to get home and deal with her.

"How about a honey rosemary mule?" I ask brightly instead of turning and running out the door like I want to. "It's one of my specialties."

She sniffs. "No, thank you."

Steve growls.

She gasps, clamping a hand to her chest. "Th-that beast just growled at me."

Yeah, he did.

Because...instincts. I'm aware that I'm inclined to not like her, solely based on what Lake has told me.

But Steve is not a beast.

He's just good at reading people.

I move over to him, scooping him up and carrying him back into the kitchen.

It's late. I'm tired. I want to crawl into bed with Lake and sleep until morning, sleep until I wake up and try this interaction over.

"Steve is friendly," I say, moving to the cabinets and searching for something that might placate her.

Wine?

Cheese and crackers?

Enough vodka so she passes out.

When in doubt, mules.

Plus, it'll give me something to do so I don't run out the door.

Using Lake. Shit.

That was...terrifying and not me. Only...wasn't it? I'm staying here and—

Stop.

I grab some lemons, start slicing them, wracking my brain for a question that won't set her off, that won't have me traversing a landscape of broken glass in bare feet.

"Did you have a nice flight?"

"God no," she snaps. "Travel is always arduous for me." A sigh. "Especially when I'm traveling and my son isn't here to greet me."

"Oh," I say, squeezing the juice into a bowl, straining out the seeds. "Did he know you were coming?"

I can't believe he wouldn't say anything, but he has been really busy lately, with travel and photoshoots and testing the next version of my mules that I'm creating.

I'm thinking cucumber and raspberry.

But...that's off topic because Lake's mom sniffs again. "No."

"Oh," I say again. "Okay."

Right.

I get that, but also—

"Did you think to tell him?"

"Did my son think to tell me he's got a whore in his house?"

I'm cutting another lemon, and the knife slips, nearly slicing my hand off. Luckily, I jerk it out of the way in time.

But I decide that maybe knives and this conversation shouldn't mix, so I set it aside, try to broach this strange, land-mine-filled gulf with his mom again.

Move forward.

Just keep moving forward.

But even as I'm thinking that, I still feel myself inching toward the road, desperate for escape.

"Maybe I should let you wait up for Lake," I say.

"Oh, I see," she snaps, crossing her legs in a jerky movement. "You think you're too good to talk to me."

"I can't do this," I whisper to the bowl of lemon juice. "I can't *do* this."

I never even had a mom, and I sure as shit am not equipped to deal with one like Lake's.

There's no map to navigate this, no app to guide me through.

That road is calling, open and free and uncomplicated and—

Absent of this feeling.

Like I'm fucking up.

Like I'm not doing all I should for Lake.

Like I *am* using him.

Steve whines, and I look down at him with stinging eyes.

I can't do this.

I scoop him up, move toward the hall, glad my boots and my coat are in the mud room.

"Hey! Where are you—?"

But I'm already at the door to the garage, already shoving my feet into my boots, already reaching for my coat.

Hooking on Steve's leash.
And escaping.
Heading for freedom...
And that open road.

FIFTY-TWO

Lake

I SCREECH INTO THE DRIVEWAY, barely able to wait for the garage door to open so I can pull inside.

On the call, my mom was screaming.

From my house.

Nonsense about Nova and—

I pull the final few feet inside and brake hard, cranking off the engine, jumping out and hustling into the house.

My mom is sobbing on the couch.

Full-on shrieking and hysterical and—

Christ.

I really don't have the patience for her bullshit right now.

"Where's Nova?" I ask, moving toward her, barely resisting the urge to shake her.

My mom looks up, tears clinging to her lashes. "You m-mean your live-in girlfriend that you haven't t-told me about?" She clamps a hand to her chest, sniffs loudly.

"Yeah, Mom. My live-in girlfriend who you don't know

about because you flit into my life with your bullshit"—she gasps—"then you flit right back out again after you've drained me dry and have to move on to someone else to play emotional vampire with."

She starts crying, even louder than before.

I shake my head, not buying it this time, not having the patience for it, just extending my hand. "Give me the spare key."

The one I forgot to relocate all those weeks before.

The one she knows about because I've had it in the same spot in every single house I've lived in.

Her tears dry up in an instant, and she scowls at me. "Why?"

"Because I'm done catering to you. I'm done walking on eggshells. I'm done feeling guilty for being borne and putting up with your bullshit because you want to punish me again and again and *again*. Now tell me," I grit out, stepping closer, holding her gaze, not giving in to her crap, not this fucking time.

This is too important.

I lean in, roar, "Where. The. Fuck. Is. The. Woman. I. Love?"

"Woof!"

I jump, head whipping to the side, seeing Nova standing in the kitchen, eyes wide, Steve in her arms.

Fuck.

She heard that.

She's going to run.

She has her boots and coat on.

And Steve.

And—

I'm moving away from my mom before I even process it, crossing to her, and doing it hurrying.

Because she can't leave.

Because I love her too fucking much to allow her to go.

But she doesn't retreat as I move toward her, doesn't turn and flee out the door like I half expect.

She just stays there and lets me approach and—

"Butterfly," I rasp.

She blinks once. Twice. Then, "You love me?"

Fuck.

"Don't leave," I beg. "Just pretend you didn't hear that. We'll keep moving like we are—slow and steady and together."

"But..." Her eyes go glassy. "You love me?"

Too fucking soon for my beautiful woman who wants to fly off because it's safer than sitting on a branch and waiting to be squashed by the world.

But I can't lie to her.

This woman has come to own my heart.

"Yeah, butterfly. I love you."

She goes still, holding Steve as her eyes slide closed, her shoulders draw up.

Then she exhales and her lids peel back.

"I was going to leave this," she whispers.

"What?"

"I was going to leave this."

I frown.

"I got all the way to the pond with Steve and was planning how to get the hell out of here, and"—a tear escapes—"I was going to leave this, leave us, leave *you*."

"Butterfly."

Another tear slides down her cheek. "I'm not sure I have the tools for this. I'm not sure I won't fuck up and hurt you. I'm not sure that I even know how to be open enough to be in a relationship, but...I love you," she whispers. "Truly, I do."

My heart does that thing.

That solely-reserved-for-Nova thing.

"Woof." Steve wiggles and I give him a scratch before tugging him out of her arms, setting him on the floor.

My mom squeals when he runs toward her, and I spin around. "You can either shut up, sit there, and wait until I'm ready to talk to you." I take a breath, release it slowly, calming my tone so she knows that I'm fucking dead serious. "Or you can get the hell out of my life."

Her lips clamp together and she leans back on the couch, kicking her shoes off and curling her legs beneath her.

Out of the pup's reach.

Or so she thinks.

I shake my head, turn back to Nova. "I don't have the playbook to figure this out. I don't have the answers, and I can't guarantee that I won't be an asshole again, that I won't hurt you. But I do know that you're the one woman in my life—past and present—who gives me what I need."

"Lake," she whispers.

"And I figure we can figure the rest out, butterfly. All the bumps and misadventures, the troublesome family and the urge to hit the road."

"But I left," she says then winces. "Things got hard and I left."

"You went to the pond—to *our* pond—and were back to figure things out in what, like thirty minutes?"

"I—" She swallows then nods. "Yeah."

"I think I can deal with you going to our place for a half hour to sort out your head." My lips twitch, and I move closer, drawing her into my arms. "Can you deal with me being a grumpy asshole when things aren't going my way?"

A long, slow breath. Her eyes coming back to mine.

Strength. Courage. Warmth.

Nova.

She smiles. "That's what mules are for."

Grinning, I bring her closer. "Damn right, they are."

"I came up with a new flavor," she tells me softly. "Cucumber and raspberry."

"Nothing beats honey rosemary." I settle my forehead against hers. "And nothing beats what I feel for you."

Her hand weaves into my hair. "I love you."

"I love—"

"Woof!"

We break apart, heads jerking to the side.

Seeing the tiny demon dog with my mom's shoe in his mouth, violently shaking the expensive leather from side to side as he growls fiercely.

"Steve!" we both cry.

But fuck if that isn't the best justice I've ever seen.

And I know Nova feels the same as she glances up at me, her lips curving.

Then she's laughing.

And I am too.

And I know that things might be complicated, might not be drama-free, that we might even have to take a detour on the open road.

But we're going to do it together.

And that's all that really matters.

Well, that and mules.

EPILOGUE

"AND THIS," I say to Ella, "is my famous—or soon to be famous, anyway—cranberry and cinnamon mule."

I present the glass to her with a flourish.

She picks it up, sniffs delicately, and takes a small sip.

I wait with bated breath, our Christmas celebration fully underway. Lake's house is crowded and noisy, things he's tolerating because I asked if we could have a get-together.

Because my grandma used to have a party on Christmas for all her friends that had become family, a raucous celebration that was less about gifts and more about games and spending time together and—

Lake needed that.

The Sierra are winning games again, but it's not fun.

So, he—and his teammates, the non-asshole ones, anyway—need this time to cut loose.

With flights of my special mules.

Cucumber and raspberry. Cranberry and cinnamon. Hibiscus and jalapeño. Strawberry and mint.

Ella sets the glass down. "Not your best."

I groan.

And, because I can't ever seem to top it, I pass over her honey and rosemary mule.

No point in fighting it.

Honey and rosemary tops all.

I move on to my next victim—I mean, friend—and I set Leo and Jolie—a woman he met at Ronnie's not long ago, who has nearly as jerky of an ex as George—up with their flights of mules.

Jolie is beyond sweet, declaring them all her favorite, while Leo stands protectively at her shoulder and only drinks the honey and rosemary variety.

I sigh.

"God," Ella says, setting her glass on the island and stretching her neck from side to side. "My arms are so sore."

I reach for her, start rubbing at her tight shoulders. "That's because your boss makes you work too much."

Jolie frowns. "How much is *too much?*"

Ella starts to shrug that off, but I've been here in the present. I've been watching her and keeping tabs.

So, I don't let her minimize it.

"Eight to ten hours a day, six days a week."

And I'm glad of Jolie's gasp of outrage on her behalf—she's a fellow hairstylist. "That's not okay, Ella. Not at all."

"I mean," Ella says on a sigh. "I can't exactly tell my boss no when the clients are booked and another stylist flakes. I won't do them dirty like that."

"I get wanting to keep your clients happy," Jolie says, leaning back against Leo. "And I get being busy—hell, this season has been a disaster with this"—she lifts her casted arm, a break that her asshole ex was indirectly responsible for—"but there's also such a thing as *too* busy."

Riggs nods.

And I haven't missed him hovering around my friend.

Watching her every move.

"I'm okay." Ella smiles and it's tense. Edgy. "I promise."

"Well," Jolie says, "if you come into the market for a new job, I'm looking for another stylist at my salon."

"I—"

"Yes! That's right, baby!" Knox calls, tossing the remote onto the couch and sweeping Steve into his arms. My pup eats that up because he loves Knox and his antics.

Hell, he loves *all* of this.

The activity. The noise. The people giving him cuddles. The opportunities to scarf down food he shouldn't be eating.

Steve kisses Knox as Ivy—a personal trainer Riggs, Knox, Leo, and Lake all work with—scowls, having ended up on the wrong side of the Mario Kart battle.

Our little family.

None of us related by blood.

But making our own memories.

Living in the present.

Eating. Drinking. Playing games. Being silly and ridiculous.

Then packing them off into Lyfts when the mules hit hard and the night grows late.

"Come here, butterfly," Lake murmurs after I finish with the dishes, my feet sore and my cheeks aching from smiling so much, my arms heavy after lifting my camera so much, trying to document as much of the night as possible.

I toss the towel on the counter, move over to him, settling on the couch.

Pride and Prejudice is playing in the background, the Kiera version, which is my favorite, and Steve is passed out on his bed in front of the fireplace, his paws in the air, his snores almost drowning out the pretty, pretty words of Mr. Darcy.

"What's up, honey?" I say, curling into him.

"You happy?" he asks.

I glance at the TV then smile back at him. "Incandescently happy."

He taps my nose lightly, mouth tipping up. "Good."

Then he surprises me, not by stealing a kiss, not by coaxing me down the hall to the bedroom. Instead, he reaches into his pocket and pulls out a small velvet box.

My throat goes tight.

"Lake," I rasp.

"No need for the open road, butterfly," he teases lightly. "It's not a ring." A beat. "Not yet, anyway."

My eyes flash to his.

But the blip of panic in my heart is there and gone in a second—because I want the ring. I want him.

Forever.

"Open it," he orders.

My hands are shaking, but I follow the command, pulling the lid of the black velvet box back and—

Immediately, my eyes fill with tears.

"Lake," I whisper, barely able to see it with my vision so glassy.

Barely able to see my butterfly charm, fully repaired, all the way down to the missing diamond.

Sniffing, I launch myself into his arms, hold him tight. "God, I love you."

He rests his head atop mine, hugs me back. "I know, butter-fly." Fingers through my hair, his warm body pressed to mine. "Because you show me that every single day."

The road is bumpy.

Surrounded by snowbanks and dangerous blind turns.

But my wings are free.

And for the first time, I feel safe enough to fly.

❄ ❄ ❄ ❄

Ella

I plaster a smile on my face as Nova and I sit in the stands, cheering on the Sierra.

That's one of the perks of having a professional hockey-playing brother.

Free tickets to pretty much any home game I want.

Access to all manner of hot and sexy hockey players.

Except the one I'm actually attracted to.

Not my brother, in case that addendum is needed for clarity's sake.

But one, Riggs Ashford.

He's tall and thick, with strong thighs, a great ass, and a broody personality.

My personal kiss of death when it comes to the opposite sex.

Unfortunately for me, Riggs is a good guy.

Strait-laced. A bit uptight. Way quieter than any man I've ever met.

And...he doesn't like me.

How have I come to this brilliant conclusion?

After throwing myself at him on Christmas, and being firmly—and a little roughly (also my personal preference)—shut down.

So, while I love watching my brother play hockey and while I love spending time with my best friend Nova, who's mooning over her boyfriend (also on the ice), sitting here while trying to feign that I'm happy and comfortable and not slowly dying inside of embarrassment...

Is a losing battle.

It makes me want to pick up the drink sitting in the cupholder at my feet, and down it.

But that's something else Riggs doesn't like about me.

He thinks I drink too much.

And maybe I do.

Maybe I drink so I don't have to think—

Tap. Tap. Tap.

I jerk and look up from the tempting cocktail, seeing that Lake is standing in front of the glass, smiling at Nova, who—swear to fuck—just seems to blossom under his gaze.

Bright and beautiful, showing the world the gorgeous person she is inside.

She lifts her camera and fires off a couple of shots, causing Lake to wink before he skates off to finish his warmup.

My brother is on the far side of the ice, stretching and stick handling, getting ready for the game in a sure-minded focus that he doesn't have many other places, and they all involve hockey—off-ice training, studying tape, hitting the gym to be strong and explosive, practice and games and extra time at the rink.

I'll get my goofy Knox back after the game.

Right now he has laser focus.

"I'm going to sneak up to the bathroom," Nova murmurs.

"I'll hold the fort," I tell her, getting a smile before she starts making her way up the long concrete staircase.

My gaze goes back to my drink, mouth watering, throat so freaking dry.

Tap. Tap. Tap.

I jerk my head up again, expecting it to be Lake wondering where his woman went.

It's not.

Riggs is standing on the glass in front of me—brown eyes deep pools of chocolate, beard just long enough to give a woman ideas.

"What?" I mouth.

He holds up his gloved hand and I frown.

"I don't need a puck," I say, shaking my head.

I grew up with enough of them all over the house and yard and, hell, I probably have more than a few of them in my apartment even now.

Riggs can't possibly hear me, but maybe he reads my lips because he bangs his fist against the glass and holds the puck up again.

I sigh, stand up, and hold out my hands.

I don't know a lot about Riggs, but I've seen his stubborn streak.

Experienced it firsthand.

So...might as well get it over with.

He nods, makes the toss...

And the puck lands with a smack in my open palms.

I force another smile, start to shove the puck into my purse—

Tap. Tap. Tap.

Freezing, I glance up.

He nods toward the puck and I drag my brows together.

"What?" I mouth again.

He looks at his hand, pretends to flip something over.

Brows dragging together, I frown, but I mirror his miming, glance down at my hand, and—

Flip the puck over

My mouth drops open, my eyes go wide, my head jerks up—

He raises his brows in question.

I look from the puck to him, back down to the scrawled-out words on the black rubber. "I—"

But I don't get further than that because he winks and skates off.

I stare down at the words, my belly heating because—

Holy shit, had quiet, strait-laced Riggs Ashford just written *that?*

❄ ❄ ❄ ❄

THANK YOU FOR READING! I hope you enjoyed Nova and Lake's story as much as I loved writing their happy ending! Ella and Riggs will get their chance in CAUGHT FROM BEHIND. **It's always the quiet ones you have to watch out for...**

CLICK HERE TO READ CAUGHT FROM BEHIND NOW>

❄ ❄ ❄ ❄

AND IF YOU loved OVER THE LINE and need more Sierra hockey boys, check out SNOWED, featuring Leo and Jolie. **Leo West saves me from the floor of the bar. But he also saves me from the boring loneliness of my life. The only question is if he's going to let me save him right back.**

CLICK HERE TO READ SNOWED NOW>

❄ ❄ ❄ ❄

PLUS, you'll love finding out what happens to Rome Dawson in BROKEN LACES, book 1 of my new series, the Eagles

Hockey series. **This team of misfits and bad boys are going to puck you in the best possible way.**

❄ ❄ ❄ ❄

I so appreciate your help in spreading the word about my books, including sharing with friends! Please leave a review on your favorite book site!

You can also join my Facebook group, the Fabinators, for exclusive giveaways and sneak peeks of future books.

If you'd like to receive emails from me for new releases and monthly giveaway sign up for my newsletter at https://www.elisefaber.com/newsletter

ALSO BY ELISE FABER

***Gold Hockey* (all stand alone)**

Blocked

Backhand

Boarding

Benched

Breakaway

Breakout

Checked

Coasting

Centered

Charging

Caged

Crashed

A Gold Christmas

Cycled

Caught

Cap

Covered

Crushed

Changed

Scored

Breakers Hockey (all stand alone)

<u>Broken</u>

<u>Boldly</u>

<u>Breathless</u>

<u>Ballsy</u>

<u>Bewitched</u>

Blowout

Breathe

Blazed

Sierra Hockey Series

Over the Line

Caught from Behind

On the Fly

The Big Skate

Rush Hockey Trilogy #1

Big Puck Energy

Filthy Puckboy

So Pucking Over It

Rush Hockey Trilogy #2

Love, Pucks, and Other Stories

All's Fair in Pucks and War

No Pucks Lost Between Us

Rush Hockey Trilogy #3

Puck and Make Up

Blinded By Pucks

Match Made in Pucks

Eagles Hockey Series (all stand alone)

Broken Laces

Knotted Laces

Lace 'em Up

Sinful Bosses (all stand alone)

Ruthless Billionaire

***Billionaire's Club* (all stand alone)**

Bad Night Stand

Bad Breakup

Bad Husband

Bad Hookup

Bad Divorce

Bad Fiancé

Bad Boyfriend

Bad Blind Date

Bad Wedding

Bad Engagement

Bad Bridesmaid

Bad Swipe

Bad Girlfriend

Bad Best Friend

Bad Rebound

Bad Romance

Bad Business

Bad Billionaire's Quickies

Love, Action, Camera (all stand alone)

Dotted Line

Action Shot

Close-Up

End Scene

Meet Cute

***Love After Midnight* (all stand alone)**

Rum And Notes

Virgin Daiquiri

On The Rocks

Sex On The Seats

Life Sucks Series

Train Wreck

Hot Mess

Dumpster Fire

Clusterf*@k

FUBAR

Perfect Storm

Free Fall

Lost Cause

***Roosevelt Ranch Series* (all stand alone, series complete)**

Disaster at Roosevelt Ranch

Heartbreak at Roosevelt Ranch

Collision at Roosevelt Ranch

Regret at Roosevelt Ranch

Desire at Roosevelt Ranch

***Phoenix Series* (read in order)**

Phoenix Rising

Dark Phoenix

Phoenix Freed

***Phoenix: LexTal Chronicles* (rereleasing soon, stand alone, Phoenix world)**

From Ashes

In Flames

To Smoke

***KTS Series* (all stand alone, series complete)**

Riding The Edge

Crossing The Line

Leveling The Field

Scorching The Earth

Cocky Heroes World

Tattooed Troublemaker

ABOUT THE AUTHOR

USA Today bestselling author, Elise Faber, loves chocolate, Star Wars, Harry Potter, and hockey (the order depending on the day and how well her team -- the Sharks! -- are playing). She and her husband also play as much hockey as they can squeeze into their schedules, so much so that their typical date night is spent on the ice. Elise is the mom to two exuberant boys and lives in Northern California. Connect with her in her Facebook group, the Fabinators or find more information about her books at www.elisefaber.com.

facebook.com/elisefaberauthor

amazon.com/author/elisefaber

bookbub.com/profile/elise-faber

instagram.com/elisefaber

tiktok.com/@elisefaberauthor

goodreads.com/elisefaber

www.ingramcontent.com/pod-product-compliance
Lightning Source LLC
Chambersburg PA
CBHW060620100726
47907CB00006B/1705